KT-524-182

For Francesca

CONTENTS

Diana Wynne Jones

Castle in the Air

Illustrated by Tim Stevens

HarperCollins *Children's Books*

First published by Methuen Children's Books Ltd 1990
First published in Great Britain by HarperCollins *Children's Books* 2000
This edition published 2009
Harper Collins *Children's Books* is a division of HarperCollins *Publishers* Ltd
1 London Bridge Street, London, SE1 9GF

www.harpercollins.co.uk

25

Text copyright © Diana Wynne Jones 1990
Illustrations copyright © Tim Stevens 2000

ISBN 13: 978 0 00 675530 2

The author and the illustrator assert the moral right to be
identified as the author and illustrator of the work.

Printed and bound in Great Britain by
CPI Group (UK) Ltd, Croydon, CR0 4YY

Conditions of Sale
This book is sold subject to the condition that it shall not, by way of trade
or otherwise, be lent, re-sold, hired out or otherwise circulated without
the publisher's prior written consent in any form of binding or cover other
than that in which it is published and without a similar condition including
this condition being imposed on the subsequent purchaser.

Mixed Sources
Product group from well-managed
forests and other controlled sources
www.fsc.org Cert no. SW-COC-1806
© 1996 Forest Stewardship Council

FSC is a non-profit international organisation established to promote the
responsible management of the world's forests. Products carrying the FSC
label are independently certified to assure consumers that they come
from forests that are managed to meet the social, economic and
ecological needs of present and future generations.

Find out more about HarperCollins and the environment at
www.harpercollins.co.uk/green

CHAPTER ONE

In which Abdullah buys a carpet

Far to the south of the land of Ingary, in the Sultanates of Rashpuht, a young carpet merchant called Abdullah lived in the city of Zanzib. As merchants go, he was not rich. His father had been disappointed in him and, when he died, he had only left Abdullah just enough money to buy and stock a modest booth in the north-west corner of the Bazaar. The rest of his father's money, and the large carpet emporium in the centre of the Bazaar, had all gone to the relatives of his father's first wife.

Abdullah had never been told why his father was disappointed in him. A prophecy made at Abdullah's birth had something to do with it. But Abdullah had never bothered to find out more. Instead, from a very early age, he had simply made up daydreams about it. In his daydreams, he was really the long-lost son of a great prince, which meant, of course, that his father was not really his father. It was a complete castle in the air and Abdullah knew it was. Everyone told him he had inherited his father's looks. When he looked in a mirror, he saw a decidedly handsome young man, in a thin, hawk-faced way, and knew he looked very like the portrait of his father as a young man – always allowing for the fact that his father wore a flourishing moustache, whereas Abdullah was still scraping together the six hairs on his upper lip and hoping they would multiply soon.

Unfortunately, as everyone also agreed, Abdullah had inherited his character from his mother – his father's second wife. She had been a dreamy and timorous woman, and a great disappointment to everyone. This did not bother Abdullah particularly. The life of a carpet merchant holds few opportunities for bravery and he was, on the whole, content with it. The booth he had bought, though small, turned out to be rather well placed. It was not far from the West Quarter where the rich people lived in their big houses surrounded by beautiful gardens. Better still, it was the first part of the Bazaar the carpet-makers came to when they came into Zanzib from the desert to the north. Both the rich people and the carpet-makers were usually seeking the bigger shops in the centre of the Bazaar, but a surprisingly large number of them were ready to pause at the booth of a young carpet merchant when that young merchant rushed out into their paths and offered them bargains and discounts with most profuse politeness.

In this way, Abdullah was quite often able to buy best quality carpets before anyone else saw them, and sell them at a profit too. In between buying and selling he could sit in his booth and continue with his daydream, which suited him very well. In fact, almost the only trouble in his life came from his father's first wife's relations, who would keep visiting him once a month in order to point out his failings.

"But you're not saving any of your profits!" cried Abdullah's father's first wife's brother's son, Hakim (whom Abdullah detested), one fateful day.

Abdullah explained that, when he made a profit, his custom was to use that money to buy a better carpet. Thus, although all his money was bound up in his stock, it was getting to be better and better stock. He had enough to live on. And, as he told his father's relatives, he had no need of more, since he was not married.

"Well you *should* be married!" cried Abdullah's father's first wife's sister, Fatima (whom Abdullah detested even more). "I've said it once and I'll say it again – a young man like you should have at least two wives by now!" And, not content with simply saying so, Fatima declared that this time she was going to look out for some wives for him – an offer which made Abdullah shake in his shoes.

"And the more valuable your stock gets, the more likely

you are to be robbed, or the more you'll lose if your booth catches fire – have you thought of that?" nagged Abdullah's father's first wife's uncle's son, Assif (a man whom Abdullah hated more than the first two put together).

He assured Assif that he always slept in the booth and was very careful of the lamps. At which all three of his father's first wife's relatives shook their heads, tut-tutted and went away. This usually meant they would leave him in peace for another month. Abdullah sighed with relief and plunged straight back into his daydream.

The daydream was enormously detailed by now. In it, Abdullah was the son of a mighty prince who lived so far to the east that his country was unknown in Zanzib. But Abdullah had been kidnapped at the age of two by a villainous bandit called Kabul Aqba. Kabul Aqba had a hooked nose like the beak of a vulture and wore a gold ring clipped into one of its nostrils. He carried a pistol with a silver-mounted stock with which he menaced Abdullah, and there was a bloodstone in his turban which seemed to give him more than human power. Abdullah was so frightened that he ran away into the desert, where he was found by the man he called his father now. The daydream took no account of the fact that Abdullah's father had never ventured into the desert in his life: indeed, he had often said that anyone who ventured beyond Zanzib must be mad. Nevertheless, Abdullah could picture every nightmare inch of the dry, thirsty, footsore journey he had made before the good carpet merchant found him. Likewise, he could picture in great detail the palace he had been kidnapped from, with its pillared throne room floored in green porphyry, its women's quarters and its kitchens, all of the utmost richness. There were seven domes on its roof, each one covered with beaten gold.

Lately, however, the daydream had been concentrating on the princess to whom Abdullah had been betrothed at his birth. She was as highborn as Abdullah and had grown up in his absence into a great beauty with perfect features and huge misty dark eyes. She lived in a palace as rich as Abdullah's own. You approached it along an avenue lined with angelic statues and entered by way of seven marble courts, each with a fountain in the middle more precious than the last, starting with one made of chrysolite and ending with one of platinum studded with emeralds.

But that day Abdullah found he was not quite satisfied with this arrangement. It was a feeling he often had after a visit from his father's first wife's relations. It occurred to him that a good palace ought to have magnificent gardens. Abdullah loved gardens though he knew very little about them. Most of his experience had come from the public parks of Zanzib – where the turf was somewhat trampled and the flowers few – in which he sometimes spent his lunch hour when he could afford to pay one-eyed Jamal to watch his booth. Jamal kept the fried-food stall next door and would, for a coin or so, tie his dog to the front of Abdullah's booth. Abdullah was well aware that this did not really qualify him to invent a proper garden, but since anything was better than thinking of two wives chosen for him by Fatima, he lost himself in waving fronds and scented walkways in the gardens of his princess.

Or nearly. Before Abdullah was fairly started, he was interrupted by a tall dirty man with a dingy-looking carpet in his arms.

"You buy carpets for selling, son of a great house?" this stranger asked, bowing briefly.

For someone trying to sell a carpet in Zanzib, where buyers and sellers always spoke to one another in the most formal and flowery way, this man's manner was shockingly abrupt. Abdullah was annoyed anyway because his dream garden was falling to pieces at this interruption from real life. He answered curtly, "That is so, oh king of the desert. You wish to trade with this miserable merchant?"

"Not trade – sell, oh master of a stack of mats," the stranger corrected him.

Mats! thought Abdullah. This was an insult. One of the carpets on display in front of Abdullah's booth was a rare floral tufted one from Ingary – or Ochinstan, as they called that land in Zanzib – and there were at least two inside, from Inhico and Farqtan, which the Sultan himself would not have disdained for one of the smaller rooms of his palace. But of course Abdullah could not say this. The manners of Zanzib did not let you praise yourself. Instead, he bowed a coldly shallow bow.

"It is possible that my low and squalid establishment might provide that which you seek, oh pearl of wanderers," he said, and cast his eye critically over the stranger's dirty desert robe, the corroded stud in the side of the man's nose and his tattered headcloth, as he said it.

"It is worse than squalid, mighty seller of floor-coverings," the stranger agreed. He flapped one end of his dingy carpet towards Jamal, who was frying squid just then in clouds of blue fishy smoke. "Does not the honourable activity of your neighbour penetrate your wares," he asked, "even to a lasting aroma of octopus?"

Abdullah seethed with such rage inside that he was forced to rub his hands together slavishly to hide it. People were not supposed to mention this sort of thing. And a slight smell of squid might even improve that thing the stranger wanted to sell, he thought, eyeing the drab and threadbare rug in the man's arms.

"Your humble servant takes care to fumigate the interior of his booth with lavish perfumes, oh prince of wisdom," he said. "Perhaps the heroic sensitivity of the prince's nose will nevertheless allow him to show this beggarly trader his merchandise?"

"Of course it does, oh lily among mackerel," the stranger retorted. "Why else should I stand here?"

Abdullah reluctantly parted the curtains and ushered the man inside his booth. There he turned up the lamp which hung from the centre pole, but, upon sniffing, decided that he was not going to waste incense on this person. The interior smelt quite strongly enough of yesterday's scents. "What magnificence have you to unroll before my unworthy eyes?" he asked dubiously.

"This, buyer of bargains!" the man said and, with a deft thrust of one arm, he caused the carpet to unroll across the floor.

Abdullah could do this too. A carpet merchant learnt these things. He was not impressed. He stuck his hands in his sleeves in a primly servile attitude and surveyed the merchandise. The carpet was not large. Unrolled, it was even dingier than he had thought – although the pattern was unusual, or it would have been if most of it had not been worn away. What was left was dirty and its edges were frayed.

"Alas, this poor salesman can only stretch to three copper coins for this most ornamental of rugs," he observed. "It is the limit of my slender purse. Times are hard, oh captain of many camels. Is the price acceptable in any way?"

"I'll take FIVE HUNDRED," said the stranger.

"*What?*" said Abdullah.

"GOLD coins," added the stranger.

"The king of all desert bandits is surely pleased to jest?" said Abdullah. "Or maybe, having found my small booth lacking in anything but the smell of frying squid, he wishes to leave and try a richer merchant?"

"Not particularly," said the stranger. "Although I will leave if you are not interested, oh neighbour of kippers. It is of course a magic carpet."

Abdullah had heard that one before. He bowed over his tucked-up hands. "Many and various are the virtues said to reside in carpets," he agreed. "Which one does the poet of the sands claim for this? Does it welcome a man home to his tent? Does it bring peace to the hearth? Or maybe," he said, poking the frayed edge suggestively with one toe, "it is said never to wear out?"

"It flies," said the stranger. "It flies wherever the owner commands, oh smallest of small minds."

Abdullah looked up into the man's sombre face, where the desert had entrenched deep lines down each cheek. A sneer made those lines deeper still. Abdullah found he disliked this person almost as much as he disliked his father's first wife's uncle's son. "You must convince this unbeliever," he said. "If the carpet can be put through its paces, oh monarch of mendacity, then some bargain might be struck."

"Willingly," said the tall man and stepped upon the carpet.

At this moment, one of the regular upsets happened at the fried-food stall next door. Probably some street boys had tried to steal some squid. At any rate, Jamal's dog burst out barking; various people, Jamal included, began yelling, and both sounds were nearly drowned by the clash of saucepans and the hissing of hot fat.

Cheating was a way of life in Zanzib. Abdullah did not allow his attention to be distracted for one instant from the stranger and his carpet. It was quite possible the man had bribed Jamal to cause a distraction. He had mentioned Jamal rather often, as if Jamal were on his mind. Abdullah kept his eyes sternly on the tall figure of the man and particularly on the dirty feet planted on the carpet. But he spared a corner of one eye for the man's face and he saw the man's lips move. His alert ears even caught the words "two feet upwards" despite the din from next door. And he looked even more carefully when the carpet rose smoothly from the floor and hovered about level with Abdullah's knees, so that the stranger's tattered headgear was not quite brushing the roof of the booth. Abdullah looked for rods underneath. He searched for wires that might have been deftly hooked to the roof. He took hold of the lamp and tipped it about, so that its light played both over and under the carpet.

The stranger stood with his arms folded and the sneer entrenched on his face while Abdullah performed these tests. "See?" he said. "Is the most desperate of doubters now convinced? Am I standing in the air, or am I not?" He had to shout rather. The noise was still deafening from next door.

Abdullah was forced to admit that the carpet did appear to be up in the air without any means of support that he could find. "Very nearly," he shouted back. "The next part of the demonstration is for you to dismount and for me to ride that carpet."

The man frowned. "Why so? What have your other senses to add to the evidence of your eyes, oh dragon of dubiety?"

"It could be a one-man carpet," Abdullah bawled. "As

some dogs are." Jamal's dog was still bellowing away outside, so it was natural to think of this. Jamal's dog bit anyone who touched it, except Jamal.

The stranger sighed. "Down," he said, and the carpet sank gently to the floor. The stranger stepped off and bowed Abdullah towards it. "It is yours to test, oh sheik of shrewdness."

With considerable excitement, Abdullah stepped on to the carpet. "Go up two feet," he said to it – or rather yelled. It sounded as if the constables of the City Watch had arrived at Jamal's stall now. They were clashing weapons and bawling to be told what had happened.

And the carpet obeyed Abdullah. It rose two feet in a smooth surge which left Abdullah's stomach behind it. He sat down rather hastily. The carpet was perfectly comfortable to sit on. It felt like a very tight hammock. "This woefully sluggish intellect is becoming convinced," he confessed to the stranger. "What was your price again, oh paragon of generosity? Two hundred silver?"

"Five hundred *gold*," said the stranger. "Tell the carpet to descend and we will discuss the matter."

Abdullah told the carpet, "Down, and land on the floor," and it did so, thus removing a slight nagging doubt in Abdullah's mind that the stranger had said something extra when Abdullah first stepped on it, which had been drowned in the din from next door. He bounced to his feet and the bargaining commenced.

"The utmost of my purse is one hundred and fifty gold,"

he explained, "and that is when I shake it out and feel all round the seams."

"Then you must fetch out your other purse or even feel under your mattress," the stranger rejoined. "For the limit of my generosity is four hundred and ninety-five gold and I would not sell at all but for the most pressing need."

"I might squeeze another forty-five gold from the sole of my left shoe," Abdullah replied. "That I keep for emergencies, and it is my pitiful all."

"Examine your right shoe," the stranger answered. "Four-fifty."

And so it went on. An hour later the stranger departed from the booth with two hundred and ten gold pieces, leaving Abdullah the delighted owner of what seemed to be a genuine – if threadbare – magic carpet. He was still mistrustful. He did not believe that anyone, even a desert wanderer with few needs, would part with a real flying carpet – albeit nearly worn out – for less than four hundred gold pieces. It was too useful – better than a camel, because it did not need to eat – and a good camel cost at least four hundred and fifty in gold.

There had to be a catch. And there was one trick Abdullah had heard of. It was usually worked with horses or dogs. A man would come and sell a trusting farmer or hunter a truly superb animal for a surprisingly small price, saying that it was all that stood between himself and starvation. The delighted farmer (or hunter) would put the horse in a stall (or the dog in a kennel) for the night. In the morning it would be gone, being trained to slip its halter (or collar) and return to its owner in the night. It seemed to Abdullah that a suitably obedient carpet could be trained to do the same. So, before he left his booth, he very carefully wrapped the magic carpet round one of the poles that supported the roof and bound it there, round and round, with a whole reel of twine, which he then tied to one of the iron stakes at the base of the wall.

"I think you'll find it hard to escape from that," he told it, and went out to discover what had been going on at the food stall.

The stall was quiet now, and tidy. Jamal was sitting on its counter, mournfully hugging his dog.

"What happened?" asked Abdullah.

"Some thieving boys spilt all my squid," Jamal said. "My whole day's stock down in the dirt, lost, gone!"

Abdullah was so pleased with his bargain that he gave Jamal two silver pieces to buy more squid. Jamal wept with gratitude and embraced Abdullah. His dog not only failed to bite Abdullah: it licked his hand. Abdullah smiled. Life was good. He went off whistling to find a good supper while the dog guarded his booth.

When the evening was staining the sky red behind the domes and minarets of Zanzib, Abdullah came back, still whistling, full of plans to sell the carpet to the Sultan himself for a very large price indeed. He found the carpet exactly where he had left it. Or would it be better to approach the Grand Vizir, he wondered while he was washing, and suggest that the Vizir might wish to make the Sultan a present of it? That way, he could ask for even more money. At the thought of how valuable that made the carpet, the story of the horse trained to slip its halter began to nag at him again. As he got into his nightshirt, Abdullah began to visualise the carpet wriggling free. It was old and pliable. It was probably very well trained. It could certainly slither out from behind the twine. Even if it did not, he knew the idea would keep him awake all night.

In the end, he carefully cut the twine away and spread the carpet on top of the pile of his most valuable rugs, which he always used as a bed. Then he put on his nightcap – which was necessary, because the cold winds blew off the desert and filled the booth with draughts – spread his blanket over him, blew out his lamp and slept.

CHAPTER TWO

In which Abdullah is mistaken for a young lady

He woke to find himself lying on a bank, with the carpet still underneath him, in a garden more beautiful than any he had imagined.

Abdullah was convinced that this was a dream. Here was the garden he had been trying to imagine when the stranger so rudely interrupted him. Here the moon was nearly full and riding high above, casting light as white as paint on a hundred small fragrant flowers in the grass around him. Round yellow lamps hung in the trees, dispelling the dense black shadows from the moon. Abdullah thought this was a very pleasing idea. By the two lights, white and yellow, he could see an arcade of creepers supported on elegant pillars, beyond the lawn where he lay; and from somewhere behind that, hidden water was quietly trickling.

It was so cool and so heaven-like that Abdullah got up and went in search of the hidden water, wandering down the arcade, where starry blooms brushed his face, all white and hushed in the moonlight, and bell-like flowers breathed out the headiest and gentlest of scents. As one does in dreams, Abdullah fingered a great waxy lily here, and detoured deliciously there into a dell of pale roses. He had never before had a dream that was anything like so beautiful.

The water, when he found it beyond some big fern-like bushes dripping dew, was a simple marble fountain in another lawn, lit by strings of lamps in the bushes which made the rippling water into a marvel of gold and silver crescents. Abdullah wandered towards it raptly.

There was only one thing needed to complete his rapture and, as in all the best dreams, it was there. An extremely lovely girl came across the lawn to meet him, treading softly on the damp grass with bare feet. The gauzy garments floating round her showed her to be slender, but not thin, just like the princess from Abdullah's daydream. When she was near Abdullah, he saw that her face was not quite a perfect oval as the face of his dream princess should have been, and nor were her huge dark eyes at all misty. In fact, they examined his face keenly, with evident interest. Abdullah hastily adjusted his dream, for she was certainly very beautiful. And when she spoke, her voice was all he could have desired, being light and merry as the water in the fountain and the voice of a very definite person too.

"Are you a new kind of servant?" she said.

People always did ask strange things in dreams, Abdullah thought. "No, masterpiece of my imagination," he said. "Know that I am really the long-lost son of a distant prince."

"Oh," she said. "Then that may make a difference. Does that mean you're a different kind of woman from me?"

Abdullah stared at the girl of his dreams in some perplexity. "*I'm* not a woman!" he said.

"Are you sure?" she asked. "You *are* wearing a dress."

Abdullah looked down and discovered that, in the way of dreams, he was wearing his nightshirt. "This is just my strange foreign garb," he said hastily. "My true country is far from here. I assure you that I am a man."

"Oh no," she said decidedly. "You can't be a man. You're quite the wrong shape. Men are twice as thick as you all over and their stomachs come out in a fat bit that's called a belly. And they have grey hair all over their faces and nothing but shiny skin on their heads. You've got hair on your head like me and almost none on your face." Then, as Abdullah put his hand rather indignantly to the six hairs on his upper lip, she asked, "Or have you got bare skin under your hat?"

"Certainly not," said Abdullah, who was proud of his thick wavy hair. He put his hand to his head and removed what turned out to be his nightcap. "Look," he said.

"Ah," she said. Her lovely face was puzzled. "You have hair that's almost as nice as mine. I don't understand."

"I'm not sure I do either," said Abdullah. "Could it be that you have not seen very many men?"

"Of course not," she said. "Don't be silly – I've only seen my father! But I've seen quite a lot of him, so I *do* know."

"But – don't you ever go out at all?" Abdullah asked helplessly.

She laughed. "Yes, I'm out now. This is my night garden. My father had it made so that I wouldn't ruin my looks going out in the sun."

"I mean, out into the town, to see all the people," Abdullah explained.

"Well, no, not yet," she admitted. As if that bothered her a little, she twirled away from him and went to sit on the edge of the fountain. Turning to look up at him, she said, "My father tells me I *might* be able to go out and see the town sometimes after I'm married – if my husband allows me to – but it won't be *this* town. My father's arranging for me to marry a prince from Ochinstan. Until then I have to stay inside these walls of course."

Abdullah had heard that some of the very rich people in Zanzib kept their daughters – and even their wives too – almost like prisoners inside their grand houses. He had many times wished someone would keep his father's first wife's sister Fatima that way. But now, in this dream, it seemed to him that this custom was entirely unreasonable and not fair on this lovely girl at all. Fancy not knowing what a normal young man looked like!

"Pardon my asking, but is the prince from Ochinstan perhaps old and a little ugly?" he said.

"Well," she said, evidently not quite sure, "my father says he's in his prime, just like my father is himself. But I believe the problem lies in the brutal nature of men. If another man saw me before the prince did, my father says he would instantly fall in love with me and carry me off, which would ruin all my father's plans, naturally. He says most men are great beasts. Are you a beast?"

"Not in the least," said Abdullah.

"I thought not," she said, and looked up at him with great concern. "You do not seem to me to be a beast. This makes me quite sure that you can't really be a man." Evidently she was one of those people who like to cling to a theory once they have made it. After considering a moment, she asked, "Could your family, perhaps, for reasons of their own, have brought you up to believe a falsehood?"

Abdullah would have liked to say that the boot was on the other foot, but, since that struck him as impolite, he simply shook his head and thought how generous of her it was to be so worried about him, and how the worry on her face only made it more beautiful – not to speak of the way her eyes shone compassionately in the gold and silver light reflecting from the fountain.

"Perhaps it has something to do with the fact that you are from a distant country," she said, and patted the edge of the fountain beside her. "Sit down and tell me all about it."

"Tell me your name first," said Abdullah.

"It's rather a silly name," she said nervously. "I'm called Flower-in-the-Night."

It was the perfect name for the girl of his dreams, Abdullah thought. He gazed down at her admiringly. "My name is Abdullah," he said.

"They even gave you a man's name!" Flower-in-the-Night exclaimed indignantly. "Do sit down and tell me."

Abdullah sat on the marble kerb beside her and thought that this was a very real dream. The stone was cold. Splashes from the fountain soaked into his nightshirt, while the sweet smell of rosewater from Flower-in-the-Night mingled most realistically with scents from the flowers in the garden. But since it was a dream, it followed that his daydreams were true here too. So Abdullah told her all about the palace he had lived in as a prince and how he was kidnapped by Kabul Aqba and escaped into the desert, where the carpet merchant found him.

Flower-in-the-Night listened with complete sympathy. "How terrifying! How exhausting!" she said. "Could it be that your foster father was in league with the bandits to deceive you?"

Abdullah had a growing feeling, despite the fact that he was only dreaming, that he was getting her sympathy on false pretences. He agreed that his father could have been in the pay of Kabul Aqba, and then changed the subject. "Let us get back to *your* father and his plans," he said. "It seems to me a little awkward that you should marry this prince from Ochinstan without having seen any other men to compare him to. How are you going to know whether you love him or not?"

"You have a point," she said. "This worries me too sometimes."

"Then I tell you what," Abdullah said. "Suppose I come back tomorrow night and bring you pictures of as many men as I can find? That should give you some standard to compare the prince with." Dream or not, Abdullah had absolutely no doubt that he would be back tomorrow. This would give him a proper excuse.

Flower-in-the-Night considered this offer, swaying dubiously back and forth with her hands clasped round her knees. Abdullah could almost see rows of fat bald men with grey beards passing in front of her mind's eye.

"I assure you," he said, "that men come in every sort of size and shape."

"Then that would be very instructive," she agreed. "At least it would give me an excuse to see you again. You're one of the nicest people I've ever met."

This made Abdullah even more determined to come back tomorrow. He told himself it would be unfair to leave her in such a state of ignorance. "And I think the same about you," he said shyly.

At this, to his disappointment, Flower-in-the-Night got up to leave. "I have to go indoors now," she said. "A first visit must last no longer than half an hour, and I'm almost sure you've been here twice as long as that. But now we know one another, you can stay at least two hours next time."

"Thank you. I shall," said Abdullah.

She smiled and passed away like a dream, beyond the fountain and behind two frondy flowering shrubs.

After that, the garden, the moonlight and the scents seemed rather tame. Abdullah could think of nothing better to do than wander back the way he had come. And there, on the moonlit bank, he found the carpet. He had forgotten about it completely. But since it was there in the dream too, he lay down on it and fell asleep.

He woke up some hours later with blinding daylight streaming in through the chinks in his booth. The smell of the day before yesterday's incense hanging about in the air struck him as cheap and suffocating. In fact the whole booth was fusty and frowsty and cheap. And he had earache because his nightcap seemed to have fallen off in the night. But at least, he found while he hunted for the nightcap, the carpet had not made off in the night. It was still underneath him. This was the one good thing he could see in what suddenly struck him as a thoroughly dull and depressing life.

Here Jamal, who was still grateful for the silver pieces, shouted outside that he had breakfast ready for both of them. Abdullah gladly flung back the curtains of the booth. Cocks crowed in the distance. The sky was glowing blue, and shafts of strong sunlight sliced through the blue dust and old incense inside the booth. Even in that strong light,

Abdullah failed to discover his nightcap. And he was more depressed than ever.

"Tell me, do you sometimes find yourself unaccountably sad on some days?" he asked Jamal as the two of them sat cross-legged in the sun outside to eat.

Jamal tenderly fed a piece of sugar pastry to his dog. "I would have been sad today," he said, "but for you. I think someone paid those wretched boys to steal. They were so thorough. And on top of that, the Watch fined me. Did I say? I think I have enemies, my friend."

Though this confirmed Abdullah's suspicions of the stranger who sold him the carpet, it was not much help. "Maybe," he said, "you should be more careful about whom you let your dog bite."

"Not I!" said Jamal. "I am a believer in free will. If my dog chooses to hate the whole human race except myself, it must be free to do so."

After breakfast, Abdullah looked for his nightcap again. It was simply not there. He tried thinking carefully back to the last time he truly remembered wearing it. That was when he lay down to sleep the previous night, when he was thinking of taking the carpet to the Grand Vizir. After that came the dream. He had found he was wearing the nightcap then. He remembered taking it off to show Flower-in-the-Night (what a lovely name!) that he was not bald. From then on, as far as he could recall, he had carried the nightcap in his hand until the moment when he had sat down beside her on the edge of the fountain. After that, when he recounted the history of his kidnapping by Kabul Aqba, he had a clear memory of waving both hands freely as he talked and he knew that the nightcap had not been in either one. Things did disappear like that in dreams, he knew, but the evidence pointed, all the same, to his having dropped it as he sat down. Was it possible he had left it lying on the grass beside the fountain? In which case—

Abdullah stood stock-still in the centre of the booth, staring into the rays of sunlight which, oddly enough, no longer seemed full of squalid motes of dust and old incense. Instead, they were pure golden slices of heaven itself.

"It was *not a dream*!" said Abdullah.

Somehow, his depression was clean gone. Even breathing was easier.

"It was *real*!" he said.

He went to stand thoughtfully looking down at the magic carpet. That had been in the dream too. In which case— "It follows that you transported me to some rich man's garden while I slept," he said to it. "Perhaps I spoke and ordered you to do so in my sleep. Very likely. I was thinking of gardens. You are even more valuable than I realised!"

CHAPTER THREE

In which Flower-in-the-Night discovers several important facts

Abdullah carefully tied the carpet round the roof pole again and went out into the Bazaar, where he sought out the booth of the most skilful of the various artists who traded there.

After the usual opening courtesies, in which Abdullah called the artist prince of the pencil and enchanter with chalks, and the artist retorted by calling Abdullah cream of customers and duke of discernment, Abdullah said, "I want drawings of every size, shape and kind of man that you have ever seen. Draw me kings and paupers, merchants and workmen, fat and thin, young and old, handsome and ugly, and also plain average. If some of these are kinds of men that you have never seen, I require you to invent them, oh paragon of the paintbrush. And if your invention fails, which I hardly think likely, oh aristocrat of artists, then all you need do is turn your eyes outward, gaze and copy!"

Abdullah flung out one arm to point to the teeming, rushing crowds shopping in the Bazaar. He was moved almost to tears at the thought that this everyday sight was something Flower-in-the-Night had never seen.

The artist drew his hand dubiously down his straggly beard. "For sure, noble admirer of mankind," he said. "This I can do easily. But could the jewel of judgement perhaps inform this humble draughtsman what these many portraits of men are needed for?"

"Why should the crown and diadem of the drawing board wish to know this?" Abdullah asked, rather dismayed.

"Assuredly, the chieftain of customers will understand that this crooked worm needs to know what medium to use," the artist replied. In fact, he was simply curious about this most unusual order. "Whether I paint in oils on wood or canvas, in pen upon paper or vellum, or even in fresco upon a wall, depends on what this pearl among patrons wishes to do with the portraits."

"Ah – paper, please," Abdullah said hastily. He had no wish to make his meeting with Flower-in-the-Night public. It was clear to him that her father must be a very rich man who would certainly object to a young carpet merchant showing her other men beside this prince of Ochinstan. "The portraits are for an invalid who has never been able to walk abroad as other men do."

"Then you are a champion of charity," said the artist, and he agreed to draw the pictures for a surprisingly small sum. "No, no, child of fortune, do not thank me," he said when Abdullah tried to express his gratitude. "My reasons are three. First, I have laid by me many portraits which I do for my own pleasure, and to charge you for those is not honest, since I would have drawn them anyway. Second, the task you set is ten times more interesting than my usual work, which is to do portraits of young women or their bridegrooms, or of horses and camels, all of whom I have to make handsome, regardless of reality; or else to paint rows of sticky children whose parents wish them to seem like angels – again regardless of reality. And my third reason is that I think you are mad, my most noble of customers, and to exploit you would be unlucky."

It became known almost immediately, all over the Bazaar, that young Abdullah the carpet merchant had lost his reason and would buy any portraits that people had for sale.

This was a great nuisance to Abdullah. For the rest of that day he was constantly being interrupted by persons arriving with long and flowery speeches about this portrait of their grandmother which only poverty would induce them to part with; or this portrait of the Sultan's racing camel which happened to fall off the back of a cart; or this locket containing a picture of their sister. It took Abdullah much time to get rid of these people – and on several occasions he did actually buy a painting or drawing, if the subject was a man. Which of course kept people coming.

"Only today. My offer extends only until sunset today," he told the gathering crowd at last. "Let all with a picture of a *man* for sale come to me an hour before sunset and I will buy. But only then."

This left him a few hours of peace in which to experiment with the carpet. He was wondering by now if he was right to think that his visit to the garden had been any more than a dream. For the carpet would not move. Abdullah had naturally tested it after breakfast by asking it to rise up two feet again, just to prove that it still would. And it simply lay on the floor. He tested it again when he came back from the artist's booth, and still it just lay there.

"Perhaps I have not treated you well," he said to it. "You have remained with me faithfully, in spite of my suspicions, and I have rewarded you by tying you round a pole. Would you feel better if I let you lie free on the floor, my friend? Is that it?"

He left the carpet on the floor, but it still would not fly. It might have been any old hearthrug.

Abdullah thought again, in between the times when people were pestering him to buy portraits. He went back to his suspicions of the stranger who had sold him this carpet and to the enormous noise that just happened to break out in Jamal's stall at the precise moment when the stranger ordered the carpet to rise. He recalled that he had seen the man's lips move both times, but had not heard all that was said.

"That is *it*!" he cried out, smashing his fist into his palm. "A code word needs to be spoken before it will move, which for reasons of his own – no doubt highly sinister – this man withheld from me. The villain! And this word I must have spoken in my sleep."

He rushed to the back of his booth and rummaged out the tattered dictionary he had once used at school. Then, standing on the carpet, he cried out, "Aardvark! Fly, please!"

Nothing happened, either then or for any word beginning with A. Doggedly, Abdullah went on to B, and when that did no good, he went on again, through the whole dictionary. With the constant interruptions from portrait sellers, this took him some time. Nevertheless, he reached *zymurgy* in the early evening without the carpet having so much as twitched.

"Then it has to be a made-up word or a foreign one!" he cried out feverishly. It was that, or believe that Flower-in-the-Night was only a dream after all. Even if she was real, his chances of getting the carpet to take him to her seemed slimmer by the minute. He stood there uttering every strange sound and every foreign word he could think of, and still the carpet made no move of any kind.

Abdullah was interrupted again an hour before sundown by a large crowd gathering outside, carrying bundles and big flat packages. The artist had to push his way through the crowd with his portfolio of drawings. The following hour was hectic in the extreme. Abdullah inspected paintings, rejected portraits of aunts and mothers, and beat down huge prices asked for bad drawings of nephews. In the course of that hour he acquired, beside the hundred excellent drawings from the artist, eighty-nine further pictures, lockets, drawings, and even a piece of a wall with a face daubed on it. He also parted with almost all the money he had left over after buying the magic carpet – if it *was* magic. By the time he finally convinced the man, who claimed that the oil painting of his fourth wife's mother was enough like a man to qualify, that this was not the case, and pushed him out of the booth, it was dark. He was by then too tired and wrought up to eat. He would have gone straight to bed had not Jamal – who had been doing a roaring trade selling snacks to the waiting crowd – arrived with tender meat on a skewer.

"I don't know what has got into you," Jamal said. "I used to think you were normal. But mad or not, you must eat."

"There is no question of madness," Abdullah said. "I have simply decided to go into a new line of business." But he ate the meat.

At last he was able to pile his hundred and eighty-nine pictures on to the carpet and lie down among them.

"Now listen to this," he told the carpet. "If by some lucky chance I happen to say your command-word in my sleep, you must instantly fly with me to the night garden of

Flower-in-the-Night." That seemed the best he could do. It took him a long time to get to sleep.

He woke to the dreamy fragrance of night flowers and a hand gently prodding him. Flower-in-the-Night was leaning over him. Abdullah saw she was far lovelier than he had been remembering her.

"You really did bring the pictures!" she said. "You are very kind."

I *did* it! Abdullah thought triumphantly. "Yes," he said. "I have one hundred and eighty-nine kinds of men here. I think this ought to give you at least a general idea."

He helped her unhook a number of the golden lamps and put them in a ring beside the bank. Then Abdullah showed her the pictures, holding them under a lamp first, and then leaning them up against the bank. He began to feel like a pavement artist.

Flower-in-the-Night inspected each man as Abdullah showed them, absolutely impartially and with great concentration. Then she picked up a lamp and inspected the artist's drawings all over again. This pleased Abdullah. The artist was a true professional. He had drawn men exactly as Abdullah asked, from a heroic and kingly person evidently taken from a statue, to the hunchback who cleaned shoes in the Bazaar, and had even included a self-portrait halfway through.

"Yes, I see," Flower-in-the-Night said at last. "Men do vary a lot, just as you said. My father is not at all typical – and neither are you of course."

"So you admit I am not a woman?" said Abdullah.

"I am forced to do so," she said. "I apologise for my error." Then she carried the lamp along the bank, inspecting certain of the pictures a third time.

Abdullah noticed, rather nervously, that the ones she had singled out were the handsomest. He watched her leaning over them with a small frown on her forehead and a curly tendril of dark hair straying over the frown, looking thoroughly intent. He began to wonder what he had started.

Flower-in-the-Night collected the pictures together and stacked them neatly in a pile beside the bank. "It is just as I thought," she said. "I prefer you to every single one of these. Some of these look far too proud of themselves and some look selfish and cruel. You are unassuming and kind. I intend to ask my father to marry me to you, instead of to the prince in Ochinstan. Would you mind?"

The garden seemed to swirl round Abdullah in a blur of gold and silver and dusky green. "I – I think that might not work," he managed to say at last.

"Why not?" she asked. "Are you married already?"

"No, no," he said. "It is not that. The law allows a man to have as many wives as he can afford, but—"

The frown came back to Flower-in-the-Night's forehead. "How many husbands are women allowed?" she asked.

"Only one!" Abdullah said, rather shocked.

"That is extremely unfair," Flower-in-the-Night observed, musingly. She sat on the bank and thought. "Would you say it is possible that the prince in Ochinstan has some wives already?"

Abdullah watched the frown grow on her forehead and the slender fingers of her right hand tapping almost irritably on the turf. He knew he had indeed started something. Flower-in-the-Night was discovering that her father had kept her ignorant of a number of important facts. "If he is a prince," Abdullah said rather nervously, "I think it entirely possible that he has quite a number of wives. Yes."

"Then he is being greedy," Flower-in-the-Night stated. "This takes a weight off my mind. Why did you say that my marrying you might not work? You mentioned yesterday that you are a prince as well."

Abdullah felt his face heating up, and he cursed himself for babbling out his daydream to her. Though he told himself that he had had every reason to believe he was dreaming when he told her, this did not make him feel any better. "True. But I also told you I was lost and far from my kingdom," he said. "As you might conjecture, I am now forced to make my living by humble means. I sell carpets in the Bazaar of Zanzib. Your father is clearly a very rich man. This will not strike him as a fitting alliance."

Flower-in-the-Night's fingers drummed quite angrily. "You speak as if it is my *father* who intends to marry you!" she said. "What is the matter? I love you. Do you not love me?"

She looked into Abdullah's face as she said this. He looked back into hers, into what seemed an eternity of big dark eyes. He found himself saying, "*Yes.*" Flower-in-the-Night smiled. Abdullah smiled. Several more moonlit eternities went by.

"I shall come with you when you leave here," Flower-in-the-Night said. "Since what you say about my father's attitude to you could well be true, we must get married first and tell my father afterwards. Then there is nothing he can say."

Abdullah, who had had some experience of rich men, wished he could be sure of that. "It may not be quite that simple," he said. "In fact, now I think about it, I am certain our only prudent course is to leave Zanzib. This ought to be easy, because I do happen to own a magic carpet – there it is, up on the bank. It brought me here. Unfortunately, it needs to be activated by a magic word which I seem only able to say in my sleep."

Flower-in-the-Night picked up a lamp and held it high so that she could inspect the carpet. Abdullah watched, admiring the grace with which she bent towards it. "It seems very old," she said. "I have read about such carpets. The command-word will probably be a fairly common word pronounced in an old way. My reading suggests these carpets were meant to be used quickly in an emergency, so the word will not be anything too out of the way. Why do you not tell me carefully everything you know about it? Between us we ought to be able to work it out."

From this Abdullah realised that Flower-in-the-Night – if you discounted the gaps in her knowledge – was both intelligent and very well educated. He admired her even more. He told her, as far as he knew them, every fact about the carpet, including the uproar at Jamal's stall which had prevented him hearing the command-word.

Flower-in-the-Night listened and nodded at each new fact. "So," she said, "let us leave aside the reason why someone should sell you a proven magic carpet and yet make sure you could not use it. That is such an odd thing to do that I feel sure we should think about it later. But let us first think about what the carpet does. You say it came down when you ordered it to. Did the stranger speak then?"

She had a shrewd and logical mind. Truly he had found a pearl among women, Abdullah thought. "I am quite sure he said nothing," he said.

"Then," said Flower-in-the-Night, "the command-word is only needed to start the carpet flying. After that, I see two possibilities. First, that the carpet will do as you say until it touches ground anywhere. Or second, that it will in fact obey your command until it is back at the place where it first started—"

"That is easily proved," Abdullah said. He was dizzy with admiration for her logic. "I think the second possibility is the correct one." He jumped on the carpet and cried experimentally, "Up, and back to my booth!"

"No, no! Don't! Wait!" Flower-in-the-Night cried out at the same instant.

But it was too late. The carpet whipped up into the air and then away sideways with such speed and suddenness that Abdullah was first thrown over on his back, with all the breath knocked out of him, and then found himself hanging half off over its frayed edge at what seemed a terrifying height in the air. The wind of its movement took his breath away as soon as he did manage to breathe. All he could do was to claw frantically for a better grip on the fringe at one end. And before he could work his way back on top of it, let alone speak, the carpet plunged downwards – leaving Abdullah's newly-gained breath high in the air above – barged its way through the curtains of the booth – half-smothering Abdullah in the process – and landed smoothly – and very finally – on the floor inside.

Abdullah lay on his face gasping, with dizzy memories of turrets whirling past him against a starry sky. Everything had happened so quickly that, at first, all he could think of was that the distance between his booth and the night garden must be quite surprisingly short. Then, as his breath did at last come back, he wanted to kick himself. What a *stupid* thing to have done! He could at least have waited until Flower-in-the-Night had had time to step on the carpet too. Now Flower-in-the-Night's own logic told him that there was no way to get back to her but to fall asleep again and, once more, hope he chanced to say the command-word in his sleep. But as he had already done it twice, he was fairly sure that he would. He was even more certain that Flower-in-the-Night would work this out for herself and wait in the garden for him. She was intelligence itself – a pearl among women. She would expect him back in an hour or so.

After an hour of alternately blaming himself and praising Flower-in-the-Night, Abdullah did manage to fall asleep. But, alas, when he woke he was still face down on the carpet in the middle of his own booth. Jamal's dog was barking outside, which was what had woken him up.

"Abdullah!" shouted the voice of his father's first wife's brother's son. "Are you awake in there?"

Abdullah groaned. This was all he needed.

CHAPTER FOUR

Which concerns marriage and prophecy

Abdullah could not think what Hakim was doing there. His father's first wife's relatives usually only came near him once a month, and they had paid that visit to him two days ago. "What do you want, Hakim?" he shouted wearily.

"To speak to you of course!" Hakim shouted back. "Urgently!"

"Then part the curtains and come in," said Abdullah.

Hakim inserted his plump body between the hangings. "I must say, if this is your vaunted security, son of my aunt's husband," he said, "I don't think much of it.

Anyone could come in here and surprise you as you slept."

"The dog outside warned me you were there," Abdullah said.

"What use is that?" asked Hakim. "What would you propose to do if I proved to be a thief? Strangle me with a carpet? No, I cannot approve the safety of your arrangements."

"What did you wish to say to me?" asked Abdullah. "Or did you only come here to find fault as usual?"

Hakim seated himself portentously on a pile of carpets. "You lack your normal scrupulous politeness, cousin by marriage," he said. "If my father's uncle's son were to hear you, he would not be pleased."

"I am not answerable to Assif for my behaviour or for anything else!" Abdullah snapped. He was thoroughly miserable. His soul cried out for Flower-in-the-Night, and he could not get to her. He had no patience with anything else.

"Then I shall not trouble you with my message," Hakim said, getting up haughtily.

"Good!" said Abdullah. He went to the back of his booth to wash.

But it was clear that Hakim was not going away without delivering his message. When Abdullah turned round from washing, Hakim was still standing there. "You would do well to change clothes and visit a barber, cousin by marriage," he told Abdullah. "At present you do not look a suitable person to visit our emporium."

"And why should I visit there?" Abdullah asked,

somewhat surprised. "You all made it clear long ago that I am not welcome."

"Because," said Hakim, "the prophecy made at your birth has come to light in a box long thought to contain incense. If you care to present yourself at the emporium in proper apparel, this box will be handed over to you."

Abdullah had not the slightest interest in this prophecy. Nor did he see why he had to go himself to collect it when Hakim could just as easily have brought it with him. He was about to refuse, when it occurred to him that if he succeeded in uttering the correct word in his sleep tonight (which he was confident he would, having done it twice before), then he and Flower-in-the-Night would in all probability be eloping together. A man should go to his wedding correctly clothed and washed and shaved. So, since he would be going to baths and barber anyway, he might as well drop in and collect the silly prophecy on his way back.

"Very well," he said. "You may expect me two hours before sunset."

Hakim frowned. "Why so late?"

"Because I have things to do, cousin by marriage," Abdullah explained. The thought of his coming elopement so overjoyed him that he smiled at Hakim and bowed with extreme politeness. "Though I lead a busy life that has little time left in it for obeying your orders, I shall be there, never fear."

Hakim continued to frown, and turned that frown on Abdullah back over his shoulder as he left. He was obviously both displeased and suspicious. Abdullah could not have cared less. As soon as Hakim was out of sight, he joyfully gave Jamal half his remaining money to guard his booth for the day. In return, he was forced to accept from the increasingly grateful Jamal a breakfast consisting of every delicacy on Jamal's stall. Excitement had taken away Abdullah's appetite. There was so much food that, in order not to hurt Jamal's feelings, Abdullah gave most of it secretly to Jamal's dog – which he did warily, because the dog was a snapper as well as a biter. The dog, however, seemed to share its master's gratitude. It thumped its tail politely, ate everything Abdullah offered, and then tried to lick Abdullah's face.

Abdullah dodged that piece of politeness. The dog's breath was laden with the scent of elderly squid. He patted it gingerly on its gnarled head, thanked Jamal, and hurried off into the Bazaar. There he invested his remaining cash in the hire of a handcart. This cart he loaded carefully with his best and most unusual carpets – his floral Ochinstan, the glowing mat from Inhico, the golden Farqtans, the glorious patterned ones from the deep desert, and the matched pair from distant Thayack – and wheeled them along to the big booths in the centre of the Bazaar where the richest merchants traded. For all his excitement, Abdullah was being practical. Flower-in-the-Night's father was clearly very rich. None but the wealthiest of men could afford the dowry for marrying a prince. It was therefore clear to Abdullah that he and Flower-in-the-Night would have to go very far away, or her father could make things very unpleasant for them. But it was also clear to Abdullah that Flower-in-the-Night was used to having the best of everything. She would not be happy roughing it. So Abdullah had to have money. He bowed before the merchant in the richest of the rich booths and, having called him treasure among traders and most majestic of merchants, offered him the floral Ochinstan carpet for a truly tremendous sum.

The merchant had been a friend of Abdullah's father. "And why, son of the Bazaar's most illustrious," he asked, "should you wish to part with what is surely, by its price, the gem of your collection?"

"I am diversifying my trade," Abdullah told him. "As you may have heard, I have been buying pictures and other forms of artwork. In order to make room for these, I am forced to dispose of the least valuable of my carpets. And it occurred to me that a seller of celestial weavings like yourself might consider helping the son of his old friend by taking off my hands this miserable flowery thing, at a bargain price."

"The contents of your booth should in future be choice indeed," the merchant said. "Let me offer you half what you ask."

"Ah, shrewdest of shrewd men," Abdullah said. "Even a bargain costs money. But for you I will reduce my price by two coppers."

It was a long hot day. But by the early evening,

Abdullah had sold all his best carpets for nearly twice as much as he had paid for them. He reckoned that he now had enough ready money to keep Flower-in-the-Night in reasonable luxury for three months or so. After that, he hoped either that something else would turn up, or that the sweetness of her nature would reconcile her to poverty. He went to the baths. He went to the barber. He called at the scent-maker and had himself perfumed with oils. Then he went back to his booth and dressed in his best clothes. These clothes, like the clothes of most merchants, had various cunning insets, pieces of embroidery and ornamental twists of braid that were not ornaments at all, but cleverly concealed purses for money. Abdullah distributed his newly earned gold among these hiding places and was ready at last. He went, not very willingly, along to his father's old emporium. He told himself that it would pass the time between now and his elopement.

It was a curious feeling to go up the shallow cedar steps and enter the place where he had spent so much of his childhood. The smell of it, the cedarwood and the spices and the hairy, oily scent of carpets, was so familiar that, if he shut his eyes, he could imagine he was ten years old again, playing behind a roll of carpet while his father bargained with a customer. But, with his eyes open, Abdullah had no such illusion. His father's first wife's sister had a regrettable fondness for bright purple. The walls, the trellis screens, the chairs for customers, the cashier's table and even the cash box had all been painted Fatima's favourite colour. Fatima came to meet him in a dress of the same colour.

"Why, Abdullah! How prompt you are and how smart you look!" she said, and her manner said she had expected him to arrive late and in rags.

"He looks almost as if he was dressed for his wedding!" Assif said, advancing too, with a smile on his thin bad-tempered face.

It was so rare to see Assif smiling that Abdullah thought for a moment that Assif had ricked his neck and was grimacing with pain. Then Hakim sniggered, which made Abdullah realise what Assif had just said. To his annoyance, he found he was blushing furiously. He was forced to bow politely in order to hide his face.

"There's no need to make the boy blush!" Fatima cried. Which of course made Abdullah's blush worse. "Abdullah, what is this rumour we hear that you are suddenly planning to deal in pictures?"

"And selling the best of your stock to make room for the pictures," added Hakim.

Abdullah ceased to blush. He saw he had been summoned here to be criticised. He was sure of it when Assif added reproachfully, "Our feelings are somewhat hurt, son of my father's niece's husband, that you did not seem to think *we* could oblige you by taking a few carpets off your hands."

"Dear relatives," said Abdullah, "I could not, of course, sell you my carpets. My aim was to make a profit and I could hardly mulct you, whom my father loved."

He was so annoyed that he turned round to go away again, only to find that Hakim had quietly shut and barred the doors.

"No need to stay open," Hakim said. "Let us be just family here."

"The poor boy!" said Fatima. "Never has he had more need of a family to keep his mind in order!"

"Yes, indeed," said Assif. "Abdullah, some rumours on the Bazaar state that you have gone mad. We do not like this."

"He's certainly behaving oddly," Hakim agreed. "We don't like such talk connected to a respectable family like ours."

This was worse than usual. Abdullah said, "There is nothing *wrong* with my mind. I know just what I am doing. And my aim is to cease giving you any chance to criticise me, probably by tomorrow. Meanwhile, Hakim told me to come here because you have found the prophecy that was made at my birth. Is this correct, or was it merely an excuse?" He had never been so rude to his father's first wife's relations before, but he was angry enough to feel they deserved it.

Oddly enough, instead of being angry with Abdullah in return, all three of his father's first wife's relations began hurrying excitedly round the emporium.

"Now where *is* that box?" said Fatima.

"Find it, find it!" said Assif. "It is the very words of the fortune teller his poor father brought to the bedside of his second wife an hour after Abdullah's birth. He must see it!"

"Written in your own father's hand," Hakim said to Abdullah. "The greatest treasure for you."

"*Here* it is!" said Fatima, triumphantly pulling a carved wooden box off a high shelf. She gave the box to Assif, who thrust it into Abdullah's hands.

"Open it, open it!" they all three cried excitedly.

Abdullah put the box down on the purple cashier's table and sprung the catch. The lid went back, bringing a musty smell from inside, which was perfectly plain and empty apart from a folded yellowish paper.

"Get it out! Read it!" said Fatima, in even greater excitement.

Abdullah could not see what the fuss was about, but he unfolded the paper. It had a few lines of writing on it, brown and faded, and definitely his father's. He turned towards the hanging lamp with it. Now that Hakim had shut the main doors, the general purpleness of the emporium made it hard to see in there.

"He can barely see!" said Fatima.

Assif said, "No wonder. There's no light in here. Bring him into the room at the back. The overhead shutters are open there."

He and Hakim took hold of Abdullah's shoulders and pushed and hustled him towards the back of the shop. Abdullah was so busy trying to read the pale and scribbly writing of his father that he let them push him until he was positioned under the big overhead louvres in the living room behind the emporium. That was better. Now he knew why his father had been so disappointed in him. The writing said:

> *These are the words of the wise fortune teller.*
> *"This son of yours will not follow you in your trade.*
> *Two years after your death, while he is still a very*
> *young man, he will be raised above all others in this*
> *land. As Fate decrees it, so I have spoken."*
> *My son's fortune is a great disappointment to me.*
> *Let Fate send me other sons to follow in my trade, or*
> *I have wasted forty gold pieces on this prophecy.*

"As you see, a great future awaits you, dear boy," said Assif.
Somebody giggled.

Abdullah looked up from the paper, a little bemused. There seemed to be a lot of scent in the air.

The giggle came again, two of it, from in front of him.

Abdullah's eyes snapped forward. He felt them bulge. Two extremely fat young women stood in front of him. They met his bulging eyes and giggled again, coyly. Both were dressed to kill in shiny satin and ballooning gauze – pink on the right, yellow on the left one – and hung with more necklaces and bracelets than seemed probable. In addition, the pink one, who was fattest, had a pearl dangling on her forehead, just below her carefully frizzed hair. The yellow one, who was only just not fattest, wore a sort of amber tiara and had even frizzier hair. Both wore a very large amount of make-up, which was, in both cases, a severe error.

As soon as they were sure Abdullah's attention was on them – and it was: he was riveted with horror – each girl drew a veil from behind her ample shoulders – a pink veil on the left and a yellow on the right – and draped it chastely across her head and face. "Greetings, dear husband!" they chorused from beneath the veils.

"*What!*" exclaimed Abdullah.

"We veil ourselves," said the pink one.

"Because you should not look at our faces," said the yellow one.

"Until we are married," finished the pink.

"There must be some mistake!" said Abdullah.

"Not in the least," said Fatima. "These are my niece's two nieces who are here to marry you. Didn't you hear me say I was going to look out for a couple of wives for you?"

The two nieces giggled again. "He's ever so handsome," said the yellow one.

After a fairly long pause, in which he swallowed hard and did his best to control his feelings, Abdullah said politely, "Tell me, oh relatives of my father's first wife, have you known of the prophecy which was made at my birth for a long time?"

"Ages," said Hakim. "Do you take us for fools?"

"Your dear father showed it to us," said Fatima, "at the time he made his will."

"And naturally we are not prepared to let your great good fortune take you away from the family," Assif explained. "We waited only for the moment when you ceased to follow your good father's trade – this surely being the signal for the Sultan to make you a Vizir or invite you to command his armies, or maybe to elevate you in some other way. Then we took steps to ensure that we shared in your good fortune. These two brides of yours are closely related to all three of us. You will naturally not neglect us as you rise. So, dear boy, it only remains for me to introduce you to the magistrate who, as you see, stands ready to marry you."

Abdullah had, up to now, been unable to look away from the billowing figures of the two nieces. Now he raised his eyes and met the cynical look of the Justice of the Bazaar, who was just stepping out from behind a screen with his Register of Marriages in his hands. Abdullah wondered how much he was being paid.

Abdullah bowed politely to the Justice. "I am afraid this is not possible," he said.

"Ah, I *knew* he would be unkind and disagreeable!" said Fatima. "Abdullah, think of the disgrace and disappointment to these poor girls, if you refuse them now! After they've come all this way, expecting to be married, and got all dressed up! How could you, nephew!"

"Besides, I've locked all the doors," said Hakim. "Don't think you can get away."

"I am sorry to hurt the feelings of two such spectacular young ladies—" Abdullah began.

The feelings of the two brides were hurt anyway. Each girl uttered a wail. Each put her veiled face in her hands and sobbed heavily.

"This is awful!" wept the pink one.

"I *knew* they should have asked him first!" cried the yellow one.

Abdullah discovered that the sight of females crying – particularly such large ones, who wobbled with it everywhere – made him feel terrible. He knew he was an oaf and a beast. He was ashamed. The situation was not the girls' fault. They had been used by Assif, Fatima and Hakim, just as Abdullah had been. But the chief reason he felt so beastly, and which made him truly ashamed, was that he just wanted them to stop, to shut up and stop wobbling. Otherwise he did not care two hoots for their feelings. If he compared them to Flower-in-the-Night, he knew they revolted him. The idea of marrying them stuck in his craw. He felt sick. But, just because they were whimpering and sniffing and flubbering in front of him, he found himself considering that three wives was perhaps not so many after all. The two of them would make companions for Flower-in-the-Night when they were all far from Zanzib and home. He would have to explain the situation to them and load them on to the magic carpet—

That brought Abdullah back to reason. With a bump. With the sort of bump a magic carpet might make if loaded with two such weighty females – always supposing it could even get off the ground with them on it in the first place. They were so very fat. As for thinking they would make companions for Flower-in-the-Night – phooey! She was intelligent, educated and kind, as well as being beautiful (and thin). These two had yet to show him that they had a brain cell between them. They wanted to be married and their crying was a way of bullying him into it. And they giggled. He had never heard Flower-in-the-Night giggle.

Here Abdullah was somewhat amazed to discover that he, really and truly, did love Flower-in-the-Night just as ardently as he had been telling himself he did – or more, because he now saw he respected her. He knew he would die without her. And if he agreed to marry these two fat nieces, he *would* be without her. She would call him greedy, like the prince in Ochinstan.

"I am very sorry," he said, above the loud sobbings. "You should really have consulted me first about this, oh relatives of my father's first wife, oh much honoured and most honest Justice. It would have saved this misunderstanding. I cannot marry yet. I have made a vow."

"*What* vow?" demanded everyone else, the fat brides included, and the Justice added, "Have you registered this vow? To be legal, all vows must be registered with a magistrate."

This was awkward. Abdullah thought rapidly. "Indeed, it *is* registered, oh veritable weighing-scale of judgement," he said. "My father took me to a magistrate to register the vow when he ordered me to make it. I was but a small child at the time. Though I did not understand then, I see now it was because of the prophecy. My father, being a prudent man, did not wish to see his forty gold coins wasted. He made me vow that I would never marry until Fate had placed me above all others in this land. So you see—" Abdullah put his hands in the sleeves of his best suit and bowed regretfully to the two fat brides, "I cannot yet marry you, twin plums of candied sugar, but the time will come."

Everyone said, "Oh, in *that* case—!" in various tones of discontent and, to Abdullah's profound relief, most of them turned away from him.

"I always thought your father was a rather grasping man," Fatima added.

"Even from beyond the grave," Assif agreed. "We must wait for this dear boy's elevation, then."

The Justice, however, stood his ground. "And which magistrate was it, before whom you made this vow?" he asked.

"I do not know his name," Abdullah invented, speaking with intense regret. He was sweating rather. "I was a tiny child, and he appeared to me an old man with a long white beard." That, he thought, would serve as a description of every magistrate there ever was, including the Justice standing before him.

"I shall have to check all records," the Justice said irritably. He turned to Assif, Hakim and Fatima and – rather coldly – made his formal goodbyes.

Abdullah left with him, almost clinging to the Justice's official sash in his hurry to get away from the emporium and the two fat brides.

CHAPTER FIVE

Which tells how Flower-in-the-Night's father wished to raise Abdullah above all others in the land

"What a day!" Abdullah said to himself, when he was back inside his booth at last. "If my luck goes on this way, I will not be surprised if I never get the carpet to move again!" Or, he thought as he lay down on the carpet, still dressed in his best, he might get to the night garden only to find that Flower-in-the-Night was too annoyed at his stupidity last night to love him any more. Or she might love him still, but have decided not to fly away with him. Or...

It took him a while to get to sleep.

But when he woke, everything was perfect. The carpet was just gliding to a gentle landing on the moonlit bank. So Abdullah knew he had said the command-word after all, and it was such a short while since he had said it that he *almost* had a memory of what it was. But it went clean out of his head when Flower-in-the-Night came running eagerly towards him, among the white scented flowers and the round yellow lamps.

"You're here!" she called as she ran. "I was quite worried!"

She was not angry. Abdullah's heart sang. "Are you ready to leave?" he called back. "Jump on beside me."

Flower-in-the-Night laughed delightedly – it was definitely no giggle – and came running on across the lawn. The moon seemed just then to go behind a cloud, because Abdullah saw her lit entirely by the lamps for a moment, golden and eager, as she ran. He stood up and held out his hands to her.

As he did so, the cloud came right down into the lamplight. And it was not a cloud but great black leathery wings, silently beating. A pair of equally leathery arms, with hands that had long fingernails like claws, reached from the shadow of those fanning wings and wrapped themselves round Flower-in-the-Night. Abdullah saw her jerk as those arms stopped her running. She looked round and up. Whatever she saw made her scream, one single, wild, frantic scream, which was cut off when one of the leathery arms changed position to clap its huge taloned hand over her face.

Flower-in-the-Night beat at the arm with her fists, and kicked and struggled, but all quite uselessly. She was lifted up, a small white figure against the huge blackness. The great wings silently beat again. A gigantic foot, with talons like the hands, pressed the turf a yard or so from the bank where Abdullah was still in the act of standing up, and a leathery leg flexed mighty calf muscles as the thing – whatever it was – sprang upright. For the merest instant, Abdullah found himself staring into a hideous leathery face with a ring through its hooked nose and long, upslanting eyes, remote and cruel. The thing was not looking at him. It was simply concentrating on getting itself and its captive airborne.

The next second, it was aloft. Abdullah saw it overhead for a heartbeat longer, a mighty flying djinn dangling a tiny pale human girl in its arms. Then the night swallowed it up. It all happened unbelievably quickly.

"After it! Follow that djinn!" Abdullah ordered the carpet.

The carpet seemed to obey. It bellied up from the bank. Then, almost as if someone had given it another command, it sank back and lay still.

"You moth-eaten doormat!" Abdullah screamed at it.

There was a shout from further down the garden. "This way, men! That scream came from up there!"

Along the arcade, Abdullah glimpsed moonlight on metal helmets and – worse still – golden lamplight on swords and crossbows. He did not wait to explain to these people why he had screamed. He flung himself flat on the carpet.

"Back to the booth!" he whispered to it. "Quickly! Please!"

This time the carpet obeyed, as quickly as it had the night before. It was up off the bank in an eyeblink and then hurtling sideways across a forbiddingly high wall. Abdullah had just a glimpse of a large party of northern mercenaries milling around in the lamplit garden, before he was speeding above the sleeping roofs and moonlit towers of Zanzib. He had barely time to reflect that Flower-in-the-Night's father must be even richer than he had thought – few people could afford that many hired soldiers, and mercenaries from the north were the most expensive kind – before the carpet planed downwards and brought him smoothly in through the curtains to the middle of his booth.

There he gave himself up to despair.

A djinn had stolen Flower-in-the-Night and the carpet refused to follow. He knew that was not surprising. A djinn, as everyone in Zanzib knew, commanded enormous powers in the air and the earth. No doubt the djinn had, as a precaution, ordered everything in the garden to stay where it was while he carried Flower-in-the-Night away. It had probably not even noticed the carpet, or Abdullah on it, but the carpet's lesser magic had been forced to give way to the djinn's command. So the djinn had stolen away Flower-in-the-Night, whom Abdullah loved more than his own soul, just at the moment when she was about to run into his arms, and there seemed nothing he could do.

He wept.

After that, he vowed to throw away all the money hidden

in his clothes. It was useless to him now. But before he did, he gave himself over to grief again, noisy misery at first, in which he lamented out loud and beat his breast in the manner of Zanzib; then, as cocks crew and people began moving about, he fell into silent despair. There was no point even in moving. Other people might bustle about and whistle and clank buckets, but Abdullah was no longer part of that life. He stayed crouching on the magic carpet, wishing he was dead.

So miserable was he, that it never occurred to him that he might be in any danger himself. He paid no attention when all the noises in the Bazaar stopped, like birds when a hunter enters a wood. He did not really notice the heavy marching of feet, nor the regular clank, clank, clank of mercenary armour that went with it. When someone barked, "*Halt!*" outside his booth, he did not even turn his head. But he did turn round when the curtains of the booth were torn down. He was sluggishly surprised. He blinked his swollen eyes against the powerful sunlight and wondered vaguely what a troop of northern soldiers was doing coming in here.

"That's him," said someone in civilian clothes, who might have been Hakim, and then faded prudently away before Abdullah's eyes could focus on him.

"You!" snapped the squad leader. "Out. With us."

"What?" said Abdullah.

"Fetch him," said the leader.

Abdullah was bewildered. He protested feebly when they dragged him to his feet and twisted his arms to make him walk. He went on protesting as they marched him at the double – clank-clank, clank-clank – out of the Bazaar and into the West Quarter. Before long, he was protesting very strongly indeed. "What is this?" he panted. "I demand – as a citizen – where we are – going!"

"Shut up. You'll see," they answered. They were too fit to pant.

A short while after, they ran Abdullah in under a massive stone gate, made of blocks of stone that glared white in the sun, into a blazing courtyard, where they spent five minutes outside an oven-like smithy loading Abdullah with chains. He protested even more. "What is this for? Where *is* this? I demand to know!"

"Shut *up*!" said the squad leader. He remarked to his second-in-command, in his barbarous northern accent, "They always *whinge* so, these Zanzibbeys. Got no notion of dignity."

While the squad leader was saying this, the smith, who was from Zanzib too, murmured to Abdullah, "The Sultan wants you. I don't think much to your chances, either. Last one I chained like this got crucified."

"*But I haven't done anyth—!*" protested Abdullah.

"SHUT UP!" screamed the squad leader. "Finished, smith? Right. *At* the double!" And they ran Abdullah off again, across the glaring yard and into the large building beyond.

Abdullah would have said it was impossible even to walk in those chains. They were so heavy. But it is wonderful what you can do if a party of grim-faced soldiers are quite set on making you do it. He ran, clank-chankle, clank-chankle, clash, until at last, with an exhausted jingle, he arrived at the foot of a high raised seat made of cool blue and gold tiles and piled with cushions. There the soldiers all went down on one knee, in a distant, decorous way, as northern soldiers did to the person who was paying them.

"Present prisoner Abdullah, m'lord Sultan," the squad leader said.

Abdullah did not kneel. He followed the customs of Zanzib and fell on his face. Besides, he was exhausted and it was easier to fall down with a mighty clatter than do anything else. The tiled floor was blessedly, wonderfully cool.

"Make the son of a camel's excrement kneel," said the Sultan. "Make the creature look us in the face." His voice was low, but it trembled with anger.

A soldier hauled on the chains and two others pulled on Abdullah's arms until they had got him sort of bent on his knees. They held him that way and Abdullah was glad. He would have crumpled up in horror otherwise. The man lounging on the tiled throne was fat and bald and wore a bushy grey beard. He was slapping at a cushion in a way that looked idle, but was really bitterly angry, with a white cotton thing that had a tassel on top. It was this tasselled thing that made Abdullah see what trouble he was in. The thing was his own nightcap.

"Well, dog from a muck heap?" said the Sultan. "Where is my daughter?"

"I have no idea," Abdullah said miserably.

"Do you deny," said the Sultan, dangling the nightcap as if it were a severed head he was holding up by its hair, "do you *deny* that this is your nightcap? Your name is inside it, you miserable salesman! It was found by me – by *us* in person! – inside my daughter's trinket box, along with eighty-two portraits of common persons, which had been hidden by my daughter in eighty-two cunning places. Do you deny that you crept into my night garden and presented my daughter with these portraits? Do you deny that you then stole my daughter away?"

"Yes, I do deny that!" said Abdullah. "I do not deny, oh most exalted defender of the weak, the nightcap or the pictures – although I must point out that your daughter is cleverer in hiding than you are in finding, great wielder of wisdom, for I gave her in fact one hundred and seven more pictures than you have discovered – but I have most certainly not stolen Flower-in-the-Night away. She was snatched from before my very eyes by a huge and hideous djinn. I have no more idea than your most celestial self where she is now."

"A likely story!" said the Sultan. "Djinn indeed! Liar! Worm!"

"I swear it is true!" Abdullah cried out. He was in such despair by now that he hardly cared what he said. "Get any holy object you like and I swear to the djinn on it. Have me enchanted to tell the truth and I will still say the same, oh mighty crusher of criminals. For it is the truth. And since I am probably far more desolated than yourself by the loss of your daughter, great Sultan, glory of our land, I implore you to kill me now and spare me a life of misery!"

"I will willingly have you executed," said the Sultan. "But first tell me where she is."

"But I have *told* you, wonder of the world!" said Abdullah. "I do not know where she is."

"Take him away," the Sultan said with great calmness to his kneeling soldiers. They sprang up readily and pulled Abdullah to his feet. "Torture the truth out of him," the Sultan added. "When we find her, you can kill him, but have him linger until then. I daresay the Prince of Ochinstan will accept her as a widow if I double the dowry."

"You mistake, sovereign of sovereigns!" Abdullah gasped as the soldiers clattered him across the tiles. "I have no idea where the djinn went, and my great sorrow is that he took her before we had any chance to get married."

"*What?*" shouted the Sultan. "Bring him back!" The soldiers at once trailed Abdullah and his chains back to the tiled seat, where the Sultan was now leaning forwards and glaring. "Did my clean ear become soiled by hearing you say you are *not* married to my daughter, filth?" he demanded.

"That is correct, mighty monarch," said Abdullah. "The djinn came before we could elope."

The Sultan glared down at him in what seemed to be horror. "This is the truth?"

"I swear," said Abdullah, "that I have not yet so much as kissed your daughter. I had intended to seek out a magistrate as soon as we were far from Zanzib. I know what is proper. But I also felt it proper to make sure first that Flower-in-the-Night indeed wished to marry me. Her decision struck me as made in ignorance, despite the hundred and eighty-nine pictures. If you will forgive me saying so, protector of patriots, your method of bringing up your daughter is decidedly unsound. She took me for a woman when she first saw me."

"So," said the Sultan musingly, "when I set soldiers to catch and kill the intruder in the garden last night, it could have been disastrous. You fool," he said to Abdullah, "slave and mongrel who dares to criticise! Of course I had to bring my daughter up as I did. The prophecy made at her birth was that she would marry the first man, apart from me, that she saw!"

Despite the chains, Abdullah straightened up. For the first time that day he felt a twinge of hope.

The Sultan was staring down the gracefully tiled and ornamented room, thinking. "The prophecy suited me very well," he remarked. "I had long wished for an alliance with the countries of the north, for they have better weapons than we can make here, some of those weapons being truly sorcerous, I understand. But the princes of Ochinstan are very hard to pin down. So all I had to do – so I thought – was to isolate my daughter from any possibility of seeing a man – and naturally give her the best of educations otherwise, to make sure she could sing and dance and make herself pleasing to a prince. Then, when my daughter was of marriageable age, I invited the prince here on a visit of state. He was to come here next year, when he had finished subduing a land he had just conquered with those same excellent weapons. And I knew that as soon as my daughter set eyes on him, the prophecy would make sure that I had him!" His eyes turned balefully down on Abdullah. "Then my plans are upset by an insect like you!"

"That is unfortunately true, most prudent of rulers," Abdullah admitted. "Tell me, is this prince of Ochinstan by any chance somewhat old and ugly?"

"I believe him to be hideous in the same northern fashion as these mercenaries," the Sultan said, at which Abdullah sensed the soldiers, most of whom ran to freckles and reddish hair, stiffened rather. "Why do you ask, dog?"

"Because, if you will forgive further criticism of your great wisdom, oh nurturer of our nation, this seems somewhat unfair on your daughter," Abdullah observed. He felt the eyes of the soldiers turn to him, wondering at his daring. Abdullah did not care. He felt he had little to lose.

"Women do not count," said the Sultan. "Therefore it is impossible to be unfair to them."

"I disagree," said Abdullah, at which the soldiers stared even harder.

The Sultan glowered down at him. His powerful hands wrung the nightcap as if it were Abdullah's neck. "Be silent, you diseased toad!" he said. "Or you will make me forget myself and order your instant execution!"

Abdullah relaxed a little. "Oh absolute sword among

the citizens, I implore you to kill me now," he said. "I have transgressed and I have sinned and I have trespassed in your night garden—"

"Be quiet," said the Sultan. "You know perfectly well I *can't* kill you until I have found my daughter and made sure she marries you."

Abdullah relaxed further. "Your slave does not follow your reasoning, oh jewel of judgement," he protested. "I demand to die now."

The Sultan practically snarled at him. "If I have learnt one thing," he said, "from this sorry business, it is that even I, Sultan of Zanzib though I am, cannot cheat Fate. That prophecy will get itself fulfilled somehow, I know that. Therefore, if I wish my daughter to marry the Prince of Ochinstan, I must first go along with the prophecy."

Abdullah relaxed almost completely. He had naturally seen this straight away, but he had been anxious to make sure the Sultan had worked it out too. And he had. Clearly Flower-in-the-Night inherited her logical mind from her father.

"So where is my daughter?" asked the Sultan.

"I have told you, oh sun shining upon Zanzib," said Abdullah. "The djinn—"

"I do not for a moment believe in the djinn," said the Sultan. "It is far too convenient. You must have hidden the girl somewhere. Take him away," he said to the soldiers, "and shut him in the safest dungeon we have. Leave the chains on him. He must have used some form of enchantment to get into the garden and he can probably use it to escape unless we are careful."

Abdullah was unable to avoid flinching at this. The Sultan noticed. He smiled nastily. "Then," he said, "I want a house-to-house search made for my daughter. She is to be brought to the dungeon for the wedding as soon as she is found." His eyes turned musingly back to Abdullah. "Until then," he said, "I shall entertain myself by inventing new ways to kill you. At the moment, I favour impaling you upon a forty-foot stake and then loosing vultures to eat bits off you. But I could change my mind if I think of something worse."

As the soldiers dragged him away, Abdullah nearly despaired again. He thought of the prophecy made at his own birth. A forty-foot stake would raise him above all others in the land very nicely.

Chapter Six

Which shows how Abdullah went from the frying pan into the fire

They put Abdullah in a deep and smelly dungeon where the only light came through a tiny grating high up in the ceiling – and that light was not daylight. It probably came from a distant window at the end of a passage on the floor above, where the grating was part of the floor.

Knowing that this was what he had to look forward to, Abdullah tried, as the soldiers dragged him away, to fill his eyes and mind with images of light. In the pause while the soldiers were unlocking the outside door to the dungeons, he looked up and around. They were in a dark little courtyard with blank walls of stone standing like cliffs all about it. But if he tipped his head right back, Abdullah could just see a slender spire in the mid-distance, outlined against the rising gold of morning. It amazed him to see that it was only an hour after dawn. Above the spire, the sky was deep blue with just one cloud standing peacefully in it. Morning was still flushing the cloud red and gold, giving it the look of a high-piled castle with golden windows. Golden light caught the wings of a white bird circling the spire. Abdullah was sure this was the last beauty he would ever see in his life. He stared backwards at it as the soldiers lugged him inside.

He tried to treasure this image when he was locked in the cold grey dungeon, but it was impossible. The dungeon was another world. For a long time he was too miserable even to notice how cramped he was in his chains. When he did notice, he shifted and clanked about on the cold floor, but it did not help very much.

"I have to look forward to a lifetime of this," he told himself. "Unless someone rescues Flower-in-the-Night, of course." That did not seem likely, since the Sultan refused to believe in the djinn.

After this, he tried to stave off despair with his daydream. But somehow, thinking of himself as a prince who had been kidnapped helped not at all. He knew it was untrue, and he kept thinking guiltily that Flower-in-the-Night had believed him when he told her. She must have decided to marry him because she thought he was a prince – being a princess herself, as he now knew. He simply could not imagine himself ever daring to tell her the truth. For a while, it seemed to him that he deserved the worst fate the Sultan could invent for him.

Then he began thinking of Flower-in-the-Night herself. Wherever she was, she was certainly at least as scared and miserable as he was himself. Abdullah yearned to comfort her. He wanted to rescue her so much that he spent some time wrenching uselessly at his chains.

"For certainly nobody *else* is likely to try," he muttered. "I must get *out* of here!"

Then, although he was sure it was another notion as silly as his daydream, he tried to summon the magic carpet. He visualised it lying on the floor of his booth and he called to it, out loud, over and over again. He said all the magic-sounding words he could think of, hoping one of them would be the command-word.

Nothing happened. And how silly to think that it would! Abdullah thought. Even if the carpet could hear him from the dungeon, supposing he got the command-word right at last, how could even a magic carpet wriggle its way in here through the tiny grating? And suppose it *did* wriggle in, how would that help Abdullah to get out?

Abdullah gave up and leant against the wall, half-dozing, half-despairing. It must now be the heat of the day, when most folk in Zanzib took at least a short rest. Abdullah himself, when he was not visiting one of the public parks, usually sat on a pile of his less good carpets in the shade in front of his stall, drinking fruit juice, or wine if he could afford it, and chatting lazily with Jamal. No longer. And this is just my first day! he thought morbidly. I'm keeping track of the hours now. How long before I lose track even of days?

He shut his eyes. One good thing. A house-to-house search for the Sultan's daughter would cause at least some annoyance to Fatima, Hakim and Assif, simply because they were known to be the only family Abdullah had. He hoped soldiers turned the purple emporium upside down. He hoped they slit the walls and unrolled all the carpets. He hoped they arrested—

Something landed on the floor beyond Abdullah's feet.

So they throw me some food, Abdullah thought, and I would rather starve. He opened his eyes lazily. They shot wide of their own accord.

There, on the dungeon floor, lay the magic carpet. Upon it, peacefully sleeping, lay Jamal's bad-tempered dog.

Abdullah stared at both of them. He could imagine how, in the heat of midday, the dog might lie down in the shade of Abdullah's booth. He could see that it would lie on the carpet because it was comfortable. But how a dog – a *dog*! – could chance to say the command-word was beyond him to understand entirely. As he stared, the dog began dreaming. Its paws worked. Its snout wrinkled, and it snuffled, as if it had caught the most delicious possible scent, and it uttered a faint whimper, as if whatever it smelt in the dream was escaping from it.

"Is it possible, my friend," Abdullah said to it, "that you were dreaming of me, and of the time I gave you most of my breakfast?"

The dog, in its sleep, heard him. It uttered a loud snore and woke up. Dog-like, it wasted no time wondering how it came to be in this strange dungeon. It sniffed, and smelt Abdullah. It sprang up with a delighted squeak, planted its paws among the chains on Abdullah's chest and enthusiastically licked his face.

Abdullah laughed and rolled his head to keep his nose out of the dog's squiddy breath. He was quite as delighted as the dog was. "So you *were* dreaming of me!" he said. "My friend, I shall arrange for you to have a bowl of squid daily. You have saved my life and possibly Flower-in-the-Night's too!"

As soon as the dog's rapture had abated a little, Abdullah began rolling and working himself along the floor in his chains, until he was lying, propped on one elbow, on top of the carpet. He gave a great sigh. Now he was safe. "Come along," he said to the dog. "Get on the carpet too."

But the dog had found the scent of what was certainly a rat in the corner of the dungeon. It was pursuing the smell with excited snorts. At each snort, Abdullah felt the carpet quiver beneath him. It gave him the answer he needed.

"Come along," he said to the dog. "If I leave you here, they will find you when they come to question me, and they will assume I have turned myself into a dog. Then my fate will be yours. You have brought me the carpet and revealed to me its secret and I cannot see you stuck on a forty-foot stake."

The dog had its nose rammed into the corner. It was not attending. Abdullah heard, unmistakable even through the thick walls of the dungeon, the tramp of feet and the rattle of keys. Someone was coming. He gave up persuading the dog. He lay flat on the carpet.

"Here, boy!" he said. "Come and lick my face!"

The dog understood that. It left the corner, jumped on Abdullah's chest and proceeded to obey him.

"Carpet," Abdullah whispered from under the busy tongue. "To the Bazaar, but do not land. Hover beside Jamal's stall."

The carpet rose and rushed sideways – which was just as well. Keys were unlocking the dungeon door. Abdullah was not any too sure how the carpet left the dungeon because the dog was still licking his face and he was forced to keep his eyes shut. He felt a dank shadow pass across him – perhaps that was when they melted through the wall – and then bright sunlight. The dog lifted its head into the sunlight, puzzled. Abdullah squinted sideways across the chains and saw a high wall rear in front of them and then fall below as the carpet rose smoothly over it. Then came a succession of towers and roofs, quite familiar to Abdullah though he had only seen them by night before. And after that the carpet went planing down towards the outer edge of the Bazaar. For the palace of the Sultan was indeed only five minutes' walk from Abdullah's booth.

Jamal's stall came into view and, beside it, Abdullah's own wrecked booth, with carpets flung all over the walkway. Obviously soldiers had searched there for Flower-in-the-Night. Jamal was dozing, with his head on his arms, between a big simmering pot of squid and a charcoal grill with skewered meat smoking on it. He raised his head and his one eye stared as the carpet came to hang in the air in front of him.

"Down, boy!" Abdullah said. "Jamal, call your dog."

Jamal was clearly very scared. It is no fun keeping the stall next door to anyone a Sultan wishes to impale on a stake. He seemed speechless. Since the dog was taking no notice of either, Abdullah struggled into sitting position, clanking, rattling and sweating. This tipped the dog off. It jumped nimbly to the stall counter, where Jamal absently seized it in his arms.

"What do you want me to do?" he asked, eyeing the chains. "Shall I fetch the blacksmith?"

Abdullah was touched at this proof of Jamal's friendship. But sitting up had given him a view down the walkway between the stalls. He could see the soles of running feet down there and flying garments. It seemed that one boothkeeper was on his way to fetch the Watch – though there was something about the running figure that reminded Abdullah rather strongly of Assif. "No," he said. "There's no time." Clanking, he wriggled his left leg over to the edge of the carpet. "Do this for me instead. Put your hand on the embroidery above my left boot."

Jamal obediently stretched out a brawny arm and, very gingerly, touched the embroidery. "Is it a spell?" he asked nervously.

"No," said Abdullah. "It's a hidden purse. Put your hand in and take the money out of it."

Jamal was puzzled, but his fingers groped, found the way into the purse and came out as a fist full of gold. "There's a fortune here," he said. "Will this buy your freedom?"

"No," said Abdullah. "Yours. They'll be after you and your dog for helping me. Take the gold and the dog and get out. Leave Zanzib. Go north to the barbarous places where you can hide."

"North!" said Jamal. "But whatever can I do in the north?"

"Buy everything you need and set up a Rashpuhti restaurant," said Abdullah. "There's enough gold to do it and you're an excellent cook. You could make your fortune there."

"Really?" said Jamal, staring from Abdullah to his handful of money. "You really think I could?"

Abdullah had been keeping a wary eye on the walkway. Now he saw the space fill, not with the Watch but with northern mercenaries, and they were running. "Only if you go now," he said.

Jamal caught the clank-clank of running soldiers. He leaned out to look and make sure. Then he whistled his dog and was gone, so swiftly and quietly that Abdullah could only admire. Jamal had even spared time to move the meat off the grill so that it would not burn. All the soldiers were going to find here was a cauldron of half-boiled squid.

Abdullah whispered to the carpet. "To the desert. Fast!"

The carpet was off at once, with its usual sideways

rush. Abdullah thought he certainly would have been thrown off it, but for the weight of his chains, which caused the carpet to bulge downwards in the centre, rather like a hammock. And speed was necessary. The soldiers shouted behind him. There were some loud bangs. For a few instants, two bullets and a crossbow bolt carved the blue sky beside the carpet, and then fell behind. The carpet hurtled on, across roofs, over walls, beside towers, and then skimming palm trees and market gardens. Finally it shot forth into hot grey emptiness, shimmering white and yellow under a huge bowl of sky, where Abdullah's chains began to grow uncomfortably warm.

The rushing of air stopped. Abdullah raised his head and saw Zanzib as a surprisingly small clump of towers on the horizon. The carpet sailed slowly past a person riding a camel, who turned his well-veiled face to watch. It began to sink towards the sand. At this, the person on the camel turned his camel too and urged it into a trot after the carpet. Abdullah could almost *see* him thinking gleefully that here was his chance to get his hands on a genuine, working magic carpet, and its owner in chains and in no position to resist him.

"Up, up!" he almost shrieked at the carpet. "Fly north!"

The carpet lumbered up into the air again. Annoyance and reluctance breathed from every thread of it. It turned in a heavy half-circle and sailed gently northwards at walking pace. The person on the camel cut across the middle of the half-circle and came on at a gallop. Since the carpet was only about nine feet in the air, it was a sitting target for someone on a galloping camel.

Abdullah saw it was time for some quick talking. "Beware!" he shouted at the camel rider. "Zanzib has cast me out in chains for fear I spread the plague I have!" The rider was not quite fooled. He reined in his camel and followed at a more cautious pace, while he wrestled a tent pole out of his baggage. Clearly he intended to tip Abdullah off the carpet with it. Abdullah turned his attention hastily to the carpet. "Oh most excellent of carpets," he said, "oh brightest coloured and most delicately woven, whose lovely textile is so cunningly enhanced with magic, I fear I have not treated you hitherto with proper respect. I have snapped commands and even shouted at you, where I now see that your gentle nature requires only the mildest of requests. Forgive, oh forgive!"

The carpet appreciated this. It stretched tighter in the air and put on a bit of speed.

"And, dog that I am," continued Abdullah, "I have caused you to labour in the heat of the desert, weighted most dreadfully with my chains. Oh best and most elegant of carpets, I think now only of you and how best I might rid you of this great weight. If you were to fly at a gentle speed – say, only a little faster than a camel might gallop – to the nearest spot in the desert northward where I can find someone to remove these chains, would this be agreeable to your amiable and aristocratic nature?"

He seemed to have struck the right note. A sort of smug

pridefulness exuded from the carpet now. It rose a foot or so, changed direction slightly, and moved forwards at a purposeful seventy miles an hour. Abdullah clung to its edge and peered backwards at the frustrated camel rider, who was soon dwindling to a dot in the desert behind.

"Oh most noble of artefacts, you are Sultan among carpets and I am your miserable slave!" he said shamelessly.

The carpet liked this so much that it went even faster.

Ten minutes later, it surged over a sand dune and came to an abrupt stop just below the summit on the other side. Slanting. Abdullah was rolled helplessly off in a cloud of sand. And he went on rolling, clattering, jingling, bounding, raising more sand, and then – after desperate efforts – tobogganing feet first in a groove of sand, down to the very edge of a small muddy pool in an oasis. A number of ragged people, who were crouching over something at the edge of this pool, sprang up and scattered as Abdullah ploughed in among them. Abdullah's feet caught the thing they were crouching over and shot it back into the pool. One man shouted indignantly and went splashing into the water to rescue it. The rest drew sabres and knives – and in one case a long pistol – and surrounded Abdullah threateningly.

"Cut his throat," said one.

Abdullah blinked sand out of his eyes and thought he had seldom seen a more villainous crew of men. They all had scarred faces, shifty eyes, bad teeth and unpleasant expressions. The man with the pistol was the most unpleasant of the lot. He wore a sort of earring through one side of his large hooked nose and a very bushy moustache. His headcloth was pinned up at one side with a flashy red stone in a gold brooch.

"Where have you sprung from?" this man said. He kicked Abdullah. "Explain yourself."

All of them, including the man who was wading out of the pool with some kind of bottle, looked at Abdullah with expressions that said his explanation had better be good.

Or else.

CHAPTER SEVEN

Which introduces the genie

Abdullah blinked more sand out of his eyes and stared earnestly at the man with the pistol. The man really was the absolute image of the villainous bandit of his daydream. It must be one of those coincidences.

"I beg your pardon a hundred times, gentlemen of the desert," he said, with great politeness, "for intruding on you in this manner, but am I addressing the most noble and world-famous bandit, the matchless Kabul Aqba?"

The other villainous men around him seemed astonished. Abdullah distinctly heard one say, "How did he know that?" But the man with the pistol simply sneered. It was something his face was particularly well designed to do. "I am indeed he," he said. "Famous, am I?"

It *was* one of those coincidences, Abdullah thought. Well, at least he knew where he was now. "Alas, wanderers in the wilderness," he said, "I am, like your noble selves, one who is outcast and oppressed. I have sworn revenge on all Rashpuht. I came here expressly to join with you and add the strength of my mind and my arm to yours."

"Did you indeed?" said Kabul Aqba. "And how did you get here? By dropping from the sky, chains and all?"

"By magic," Abdullah said modestly. He thought it was the thing most likely to impress these people. "I did indeed drop from the sky, noblest of nomads."

Unfortunately, they did not seem impressed. Most of them laughed. Kabul Aqba, with a nod, sent two of them up the sand dune to examine Abdullah's point of arrival. "So you can work magic?" he said. "Do these chains you wear have anything to do with that?"

"Certainly," said Abdullah. "Such a mighty magician am I that the Sultan of Zanzib himself loaded me with chains for very fear of what I could do. Only strike these chains apart and undo these handcuffs and you will see great things." Out of the corner of his eye, he saw the two men returning, carrying the carpet between them. He hoped very much that this was a good thing to happen. "Iron, as you know, inhibits a magician in the use of magic," he said earnestly. "Feel free to strike it off me and see a new life open before you."

The rest of the bandits looked at him dubiously. "We

haven't got a cold chisel," said one. "Or a mallet."

Kabul Aqba turned to the two men with the carpet. "There was only this," they reported. "No sign of anything to ride. No tracks."

At this, the chief bandit stroked his moustache. Abdullah found himself wondering if it ever got tangled with his nose ring. "Hm," he said. "Then I'll lay odds it's a magic carpet. I'll have it here." He turned sneeringly to Abdullah. "Sorry to disappoint you, Magician," he said, "but since you delivered yourself so conveniently in chains, I'm going to leave you that way and take charge of your carpet, just to prevent accidents. If you really want to join us, you can make yourself useful first."

Somewhat to his surprise, Abdullah found he was far more angry than frightened. Perhaps it was that he had exhausted all his fear that morning in front of the Sultan. Or perhaps it was just because he ached all over. He was sore and scraped from sliding down the sand dune, and one of his ankle bands was chafing brutally. "But I have told you," he said haughtily, "that I shall be no use to you until my chains are off."

"It is not magic we want from you. It is knowledge," said Kabul Aqba. He beckoned to the man who had gone wading into the pool. "Tell us what manner of thing this is," he said, "and we may let your legs loose as a reward."

The man who had been in the pool squatted down and held out a smoky blue bottle with a rounded belly. Abdullah levered himself to his elbows and looked at it resentfully. It seemed to be new. There was a clean new cork showing through the smoky glass of the neck, which had been sealed over with a stamped lead seal, again new-looking. It looked like a bottle of perfume that had lost its label. "It's quite light," said the squatting man, shaking the bottle about, "and it neither rattles nor sloshes."

Abdullah thought of a way he could use this to get himself unchained. "It's a genie bottle," he said. "Know, denizens of the desert, that it could be very dangerous. Do but take these chains from me and I will control the genie within and make sure he obeys your every wish. Otherwise I think no man should touch it."

The man holding the bottle dropped it nervously, but Kabul Aqba only laughed and picked it up. "It looks more like something good to drink," he said. He tossed the flask to another man. "Open it." The man laid down his sabre and got out a large knife, with which he hacked at the lead seal.

Abdullah saw his chance of getting unchained going. Worse, he was about to be exposed as a fraud. "It is really extremely dangerous, oh rubies among robbers," he protested. "Once you have broken the seal, do not on any account draw the cork."

As he spoke, the man peeled the seal away and dropped it on the sand. He began prying the cork out, while another man held the bottle steady for him. "If you must draw the cork," Abdullah babbled, "at least tap on the bottle the correct and mystical number of times and make the genie inside swear—"

The cork came out. POP. A thin mauvish vapour came

smoking out of the neck of the flask. Abdullah hoped th thing was full of poison. But the vapour almost instantl thickened to a cloud that came rushing out of the bottle lik a kettle boiling bluish-mauve steam. This steam shaped itsel into a face – large and angry and blue – and arms, and a wis of body connected to the bottle, and went on rushing fortl until it was easily ten feet tall.

"I made a vow!" the face howled, in a large windy roai "The one who lets me out shall suffer. *There!*" The mist arms gestured.

The two men holding the cork and the bottle seemed to wink out of existence. Cork and bottle both fell to th ground, forcing the genie to billow sideways from the necl of the bottle. From the midst of his blue vapour, two larg toads came crawling and seemed to gaze around i bewilderment. The genie came slowly and vaporousl upright, hovering above the bottle with his smoky arm folded and a look of utter hatred on his misty face.

By this time everyone had run away except for Abdulla and Kabul Aqba, Abdullah because he could barely move i his chains and Kabul Aqba because he was clearl unexpectedly brave. The genie glowered at the two of them

"I am the slave of the bottle," he said. "Much as I hat and detest the whole arrangement, I have to tell you tha he who owns me is allowed one wish every day and I an forced to grant it." And he added menacingly, "What i your wish?"

"I wish—" began Abdullah. Kabul Aqba quickly

ammed his hand across Abdullah's mouth. "*I* am the one wishing," he said. "Get that quite clear, genie!"

"I hear," said the genie. "What wish?"

"One moment," said Kabul Aqba. He put his face close o Abdullah's ear. His breath smelt even worse than his hand, although neither, Abdullah had to admit, was a patch on Jamal's dog. "Well, Magician," the bandit whispered, "you've proved you know what you're talking about. Advise me what to wish and I'll make you a free man and an honoured member of my band. But if you try to make a wish yourself, I kill you. Understand?" He put the muzzle of his pistol to Abdullah's head and let go of his mouth. "What shall I wish?"

"Well," said Abdullah, "the wisest and kindest wish would be to wish your two toads turned back into men."

Kabul Aqba spared a surprised glance for the two toads. They were crawling uncertainly along the muddy edge of he pool, obviously wondering whether they could swim or not. "A waste of a wish," he said. "Think again."

Abdullah racked his brain for what might please a bandit chief most. "You could ask for limitless wealth, of course," he said, "but you would then need to carry your money, so perhaps you should first wish for a team of sturdy camels. And you would need to defend this treasure. Perhaps your first wish should be for a supply of the famous weapons of the north, or—"

"But *which*?" demanded Kabul Aqba. "Hurry. The genie s becoming impatient."

This was true. The genie was not exactly tapping his foot, since he had no feet to tap, but there was something about his looming, louring blue face that suggested there would be two more toads by the pool if he had to wait much longer.

A very short burst of thought was enough to convince Abdullah that his situation, despite the chains, would be very much worse if he became a toad. "Why not wish for a feast?" he said lamely.

"*That's* better!" said Kabul Aqba. He slapped Abdullah on the shoulder and sprang up jovially. "I wish for a most lavish feast," he said.

The genie bowed, rather like a candle flame bending in a draught. "Done," he said sourly. "And much good may it do you." And he poured himself carefully back into his bottle again.

It was a very lavish feast. It arrived almost at once, with a dull whooping noise, on a long table with a striped awning above it for shade, and with it arrived liveried slaves to serve it. The rest of the bandits rather quickly got over their fear and came racing back to lounge on cushions and eat delicate food from golden dishes and to shout at the slaves for more, more, more! The servants were, Abdullah found when he got a chance to talk to some of them, the slaves of the Sultan of Zanzib himself, and the feast should have been the Sultan's.

This news made Abdullah feel just a little better. He spent the feast still in chains, hitched up against a handy palm tree. Though he had not expected anything better, from Kabul Aqba, it was still hard. At least Kabul Aqba remembered him from time to time and, with a lordly wave of his hand, sent a slave over with a golden dish or a jug of wine.

For there was plenty. Every so often, there was another muffled whoomp and a fresh course would arrive, carried by more bewildered slaves, or there would be what looked like the pick of the Sultan's wine cellar loaded on to a jewelled trolley, or an astonished group of musicians. Whenever Kabul Aqba sent a new slave over to Abdullah, Abdullah found that slave only too ready to answer questions.

"In truth, noble captive of a desert king," one told him, "the Sultan was most enraged when the first and second courses so mysteriously disappeared. On the third course, which is this roast peacock that I carry, he placed a guard of mercenaries to escort us from the kitchen, but we were snatched from beside them, even at the very door of the banquet hall, and instantly found ourselves in this oasis instead."

The Sultan, Abdullah thought, must be getting hungrier and hungrier.

Later a troupe of dancing girls appeared, snatched in the same way. Which must have enraged the Sultan even more. These dancers made Abdullah melancholy. He thought of Flower-in-the-Night, who was twice as beautiful as any of them, and tears came into his eyes. As the jollity round the table grew, the two toads sat in the shallow edge of the pond hooting mournfully. No doubt they felt at least as bad about things as Abdullah did.

The moment night fell, the slaves, the musicians and the dancing girls all vanished, though what was left of the food and wine stayed. The bandits by then had glutted themselves, and then sated themselves again after that. Most of them fell asleep where they sat. But, to Abdullah's dismay, Kabul Aqba got up – a little unsteadily – and collected the genie bottle from under the table. He made sure it was corked. Then he staggered over to the magic carpet and lay down on it with the bottle in his hand. He fell asleep almost at once.

Abdullah sat against the palm tree in increasing anxiety. If the genie had returned the stolen slaves to the palace in Zanzib – and it seemed likely that he had – then someone was going to ask them angry questions. They would all tell the same story of being forced to serve a band of robbers, while a well-dressed young man in chains sat and watched from a palm tree. The Sultan would put two and two together. He was no fool. Even now a troop of soldiers could be setting out on fast racing camels to hunt the desert for a certain small oasis.

But that was not the greatest of Abdullah's worries. He watched the sleeping Kabul Aqba in even greater anxiety. He was about to lose the magic carpet and of course an extremely useful genie with it.

Sure enough, after about half an hour, Kabul Aqba rolled over on to his back and his mouth came open. As no doubt

Jamal's dog had done, as Abdullah himself must have done – but surely not so *very* loudly? – Kabul Aqba uttered an enormous rasping snore. The carpet quivered. Abdullah saw it clearly in the light of the rising moon rise a foot or so from the ground, where it hung and waited. Abdullah conjectured that it was busy interpreting whatever dream Kabul Aqba was having just then. What a bandit chief might dream about Abdullah had no idea, but the carpet knew. It soared into the air and began to fly.

Abdullah looked up as it glided over the palm fronds above him and had one last try at influencing it. "Oh most unfortunate carpet!" he called out softly. "I would have treated you so much more kindly!"

Maybe the carpet heard him. Or maybe it was an accident. But something roundish and faintly glimmering rolled off the edge of the carpet and dropped with a light *thunk* on the sand a few feet from Abdullah. It was the genie bottle. Abdullah reached out, as quickly as he could without too much rattling and jingling of his chains, and dragged the bottle into hiding between his back and the palm tree. Then he sat and waited for morning, feeling decidedly more hopeful.

CHAPTER EIGHT

In which Abdullah's dreams
continue to come true

The moment the sun flushed the sand dunes with white-rosy light, Abdullah wrenched the cork out of the genie's bottle.

The vapour steamed forth, became a jet, and rushed upwards into the blue-mauve shape of the genie, who looked, if possible, angrier than ever. "I said one wish a day!" the windy voice announced.

"Yes, well, this is a new day, oh mauve magnificence, and I am your new owner," said Abdullah. "And this wish is simple. I wish these chains of mine gone."

"Hardly worth wasting a wish on," the genie said contemptuously and dwindled rapidly away inside the bottle again. Abdullah was just about to protest that, though this wish might seem trivial to a genie, being without chains was important to *him*, when he found himself able to move freely, without rattling. He looked down and found the chains had vanished.

He put the cork carefully back in the bottle and stood up. He was horribly stiff. Before he could move at all, he had to make himself think of fleet camels with soldiers on them speeding towards this oasis, and then of what would happen if the sleeping bandits woke to find him standing there without his chains. That got him moving. He hobbled like an old man towards the banquet table. There, very careful not to disturb the various bandits who were asleep with their faces on the cloth, he collected food and wrapped it in a napkin. He took a flask of wine and tied it and the genie bottle to his belt with two more napkins. He took a last napkin to cover his head in case he got sunstroke – travellers had told him this was a real danger in the desert – and then he set off, as swiftly as he could limp, out of the oasis and due north.

The stiffness wore off as he walked. Walking became almost pleasant then and, for the first half of the morning, Abdullah strode out with a will, thinking of Flower-in-the-Night and eating succulent pasties and swigging from the wine flask as he walked. The second half of the morning was not so good. The sun swung overhead. The sky became glaring white and everything shimmered. Abdullah started to wish that he had poured the wine away and filled the flask at the muddy pond instead. Wine did nothing for thirst except make it worse. He wetted the napkin with wine and laid it over the back of his neck, where it kept drying out far too quickly. By midday he thought he was dying. The desert swayed about before his eyes and the glare hurt. He felt like a sort of human cinder.

"It seems that Fate has decreed that I live through my entire daydream in reality!" he croaked.

Up till then he had thought he had imagined his escape from the villainous Kabul Aqba in masterly detail, but now he knew he had never even conceived of how horrible it was to stagger in blaring heat, with sweat running into his eyes. He had not imagined the way the sand somehow got into everything, including his mouth. Nor had his daydream allowed for the difficulty of steering by the sun when the sun was right overhead. The tiny puddle of shadow round his feet gave him no guide to direction. He had to keep looking behind to check that his line of footprints was straight. This worried him because it wasted time.

In the end, wasted time or not, he was forced to stop and rest, squatting in a dip in the sands where there was a small piece of shade. He still felt like a piece of meat laid out on Jamal's charcoal grill. He soaked the napkin in wine and spread it over his head, and then watched it drip red blobs on his best clothes. The only thing that convinced him he was not going to die was that prophecy about Flower-in-the-Night. If Fate had decreed that she was to marry him, then he *had* to survive because he had not yet married her. After that, he thought of the prophecy about himself, written down by his father. It could have more than one meaning. In fact, it could already have come true, for had he not risen above everyone in the land by flying on the magic carpet? Or perhaps it did refer to a forty-foot stake.

This notion forced Abdullah to get up and walk again.

The afternoon was worse still. Abdullah was young and fit, but the life of a carpet merchant does not include long walks. He ached from his heels to the top of his head – not forgetting his toes, which seemed to have worn raw. In addition, one of his boots turned out to rub where the money-pocket was. His legs were so tired he could hardly move them. But he knew he had to put the horizon between himself and the oasis before the bandits started looking for him or the line of fleet camels appeared. Since he was not sure how far it was to the horizon, he slogged on.

By evening, all that kept him going was the knowledge that he would be seeing Flower-in-the-Night tomorrow. That was to be his next wish to the genie. Apart from that, he vowed to give up drinking wine and swore never to look at a grain of sand again.

When night fell he toppled into a sandbank and slept.

At dawn, his teeth were chattering and he was anxiously wondering about frostbite. The desert was as cold by night as it was hot by day. Still, Abdullah knew his troubles were almost over. He sat on the warmer side of the sandbank, looking east into the golden flush of dawn, and refreshed himself with the last of his food and a final swig of the hateful wine. His teeth stopped chattering, though his mouth tasted as if it belonged to Jamal's dog.

Now. Smiling in anticipation, Abdullah eased the cork out of the genie's bottle.

Out gushed the mauve smoke and rolled upwards into the genie's unfriendly form. "What are you grinning about?" asked the windy voice.

"My wish, oh amethyst among genies, of colour more beautiful than pansies," Abdullah replied. "May violets scent your breath. I wish you to transport me to the side of my bride-to-be, Flower-in-the-Night."

"Oh, do you?" The genie folded his smoky arms and turned himself to look in all directions. This, to Abdullah's fascination, turned the part of him that was joined to the bottle into a neat corkscrew shape. "Where *is* this young woman?" the genie said irritably when he was facing Abdullah again. "I can't seem to locate her."

"She was carried off by a djinn from her night garden in the Sultan's palace in Zanzib," Abdullah explained.

"That accounts for it," said the genie. "I can't grant your wish. She's nowhere on earth."

"Then she must be in the realm of the djinns," Abdullah said anxiously. "Surely you, oh purple prince among genies, must know that realm like the back of your hand."

"That shows how little you know," the genie said. "A genie confined to a bottle is debarred from any of the spirit realms. If that's where your girl is, I can't take you there. I advise you to put the cork back in my bottle and be on your way. There's quite a large troop of camels coming up from the south."

Abdullah sprang to the top of the sandbank. Sure enough, there was the line of fleet camels he had been dreading, speeding towards him with smooth waltzing strides. Though distance made them visible only as indigo shadows just then, he could tell from the outlines that the riders were armed to the teeth.

"See?" said the genie, bellying upwards to the same height as Abdullah. "They might miss finding you, but I doubt it." The idea clearly gave him pleasure.

"You must grant me a different wish, quickly," said Abdullah.

"*Oh* no," said the genie. "One wish a day. You've already made one."

"Certainly I did, oh splendour of lilac vapours," Abdullah agreed with the speed of desperation, "but that was a wish you were unable to grant. And the terms, as I clearly heard when you first stated them, were that you were forced to *grant* your owner one wish a day. This you have not yet done."

"Heaven preserve me!" the genie said disgustedly. "The young man is a coffee-shop lawyer."

"Naturally I am!" said Abdullah with some heat. "I am a citizen of Zanzib, where every child learns to guard its rights, for it is certain that no one else will guard them.

And I claim you have not yet *granted* me a wish today."

"A quibble," the genie said, swaying gracefully opposite him with folded arms. "One wish has been made."

"But not granted," said Abdullah.

"It is not my fault if you choose to ask for things which are impossible," said the genie. "There are a million beautiful girls I can take you to instead. You can have a mermaid if you fancy green hair. Or can't you swim?"

The speeding line of camels was now a good deal nearer. Abdullah said hurriedly, "Think, oh puce pearl of magic, and soften your heart. Those soldiers approaching us will certainly seize your bottle from me when they reach us. If they take you back to the Sultan, he will force you to do mighty deeds daily, bringing him armies and weapons and conquering enemies for him, most exhaustingly. If they keep you for themselves – and they might, for not all soldiers are quite honest – you will be passed from hand to hand and be made to grant many wishes each day, one for each of the squad. In either case, you will be working far harder than you will work for me, who only want one small thing."

"What eloquence!' said the genie. "Though you have a point. But have you thought, on the other hand, what opportunities the Sultan or his soldiers will give me to work havoc?"

"Havoc?" asked Abdullah, with his eyes anxiously on the speeding camels.

"I never said my wishes were supposed to do anyone any good," said the genie. "In fact, I swore that they would always do as much harm as possible. Those bandits, for instance, are now all on their way to prison or worse, for stealing the Sultan's feast. The soldiers found them late last night."

"You are causing worse havoc with me for *not* granting me a wish!" said Abdullah. "And, unlike the bandits, I do not deserve it."

"Regard yourself as unlucky," said the genie. "This will make two of us. I don't deserve to be shut in this bottle, either."

The riders were now near enough to see Abdullah. He could hear shouts in the distance and see weapons being unslung. "Give me tomorrow's wish, then," he said urgently.

"That might be the solution," the genie agreed, rather to Abdullah's surprise. "What wish then?"

"Transport me to the nearest person who can help me find Flower-in-the-Night," said Abdullah, and he bounded down the sandbank and picked the bottle up. "Quickly," he added to the genie now billowing above him.

The genie seemed a little puzzled. "This is odd," he said. "My powers of divination are usually excellent, but I can't make head or tail of this."

A bullet ploughed into the sand not too far away. Abdullah ran, carrying the genie like a vast streaming mauve candle flame. "Just take me to that person!" he screamed.

"I suppose I'd better," said the genie. "Maybe you can make some sense out of it."

The earth seemed to spin past under Abdullah's running

feet. Shortly, he seemed to be taking vast loping strides across lands that were whirling forward to meet him. Though the combined speed of his own feet and the turning world made everything into a blur, except for the genie streaming placidly out of the bottle in his hand, Abdullah knew that the speeding camels were left behind in instants. He smiled and loped on, almost as placid as the genie, rejoicing in the cool wind. He seemed to lope for a long time. Then it all stopped.

Abdullah stood in the middle of a country road getting his breath. This new place took a certain amount of getting used to. It was cool, only as warm as Zanzib in springtime, and the light was different. Though the sun was shining brightly from a blue sky, it put out a light that was lower and bluer than Abdullah was used to. This might have been because there were so many very leafy trees lining the road and casting shifting green shade over everything. Or it might have been due to the green, green grass growing on the verges. Abdullah let his eyes adjust and then looked round for the person who was supposed to help him find Flower-in-the-Night.

All he could see was what seemed to be an inn on a bend in the road, set back among the trees. It struck Abdullah as a wretched place. It was made of wood and white-painted plaster, like the poorest of poor dwellings in Zanzib, and its owners only seemed able to afford a roof made of tightly packed grass. Someone had tried to beautify the place by planting red and yellow flowers by the road. The inn sign, which was swinging on a post planted among the flowers, was a bad artist's effort to paint a lion.

Abdullah looked down at the genie's bottle, intending to put the cork back into it now he had arrived. He was annoyed to find he seemed to have dropped the cork, either in the desert or on the journey. Oh well, he thought. He held the bottle up to his face. "Where is the person who can help me find Flower-in-the-Night?" he asked.

A wisp of steam smoked from the bottle, looking much bluer in the light of this strange land. "Asleep on a bench in front of the Red Lion," the wisp said irritably, and withdrew back into the bottle.

The genie's hollow voice came from inside it. "He appeals to me. He shines with dishonesty."

CHAPTER NINE

In which Abdullah encounters an old soldier

Abdullah walked towards the inn. When he got closer, he saw that there was indeed a man dozing on one of the wooden settles that had been placed outside the inn. There were tables there too, suggesting that the place also served food. Abdullah slid into a settle behind one of the tables and looked dubiously across at the sleeping man.

He looked like an outright ruffian. Even in Zanzib, or among the bandits, Abdullah had never seen such dishonest lines as there were on this man's tanned face. A big pack on the ground beside him made Abdullah think at first that he might be a tinker – except that he was clean shaven. The only other men Abdullah had seen without beards or moustaches were the Sultan's northern mercenaries. It was possible this man was a mercenary soldier. His clothes did look like the broken-down remains of some kind of uniform, and he wore his hair in a single pigtail down his back in the way the Sultan's men did. This was a fashion the men of Zanzib found quite disgusting, for it was rumoured that the pigtail was never undone or washed. Looking at this man's pigtail, draped over the back of the settle where he slept, Abdullah could believe this. Neither it, nor anything else about the man was clean. All the same, he looked strong and healthy, although he was not young. His hair under its dirt seemed to be iron grey.

Abdullah hesitated to wake the fellow. He did not look trustworthy. And the genie had openly admitted that he granted wishes in a way that would cause havoc. This man may lead me to Flower-in-the-Night, Abdullah mused, but he will certainly rob me on the way.

While he hesitated, a woman in an apron came to the inn doorway, perhaps to see if there were customers outside. Her clothes made her into a plump hourglass-shape which Abdullah found very foreign and displeasing. "Oh!" she said, when she saw Abdullah. "Were you waiting to be served, sir? You should have banged on the table. That's what they all do round here. What'll you have?"

She spoke in the same barbarous accent as the northern mercenaries. From it, Abdullah concluded that he was now in whatever country those men came from. He smiled at her.

"What are you offering, oh jewel of the wayside?" he asked her.

Evidently no one had ever called the woman a jewel before. She blushed and simpered and twisted her apron. "Well, there's bread and cheese now," she said. "But dinner's doing. If you care to wait half an hour, sir, you can have a good game pie with vegetables from our kitchen garden."

Abdullah thought this sounded perfect, far better than he would have expected from any inn with a grass roof. "Then I would most gladly wait half an hour, oh flower among hostesses," he said.

She gave him another simper. "And perhaps a drink while you wait, sir?"

"Certainly," said Abdullah, who was still very thirsty from the desert. "Could I trouble you for a glass of sherbet – or failing that the juice of any fruit?"

She looked worried. "Oh sir, I – we don't go in much for fruit juice and I never heard of the other stuff. How about a nice mug of beer?"

"What is beer?" Abdullah asked cautiously.

This flummoxed the woman. "I – well, I – it's – er—"

The man on the other bench roused himself and yawned. "Beer is the only proper drink for a man," he said. "Wonderful stuff."

Abdullah turned to look at him again. He found himself staring into a pair of round limpid blue eyes, as honest as the day is long. There was not a trace of dishonesty in the brown face now it was awake.

"Brewed from barley and hops," added the man. "While you're here, landlady, I'll have a pint of it myself."

The landlady's expression changed completely. "I've told you already," she said, "that I want to see the colour of your money before I serve you with anything."

The man was not offended. His blue eyes met Abdullah's ruefully. Then he sighed and picked up a long white clay pipe from the settle beside him, which he proceeded to fill and light.

"Shall it be beer then, sir?" the landlady said, returning to her simper for Abdullah.

"If you would, lady of lavish hospitality," he said. "Bring me some, and also bring a fitting quantity for this gentleman here."

"Very well, sir," she said and, with a strongly disapproving look at the pigtailed man, she went back indoors.

"I call that very kind of you," the man said to Abdullah. "Come far, have you?"

"A fair way from the south, worshipful wanderer," Abdullah answered cautiously. He had not forgotten how dishonest the fellow had looked in his sleep.

"From foreign parts, eh? I thought you must be, to get a sunburn like that," the man observed.

Abdullah was fairly sure the fellow was fishing for information, to see if he was worth robbing. He was therefore quite surprised when the man seemed to give up asking questions.

"I'm not from these parts either, you know," the man

said, puffing large clouds of smoke from his barbarous pipe. "I'm from Strangia myself. Old soldier. Turned loose on the world with a bounty after Ingary beat us in the war. As you saw, there's still a lot of prejudice here in Ingary about this uniform of mine."

He said this into the face of the landlady as she came back with two glasses of frothing, brownish liquid. She did not speak to him. She just banged one glass down in front of him before she put the other carefully and politely in front of Abdullah. "Dinner in half an hour, sir," she said as she went away.

"Cheers," said the soldier, lifting his glass. He drank deeply.

Abdullah was grateful to this old soldier. Thanks to him, he now knew he was in a country called Ingary. So he said, "Cheers," in return as he dubiously lifted his own glass. It seemed to him likely that the stuff in it had come from the bladder of a camel. When he sniffed it, the smell did nothing to dispel that impression. Only the fact that he was still horribly thirsty led him to try it at all. He took a careful mouthful. Well, it was wet.

"Wonderful, isn't it?" said the old soldier.

"It is most interesting, oh captain of warriors," Abdullah said, trying not to shudder.

"Funny you should call me captain," said the soldier. "I wasn't, of course. Never made it higher than corporal. Saw a lot of fighting, though, and I did have hopes of promotion, but the enemy were all over us before I got my chance.

Terrible battle it was, you know. We were still on the march. No one expected the enemy to get there so soon. I mean, it's all over now, and there's no point in crying over spilt milk, but I'll tell you straight the Ingarians didn't fight fair. Had a couple of wizards making sure they won. I mean, what can an ordinary soldier like me do against magic? Nothing. Like me to show you a plan of how the battle went?"

Abdullah understood just where the genie's malice lay now. This man who was supposed to help him was quite obviously a thundering bore. "I know absolutely nothing of military matters, oh most valiant strategist," he said firmly.

"No matter," the soldier said cheerfully. "You can take it from me we were absolutely routed. We ran. Ingary conquered us. Overran the whole country. Our royal family, bless them, had to run too, so they put the king of Ingary's brother on the throne. There was some talk of making this prince legal by having him marry our Princess Beatrice, but she'd run with the rest of her family – long life to her! – and she couldn't be found. Mind you, the new prince wasn't all bad. Gave all the Strangian army a bounty before he turned us loose. Like to know what I'm doing with my money?"

"If you wish to tell me, bravest of veterans," Abdullah said, smothering a yawn.

"I'm seeing Ingary," said the soldier. "Thought I'd take a walk through the country that conquered us. Find out what it's like before I settle down. It's a fair sum, my bounty. I can pay my way as long as I'm careful."

"My felicitations," Abdullah said.

"They paid half of it in gold," said the soldier.

"Indeed," said Abdullah.

It was a great relief to him that a few local customers arrived just then. They were farming people mostly, wearing mucky breeches and outlandish smocks that reminded Abdullah of his own nightshirt, along with great clumping boots. Very cheerful they were, talking loudly of the hay crop – which they said was doing nicely – and bashing on the tables for beer. The landlady, and a little twinkling landlord too, were kept very busy running in and out with trays of glasses because, from then on, more and more people kept arriving.

And – Abdullah did not know whether to be more relieved, or annoyed, or amused – the soldier instantly lost interest in Abdullah and began to talk earnestly to the new arrivals. They did not seem to find him boring at all. Nor did it seem to worry them that he had been an enemy soldier. One of them bought him more beer at once. As more and more people arrived, he became ever more popular. Beer glasses lined up beside him. Dinner was ordered for him before long, while out of the crowd that surrounded the soldier, Abdullah kept hearing things like, "Great battle ... Your wizards gave them the advantage, see ... our cavalry ... folded up our left wing ... overran us on the hill ... us infantry forced to run ... went on running like rabbits ... not a bad sort ... rounded us up and paid us a bounty..."

Meanwhile the landlady came to Abdullah with a

steaming tray and more beer without being asked. He was still so thirsty he was almost glad of the beer. And the dinner struck him as quite as delicious as the Sultan's feast. For a while, he was so busy attending to it that he lost track of the soldier. When he next looked, the soldier was leaning forwards over his own empty plate, blue eyes shining with earnest enthusiasm, while he moved glasses and plates about on the table to show his country listeners exactly where everything was in the Battle of Strangia.

After a while he ran out of glasses, forks and plates. Since he had already used the salt and the pepper for the king of Strangia and his general, he had nothing left to use for the king of Ingary and his brother, or for their wizards. But the soldier did not let this bother him. He opened a pouch at his belt and took out two gold coins and a number of silver ones, which he rang down on the table to stand for the king of Ingary, his wizards and his generals.

Abdullah could not help thinking this was extraordinarily silly of him. The two gold pieces caused quite a bit of comment. Four loutish-looking young men at a nearby table turned round on their settles and began to be extremely interested. But the soldier was deep into explaining the battle and quite unaware of it.

Finally, most of the folk round the soldier got up to go back to their work. The soldier got up with them, slung his pack on his shoulder, put on his head the dirty soldier's hat which was tucked into the top flap of his pack, and asked the way to the nearest town. While everyone was loudly explaining the way to the soldier, Abdullah tried to catch the landlady in order to pay his own bill. She was a little slow in coming. By the time she was ready, the soldier was out of sight round the bend in the road. Abdullah was not sorry. Whatever help the genie thought this man could give, Abdullah felt he could do without it. He was glad that Fate and he seemed to see eye to eye for once.

Not being a fool like the soldier, Abdullah paid his bill with his smallest silver coin. Even that seemed to be big money in these parts. The landlady took it indoors in order to get change. While he was waiting for her to come back, Abdullah could not help overhearing the four loutish young men. They were holding a swift and significant discussion.

"If we nip up the old bridlepath," one said, "we can catch him in the wood at the top of the hill."

"Hide in the bushes," agreed the second, "on both sides of the road, so we come at him two ways."

"Split the money four ways," insisted the third. "He's got more gold than he showed, that's certain."

"We make sure he's dead first," said the fourth. "We don't want him telling tales."

And "Right!" and "Right," and "Right, then," the other three said, and they got up and left as the landlady came hurrying to Abdullah with a double handful of copper coins.

"I do hope this is the right change, sir. We don't get much southern silver here and I had to ask my husband how much it was worth. He says it's one hundred of our coppers, and you owed us five, so—"

"Bless you, oh cream of caterers and brewer of celestial beer," Abdullah said hurriedly, and gave her one handful of the coins back instead of the nice long chat she was obviously meaning to have with him. Leaving her staring, he set off as swiftly as he was able after the soldier. The man might be a bare-faced sponger and a thundering bore, but this did not mean he deserved to be ambushed and murdered for his gold.

CHAPTER TEN

Which tells of violence and bloodshed

Abdullah found he could not go very fast. In the cooler climate of Ingary, he had stiffened abominably while he sat still and his legs ached from walking all the day before. The money-container in his left boot proved to have made a very severe blister on his left foot. He was limping before he had walked a hundred yards. Still, he was concerned enough about the soldier to keep up the best pace he could. He limped past a number of cottages with grass roofs and then out beyond the village, where the road was more open. There he could see the soldier in the distance ahead, sauntering along towards a point where the road climbed a hill covered with the dense leafy trees that seemed to grow in these parts. That would be where the loutish young men were setting their ambush. Abdullah tried to limp faster.

An irritable blue wisp came out of the bottle bouncing at his waist. "Must you *bump* so?" it said.

"Yes," panted Abdullah. "The man you chose to help me needs *my* help instead."

"Huh!" said the genie. "I understand you now. Nothing will stop you taking a romantic view of life. You'll be wanting shining armour for your next wish."

The soldier was sauntering quite slowly. Abdullah closed the gap between them and entered the wood not far behind. But the road here wound back and forth among the trees to make an easier climb, so that Abdullah lost sight of the soldier from then on, until he limped round a final corner and saw him only a few yards ahead. That happened to be the very moment when the louts chose to make their attack.

Two of them sprang from one side of the road upon the soldier's back. The two who jumped from the other side rushed him from in front. There was a moment or so of horrid drubbing and struggling. Abdullah hastened to help – though he hastened somewhat hesitantly, because he had never hit anyone in his life.

While he approached, a whole set of miracles seemed to happen. The two fellows on the soldier's back went sailing away in opposite directions, to either side of the road, where one of them hit his head on a tree and did not trouble anyone again, while the other collapsed in a sprawl. Of the two facing the soldier, one received almost at once an interesting injury, which he doubled up to contemplate. The other, to Abdullah's considerable astonishment, rose into the air and actually, for a brief instant, became draped over the branch of a tree. From there he fell with a crash and went to sleep in the road.

At this point, the doubled-up young man undoubled himself and went for the soldier with a long narrow knife. The soldier seized the wrist of the hand that held the knife. There was a moment of grunting deadlock – which Abdullah found he had every faith would soon be resolved in favour of the soldier. He was just thinking that his concern about this soldier had been completely unnecessary, when the fellow sprawled in the road behind the soldier suddenly unsprawled himself and lunged at the soldier's back with another long thin knife.

Quickly Abdullah did what was needful. He stepped up and clouted the young man over the head with the genie bottle. "OUCH!" cried the genie. And the fellow dropped like a fallen oak tree.

At the sound, the soldier swung round from apparently tying knots in the other young man. Abdullah stepped back hurriedly. He did not like the speed with which the soldier turned, nor the way he held his hands, with the fingers tightly together, like two blunt but murderous weapons.

"I heard them planning to kill you, valiant veteran," he explained quickly, "and hurried to warn or help."

He found the soldier's eyes fixed on his, very blue but no longer at all innocent. In fact, they were eyes that would have counted as shrewd even in the Bazaar at Zanzib. They seemed to sum Abdullah up in every possible way. Luckily, they seemed satisfied with what they saw. The soldier said, "Thanks then," and turned to kick the head of the young man he had been tying into knots. He stopped moving too, making the full set.

"Perhaps," suggested Abdullah, "we should report this to a constable."

"What for?" asked the soldier. He bent down and, to Abdullah's slight surprise, made a swift and expert search of the pockets of the young man whose head he had just kicked. The result of the search was quite a large handful of coppers, which the soldier stowed in his own pouch, looking satisfied. "Rotten knife, though," he said, snapping it in two. "Since you're here, why don't you search the one you clobbered, while I do the other two? Yours looks worth a silver or so."

"You mean," Abdullah said doubtfully, "that the custom of this country permits us to rob the robbers?"

"It's no custom I ever heard of," the soldier said calmly, "but it's what I aim to do all the same. Why do you think I was so careful to flash my gold about at the inn? There's always a bad'un or so who thinks a stupid old soldier worth mugging. Nearly all of them carry cash."

He stepped across the road and began to search the young man who had fallen out of the tree. After hesitating a moment, Abdullah bent to the unpleasing task of searching the one he had felled with the bottle. He found himself revising his opinion of this soldier. Apart from anything else, a man who could confidently take on four attackers at once was someone who was better as a friend than an enemy. And the pockets of the unconscious youth did indeed contain three pieces of silver. There was also the knife. Abdullah tried breaking it on the road as the soldier had done with the other knife.

"Ah no," said the soldier. "That one's a good knife. You hang on to it."

"Truthfully I have had no experience," Abdullah said, holding it out to the soldier. "I am a man of peace."

"Then you won't get far in Ingary," said the soldier. "Keep it, and use it for cutting your meat if you'd rather. I've got six more knives better than that in my pack, all off different ruffians. Keep the silver too – though from the way you didn't get interested when I talked of my gold, I guess you're quite well off, aren't you?"

Truly a shrewd and observant man, Abdullah thought, pocketing the silver. "I am not so well off that I could not do with more," he said prudently. Then, feeling that he was entering properly into the spirit of things, he removed the young man's bootlaces and used them to tie the genie bottle more securely to his belt. The young man stirred and groaned as he did so.

"Waking up. We'd best be off," said the soldier. "They'll twist it around to *we* attacked *them* when they wake up.

And seeing this is their village and we're both foreigners, they're the ones who'll get believed. I'm going to cut off across the hills. If you'll take my advice, you'll do likewise."

"I would, most gentle fighting man, feel honoured if I could accompany you," Abdullah said.

"I don't mind," said the soldier. "It'll make a change to have company I don't have to lie to." He picked up his pack and his hat – both of which he seemed to have had time to stow tidily behind a tree before the fighting began – and led the way into the woods.

They climbed steadily among the trees for some time. The soldier made Abdullah feel woefully unfit. He strode as lightly and easily as if the way were downhill. Abdullah limped after. His left foot felt raw.

At length the soldier stopped and waited for him in an upland dell. "That fancy boot hurting you?" he asked. "Sit on that rock and take it off." He unslung his pack as he spoke. "I've got some kind of unusual first-aid kit in here," he said. "Picked it up on the battlefield, I think. Found it somewhere in Strangia anyway."

Abdullah sat down and wrestled off his boot. The relief it gave him to have it off was quickly cancelled when he looked at his foot. It *was* raw. The soldier grunted and slapped some kind of white dressing on it, which clung without needing to be tied on. Abdullah yelped. Then blissful coolness spread from the dressing. "Is this some kind of magic?" he asked.

"Probably," the soldier said. "I think those Ingary

wizards gave these packs to their whole army. Put the boot on. You'll be able to walk now. We've got to be far away before those boys' dads start looking for us on horseback."

Abdullah trod cautiously into his boot. The dressing must have been magic. His foot seemed as good as new. He was almost able to keep up with the soldier – which was just as well, for the soldier marched onwards and upwards until Abdullah felt they had gone as far as he had walked in the desert yesterday. From time to time, Abdullah could not help glancing nervously behind in case horses were now pursuing them. He told himself it made a change from camels – although it would be nice not to have someone chasing him for once. Thinking about it, he saw that even in the Bazaar, his father's first wife's relatives had been pursuing him ever since his father died. He was annoyed with himself for not having seen this before.

Meanwhile, they had climbed so high that the wood was giving way to wiry shrubs among rocks. As evening drew on, they were walking simply among rocks, somewhere near the top of a range of mountains, where only a few small, strong-smelling bushes grew, clinging to crevices. This was another sort of desert, Abdullah thought, while the soldier led the way along a narrow sort of ravine between high rocks. It did not look like a place where there was any chance of finding supper.

Some way along the ravine, the soldier stopped and took off his pack. "Take care of this for a moment," he said. "There looks to be a cave of sorts up the cliff this side. I'll pop up and see if it's a good place to spend the night."

There did seem to be a dark opening in the rocks some way above their heads, when Abdullah wearily looked up. He did not fancy sleeping in it. It looked cold, and hard. But it was probably better than just lying down on the rock, he thought, as he ruefully watched the soldier swing easily up the cliff and arrive at the hole.

There was a noise like a mad metal pulley wheel.

Abdullah saw the soldier reel back from the cave with one hand clapped to his face and almost fall backwards down the cliff. He saved himself somehow, and came sliding and cursing down the rocks in a storm of rubble.

"Wild animal in there!" he gasped. "Let's move on." He was bleeding quite badly from eight long scratches. Four of them started on his forehead, crossed his hand and went on down his cheek to his chin. The other four had torn his sleeve open and scored his arm from wrist to elbow. It looked as if he had got his hand to his face only just in time to avoid losing an eye. He was so shaken that Abdullah had to pick up his hat and his pack and guide him on down the ravine – which he did rather hurriedly. Any animal that could get the better of this soldier was an animal Abdullah did not want to meet.

The ravine ended after another hundred yards. And it ended in the perfect camping place. They were now on the other side of the mountains with a wide view over the lands beyond, all golden and green and hazy in the westering sun. The ravine stopped in a broad floor of rock sloping gently up to what was almost another cave, where the rocks above hung over the slanting floor. Better still, there was a small stony stream babbling down the mountain just beyond.

Perfect though this was, Abdullah had no wish to stop anywhere so near that wild animal in the cave. But the soldier insisted. The scratches were hurting him. He threw himself down on the sloping rock and fetched out some kind of salve from the wizardly first-aid kit. "Light a fire," he said, as he smeared the stuff on his wounds. "Wild animals are scared of fire."

Abdullah gave in and scrambled about tearing up strong-smelling shrubs to burn. An eagle or something had nested in the crags above long ago. The old nest gave Abdullah armloads of twigs and quite a few dry branches, so that he soon had quite a stack of firewood. When the soldier had finished smearing himself with the salve, he brought out a tinderbox and lit a small fire halfway down the sloping rock. It crackled and leapt most cheerfully. The smoke, smelling rather like the incense Abdullah used to burn in his booth, drifted out from the end of the ravine and spread against the beginnings of a glorious sunset. If this really scared the beast in the cave off, Abdullah thought it would be almost perfect here. Only *almost* perfect, because of course there was nothing to eat for miles. Abdullah sighed.

The soldier produced a metal can from his pack. "Like to fill that with water? Unless," he said, eyeing the genie bottle tied to Abdullah's belt, "you've got something stronger in that flask of yours."

"Alas, no," Abdullah said. "It is merely an heirloom – rare fogged glass from Singispat – which I carry for sentimental reasons." He had no intention of letting someone as dishonest as the soldier know about the genie.

"Pity," said the soldier. "Fetch us water, then, and I'll get on with cooking us some supper."

This made the place almost nearly perfect. Abdullah went leaping down to the stream with a will. When he came back, he found the soldier had brought out a saucepan and was emptying packets of dried meat and dried peas into it. He added the water and a couple of mysterious cubes and set it to boil on the fire. In a remarkably short time, it had turned into a thick stew. And smelt delicious.

"More wizard's stuff?" Abdullah asked as the soldier shared half the stew on to a tin plate and passed it to him.

"I think so," said the soldier. "I picked it up off the battlefield."

He took the saucepan to eat from himself and found a couple of spoons. They sat eating companionably with the fire crackling between them, while the sky turned slowly pink and crimson and gold, and the lands below became blue. "Not used to roughing it, are you?" the soldier remarked. "Good clothes, fancy boots, you have, but they've seen a bit of wear and tear lately by the looks of them. And by your talk and your sunburn, you come from quite a way south of Ingary, don't you?"

"All that is true, oh most acutely observant campaigner," Abdullah said cagily. "And of you all I know is that you come from Strangia and are most oddly proceeding through this land, encouraging persons to rob you by flourishing the coins of your bounty—"

"Bounty be damned!" the soldier interrupted angrily. "Not one penny did I get, either from Strangia or Ingary! I sweated my guts out in those wars – we all did – and at the end of it they say, 'Right, lads, that's it, it's peacetime now!' and turn us all out to starve. So I say to myself, Right indeed! *Someone* owes me for all the work I've done and I reckon it's the folk of Ingary! *They* were the ones who brought wizards in and cheated their way to victory! So I set off to *earn* my bounty off them, the way you saw me doing it today. You may call it a scam if you like, but you saw me – you judge me. I only take money off those who up and try to rob *me*!"

"Indeed, the word scam never crossed my lips, virtuous veteran," Abdullah said sincerely. "I call it most ingenious, and a plan that few but you could succeed in."

The soldier seemed soothed by this. He stared ruminatively out at the blue distance below. "All that down there," he said, "that's Kingsbury plain. That should yield me a mort of gold. Do you know, when I started out from Strangia, all I had was a silver threepenny bit and a brass button I used to pretend was a sovereign?"

"Then your profit has been great," said Abdullah.

"And it'll be greater yet," the soldier promised. He set

the saucepan neatly aside and fished two apples out of his pack. He gave one to Abdullah and ate the other himself, lying stretched on his back, staring out at the slowly darkening land.

Abdullah assumed he was calculating the gold he would earn from it. He was surprised when the soldier said, "I always did love the evening camp. Take a look at that sunset now. Glorious!"

It was indeed glorious. Clouds had come up from the south and had spread like a ruby landscape across the sky. Abdullah saw ranges of purple mountains flushed wine-red in one part; a smoking orange rift like the heart of a volcano; a calm rosy lake. While out beyond, laid against an infinity of gold-blue sky-sea, were islands, reefs, bays and promontories. It was as if they were looking at the sea-coast of heaven, or the land that looks westward to Paradise.

"And that cloud there," the soldier said, pointing. "Doesn't that one look just like a castle?"

It did. It stood on a high headland above a sky-lagoon, a marvel of slender gold, ruby and indigo turrets. A glimpse of golden sky through the tallest tower was like a window. It reminded Abdullah poignantly of the cloud he had seen above the Sultan's palace while he was being dragged off to the dungeon. Though it was not in the least the same shape, it brought back his sorrows to him so forcefully that he cried out.

"Oh, Flower-in-the-Night, where *are* you?"

CHAPTER ELEVEN

In which a wild animal causes
Abdullah to waste a wish

The soldier turned on his elbow and stared at Abdullah.
"What's that supposed to mean?"

"Nothing," said Abdullah, "except that my life has been
full of disappointments."

"Tell," said the soldier. "Unburden. I told you about me,
after all."

"You would never believe me," said Abdullah. "My
sorrows surpass even yours, most murderous musketeer."

"Try me," said the soldier.

Somehow it was not hard to tell, what with the sunset

and the misery that sunset brought surging up in Abdullah. So, as the castle slowly spread and dissolved into sandbars in the sky-lagoon and the whole sunset faded gently to purple, to brown, and finally to three dark red streaks like the healing clawmarks on the soldier's face, Abdullah told the soldier his story. Or at any rate, he told the gist of it. He did not of course tell anything so personal as his own daydreams, or the uncomfortable way they had of coming true lately, and he was very careful to say nothing at all about the genie. He did not trust the soldier not to take the bottle and vanish with it during the night – and he was helped in this editing of the facts by a strong suspicion that the soldier had not told his whole story either. The end of the story was quite difficult to tell with the genie left out, but Abdullah thought he managed rather well. He gave the impression he had escaped from his chains and from the bandits more or less by will-power alone, and then that he had walked all the way north to Ingary.

"Hm," said the soldier, when Abdullah had done. Musingly, he put more spicy bushes on the fire, which was now the only light left. "Quite a life. But I must say it makes up for a good deal, being fated to marry a princess. It's something I always had a fancy to do myself – marry a nice quiet princess with a bit of a kingdom and a kindly nature. Bit of a daydream of mine, really."

Abdullah found he had a splendid idea. "It is quite possible you can," he said quietly. "The day I met you I was granted a dream – a vision – in which a smoky angel the colour of lavender came to me and pointed you out to me, oh cleverest of crusaders, as you slept on a bench outside an inn. He said that you could aid me powerfully in finding Flower-in-the-Night. And if you did, said the angel, your reward would be that you would marry another princess yourself." This was – or would be – almost perfectly true, Abdullah told himself. He had only to make the correct wish to the genie tomorrow. Or rather, the day *after* tomorrow, he reminded himself, since the genie had forced him to use tomorrow's wish today. "Will you help me?" he asked, watching the soldier's firelit face rather anxiously. "For this great reward."

The soldier seemed neither eager nor dismayed. He considered. "Not sure quite what I could do to help," he said at last. "I'm not an expert on djinns, for a start. We don't seem to get them this far north. You'd need to ask some of these damn Ingary wizards what djinns do with princesses when they steal them. The wizards would know. I could help you squeeze the facts out of one, if you like. It would be a pleasure. But as for a princess – they don't grow on trees, you know. The nearest one must be the king of Ingary's daughter, way off in Kingsbury. If she's what your smoky angel-friend had in mind, then I guess you and me'd better walk down that way and see. The king's tame wizards mostly live down that way too, so they tell me, so it seems to fit in. That idea suit you?"

"Excellently well, military friend of my bosom!" said Abdullah.

"Then that's settled – but I don't promise anything, mind," said the soldier. He fetched two blankets out of his pack and suggested that they build up the fire and settle down to sleep.

Abdullah unhitched the genie bottle from his belt and put it carefully on the smooth rock beside him on the other side from the soldier. Then he wrapped himself in the blanket and settled down for what proved to be rather a disturbed night. The rock was hard. And though he was nothing like as cold as he had been yesterday night in the desert, the damper air of Ingary made him shiver just as much. In addition, the moment he closed his eyes he found he became obsessed with the wild beast in the cave up the ravine. He kept imagining he could hear it prowling round the camp. Once or twice he opened his eyes and even thought he saw something moving just beyond the light from the fire. He sat up each time and threw more wood on the fire, whereupon the flames flared up and showed him that nothing was there. It was a long time before he fell properly asleep. When he did, he had a hellish dream.

He dreamed that, around dawn, a djinn came and sat on his chest. He opened his eyes to tell it to go away, and found it was not a djinn at all, but the beast from the cave. It stood with its two vast front paws planted on his chest, glaring down at him with eyes that were like bluish lamps in the velvety blackness of its coat. As far as Abdullah could tell, it was a demon in the form of a huge panther.

He sat up with a yell.

Naturally nothing was there. Dawn was just breaking. The fire was a cherry smudge in the greyness of everything, and the soldier was a darker grey hump, snoring gently on the other side of the fire. Behind him the lower lands were white with mist. Wearily, Abdullah put another bush on the fire and fell asleep again.

He was woken by the windy roaring of the genie.

"Stop this thing! *Get it OFF me!*"

Abdullah leapt up. The soldier leapt up. It was broad daylight. There was no mistaking what they both saw. A small black cat was crouching by the genie bottle, just beside the place where Abdullah's head had been. The cat was either very curious or convinced there was food in the bottle, for it had its nose delicately but firmly in the neck of the flask. Around its neat black head, the genie was gushing out in ten or twelve distorted blue wisps and the wisps kept turning into hands or faces and then turning back to smoke again.

"Help me!" he yelled in chorus. "It's trying to *eat* me or something!"

The cat ignored the genie entirely. It just went on behaving as if there was a most enticing smell in the bottle.

In Zanzib, everyone hated cats. People thought of them as very little better than the rats and mice they ate. If a cat came near you, you kicked it, and you drowned any kittens you could lay hands on. Accordingly, Abdullah ran at the cat, aiming a flying kick at it as he ran. "*Shoo!*" he yelled. "*Scat!*"

The cat jumped. Somehow it avoided Abdullah's lashing foot and fled to the top of the overhanging rock, where it spat at him and glared. It was not deaf then, Abdullah thought, staring up into its eyes. They were bluish. So *that* was what had sat on him in the night! He picked up a stone and drew back his arm to throw it.

"Don't do that!" said the soldier. "Poor little animal!"

The cat did not wait for Abdullah to throw the stone. It shot out of sight. "There is nothing poor about that beast," he said. "You must realise, gentle gunman, that the creature nearly took your eye out last night."

"I know," the soldier said mildly. "It was only defending itself, poor thing. Is that a genie in that flask of yours? Your smoky blue friend?"

A traveller with a carpet for sale had once told Abdullah that most people in the north were inaccountably sentimental about animals. Abdullah shrugged and turned sourly to the genie bottle, where the genie had vanished without a word of thanks. This would have to happen! Now he would have to watch the bottle like a hawk. "Yes," he said.

"I thought it might be," said the soldier. "I've heard tell of genies. Come and look at this, will you?" He stooped and picked up his hat, very carefully, smiling in a strange, tender way.

There seemed definitely to be something wrong with the soldier this morning – as if his brains had softened in the night. Abdullah wondered if it was those scratches, although they had almost vanished by now. Abdullah went over to him anxiously.

Instantly, the cat was standing on the overhanging rock again, making that iron pulley noise, anger and worry in every line of its small black body. Abdullah ignored it and looked into the soldier's hat. Round blue eyes stared at him out of its greasy interior. A little pink mouth hissed defiance, as the tiny black kitten inside scrambled to the back of the hat, whipping its minute bottle-brush of a tail for balance.

"Isn't it *sweet*?" the soldier said besottedly.

Abdullah glanced at the wauling cat on top of the rock. He froze, and looked again carefully. The thing was huge. A mighty black panther stood there, baring its big white fangs at him.

"These animals must belong to a witch, courageous companion," he said shakily.

"If they did, then the witch must be dead or something," the soldier said. "You saw them – they were living wild in that cave. That mother cat must have carried her kitten all the way here in the night. Marvellous, isn't it? She must have *known* we'd help her!" He looked up at the huge beast snarling on the rock and did not seem to notice the size of it. "Come on down, sweet thing!" he said wheedlingly. "You know we won't hurt you or your kitten."

The mother beast launched herself from the rock. Abdullah gave a strangled scream, dodged, and sat down heavily. The great black body hurtled past above him –

and, to his surprise, the soldier started to laugh. Abdullah looked up indignantly to find that the beast had become a small black cat again, which was most affectionately walking about on the soldier's broad shoulder and rubbing herself on his face.

"Oh, you're a wonder, little Midnight!" the soldier chuckled. "You know I'll take care of your Whippersnapper for you, don't you? That's right. You purr!"

Abdullah got up disgustedly and turned his back on this love feast. The saucepan had been cleaned out very thoroughly in the night. The tin plate was burnished. He went and washed both, meaningly, in the stream, hoping the soldier would soon forget these dangerous magical beasts and begin thinking about breakfast.

But when the soldier finally put the hat down and tenderly plucked the mother cat off his shoulder, it was breakfast for cats that he thought about. "They'll need milk," he said, "and a nice plate of fresh fish. Get that genie of yours to fetch them some."

A jet of blue-mauve spurted from the neck of the bottle and spread into a sketch of the genie's irritated face. "Oh no," said the genie. "One wish a day is all I give, and he had today's wish yesterday. Go and fish in the stream."

The soldier advanced on the genie angrily. "There won't be any fish this high in the mountain," he said. "And that little Midnight is starving, and she's got her kitten to feed."

"Too bad!" said the genie. "And don't you try to threaten me, soldier. Men have become toads for less."

The soldier was certainly a brave man – or a very foolish one – Abdullah thought. "You do that to me, and I'll break your bottle, whatever shape I'm in!" he shouted. "I'm not wanting a wish for *myself*!"

"I prefer people to be selfish," the genie retorted. "So you *want* to be a toad?"

Further blue smoke gushed out of the bottle and formed into arms making gestures that Abdullah was afraid he recognised. "No, no, stop, I implore you, oh sapphire among spirits!" he said hastily. "Let the soldier alone and consent, as a great favour, to grant me another wish a day in advance, that the animals might be fed."

"Do *you* want to be a toad too?" the genie enquired.

"If it is written in the prophecy that Flower-in-the-Night shall marry a toad, then make me a toad," Abdullah said piously. "But first fetch milk and fish, great genie."

The genie swirled moodily. "Bother the prophecy! I can't go against that. All right. You can have your wish provided you leave me in peace for the next two days."

Abdullah sighed. It was a dreadful waste of a wish. "Very well."

A crock of milk and an oval plate with a salmon on it plunked down on the rock by his feet. The genie gave Abdullah a look of huge dislike and sucked himself back inside the bottle.

"Great work!" said the soldier, and proceeded to make a large pother over poaching salmon in milk and making sure there were no bones the cat might choke on.

The cat, Abdullah noticed, had all this while been peacefully licking at her kitten in the hat. She did not seem to know the genie was there. But she knew about the salmon all right. As soon as it started cooking, she left her kitten and wound herself round the soldier, thin and urgent and mewing. "Soon, soon, my black darling!" the soldier said.

Abdullah could only suppose that the cat's magic and the genie's were so different that they were unable to perceive one another. The one good thing he could see about the situation was that there was plenty of salmon and milk for the two humans as well. While the cat daintily guzzled, and her kitten lapped, and sneezed, and did his amateur best to drink salmon-flavoured milk, the soldier and Abdullah feasted on porridge made with milk and roast salmon steak.

After such a breakfast, Abdullah felt kinder towards the whole world. He told himself that the genie could not have made a better choice of companion for him than this soldier. The genie was not so bad. And he would surely be seeing Flower-in-the-Night soon now. He was thinking that the Sultan and Kabul Aqba were not such bad fellows either, when he discovered, to his outrage, that the soldier intended to take the cat and the kitten along with them to Kingsbury.

"But, most benevolent bombadier and considerate cuirassier," he protested, "what will become of your scheme to earn your bounty? You cannot rob robbers with a kitten in your hat!"

"I reckon I won't need to do any of that now you've

promised me a princess," the soldier answered calmly. "And no one could leave Midnight and Whippersnapper to starve on this mountain. That's cruel!"

Abdullah knew he had lost this argument. He sourly tied the genie bottle to his belt and vowed never to promise the soldier anything else. The soldier repacked his pack, scattered the fire and gently picked up his hat with the kitten in it. He set off downhill beside the stream, whistling to Midnight as if she were a dog.

Midnight, however, had other ideas. As Abdullah set off after the soldier, she stood in his way, staring meaningly up at him. Abdullah took no notice and tried to edge past her. And she was promptly huge again. A black panther, if possible even larger than before, was barring his way and snarling. He stopped, frankly terrified. And the beast leapt at him. He was too frightened even to scream. He shut his eyes and waited to have his throat torn out. So much for Fate and prophecies!

A softness touched his throat instead. Small firm feet hit his shoulder and another set of such feet pricked his chest. Abdullah opened his eyes to find that Midnight was back to cat size and clinging to the front of his jacket. The green-blue eyes looking up into his said, "Carry me. Or else."

"Very well, formidable feline," Abdullah said. "But take care not to snag any more of the embroidery on this jacket. This was once my best suit. And please remember that I carry you under strong protest. I do not love cats."

Midnight calmly scrambled her way to Abdullah's shoulder, where she sat smugly balancing while Abdullah plodded and slithered his way down the mountain for the rest of that day.

CHAPTER TWELVE

In which the law catches up with Abdullah and the soldier

By evening, Abdullah was almost used to Midnight. Unlike Jamal's dog, she smelt extremely clean, and she was clearly an excellent mother. The only times she dismounted from Abdullah were to feed her kitten. If it had not been for her alarming habit of turning huge at him when he annoyed her, Abdullah felt he could come to tolerate her in time. The kitten, he conceded, was charming. It played with the end of the soldier's pigtail and tried to chase butterflies – in a wobbly way – when they stopped for lunch. The rest of the day it spent in the front of the soldier's jacket, peeping eagerly forth at the grass and the trees, and at the fern-lined waterfalls they passed on their way to the plains.

But Abdullah was entirely disgusted at the fuss the soldier made about his new pets when they stopped for the night. They decided to stay in the inn they came to in the first valley, and here the soldier decreed that his cats were to have the best of everything.

The innkeeper and his wife shared Abdullah's opinion. They were lumpish folk who had, it seemed, been put in a bad mood anyway by the mysterious theft of a crock of milk and a whole salmon that morning. They ran about with dour disapproval, fetching just the right shape of basket and a soft pillow to put in it. They hurried grimly with cream and chicken liver and fish. They grudgingly produced certain herbs which, the soldier declared, prevented canker in the ears. They stormily sent out for other herbs which were supposed to cure a cat of worms. But they were downright incredulous when they were asked to heat water for a bath because the soldier suspected that Whippersnapper had picked up a flea.

Abdullah found himself forced to negotiate. "Oh prince and princess of publicans," he said, "bear with the eccentricity of my excellent friend. When he says a bath, he means of course a bath for himself and for me. We are both somewhat travel-stained and would welcome clean hot water – for which we will of course pay whatever extra is necessary."

"What? Me? Bath?" the soldier said, when the innkeeper

and his wife had stumped off to put big kettles to boil.

"Yes. You," said Abdullah. "Or you and your cats and I part company this very evening. The dog of my friend Jamal in Zanzib was scarcely less ripe to the nose than you, oh unwashed warrior, and Whippersnapper, fleas or not, is a good deal cleaner."

"But what about my princess and your Sultan's daughter if you leave?" asked the soldier.

"I shall think of something," said Abdullah. "But I should prefer it if you got into a bath and, if you wish, took Whippersnapper into it with you. That was my aim in asking for it."

"It weakens you – having baths," the soldier said dubiously. "But I suppose I could wash Midnight as well while I'm at it."

"Pray use both cats as sponges if it pleases you, infatuated infantryman," Abdullah said and went off to revel in his own bath.

In Zanzib, people bathed a lot, because the climate was so hot. Abdullah was used to visiting the public baths at least every other day and he was missing that. Even Jamal went to the baths once a week, and it was rumoured that he took his dog into the water with him.

The soldier, Abdullah thought, becoming soothed by the hot water, was really no more besotted with his cats than Jamal was with his dog. He hoped that Jamal and his dog had managed to escape and, if they had, that they were not at this moment suffering hardships in the desert.

The soldier did not appear any weaker for his bath, although his skin had turned a much paler brown. Midnight, it seemed, had fled at the mere sight of water, but Whippersnapper, so the soldier claimed, had loved every moment. "He played with the soap bubbles!" he said dotingly.

"I hope you think you're worth all this trouble," Abdullah said to Midnight, as she sat on his bed delicately cleaning herself after her cream and chicken. Midnight turned and gave him a round-eyed scornful look – of *course* she was worth it! – before she went back to the serious business of washing her ears.

The bill, next morning, was enormous. Most of the extra charge was for hot water, but cushions, baskets and herbs figured quite largely on the list too. Abdullah paid, shuddering, and anxiously enquired how far it was to Kingsbury.

Six days, he was told, if a person went on foot.

Six days! Abdullah nearly groaned aloud. Six days at this rate of expense and he would barely be able to afford to keep Flower-in-the-Night in the state of direst poverty when he found her. And he had to look forward to six days of the soldier making this sort of fuss about the cats, before they could collar a wizard and even *start* trying to find her. No, Abdullah thought. His next wish to the genie would be to have them all transported to Kingsbury. That meant he would only have to endure two more days.

Comforted by this thought, Abdullah strode off down the

road with Midnight serenely riding his shoulders and the genie bottle bobbing at his side. The sun shone. The greenness of the countryside was a pleasure to him after the desert.

Abdullah even began to appreciate the houses with their grass roofs. They had delightful rambling gardens and many of them had roses or other flowers trained round their doors. The soldier told him that grass roofs were the custom here. It was called thatch and it did, the soldier assured him, keep out the rain, though Abdullah found this very hard to believe.

Before long, Abdullah was deep in another daydream, of himself and Flower-in-the-Night living in a cottage with a grass roof and roses round the door. He would make her such a garden that it would be the envy of all for miles around. He began to plan the garden.

Unfortunately, towards the end of the morning, his daydream was interrupted by increasing spots of rain. Midnight hated it. She complained loudly in Abdullah's ear.

"Button her in your jacket," said the soldier.

"Not I, adorer of animals," Abdullah said. "She loves me no more than I love her. She would doubtless seize the chance to make grooves in my chest."

The soldier handed his hat to Abdullah with Whippersnapper in it, carefully covered with an unclean handkerchief, and buttoned Midnight into his own jacket. They went on for half a mile. By then the rain was pouring down.

The genie draped a ragged blue wisp over the side of his

144

bottle. "Can't you *do* something about all this water that's getting in on me?"

Whippersnapper was saying much the same at the top of his small squeaky voice. Abdullah pushed wet hair out of his eyes and felt harassed.

"We'll have to find somewhere to shelter," said the soldier.

Luckily there was an inn round the next corner but one. They squelched thankfully into its taproom, where Abdullah was pleased to discover that its grass roof was keeping the rain out very well.

Here the soldier, in the way Abdullah was getting used to, demanded a private parlour with a fire, so that the cats could be comfortable, and lunch for all four of the party. Abdullah, in the way that he was also getting used to, wondered how much the bill would be this time, although he had to admit the fire was very welcome. He stood in front of it and dripped, with a glass of beer – in this particular inn the beer tasted as if it had come from a camel that was rather unwell – while they waited for lunch. Midnight washed the kitten dry, then herself. The soldier stretched his boots to the fire and let them steam, while the genie bottle stood in the hearth and also steamed faintly. Even the genie did not complain.

They heard horses outside. This was not unusual. Most people in Ingary travelled on horseback if they could. Nor was it surprising that the riders seemed to be stopping at the inn. They must be wet too. Abdullah was just thinking that he should firmly have asked the genie to provide horses instead of milk and salmon yesterday, when he heard the horsemen shouting at the innkeeper outside the parlour window.

"Two men – a Strangian soldier and a dark chap in a fancy suit – wanted for assault and robbery – have you seen them?"

Before the riders had finished shouting, the soldier was over by the parlour window, with his back to the wall so that he could look sideways through the window without being seen, and somehow he had his pack in one hand and his hat in the other.

"Four of them," he said. "They're constables, by the uniform."

All Abdullah could think to do was stand gaping in dismay, thinking that this was what came of fussing for cat baskets and bathwater and giving innkeepers reason to remember you. *And* demanding private parlours, he thought, as he heard the voice of this innkeeper in the distance saying smarmily that yes indeed both fellows were here, in the small parlour.

The soldier held out his hat to Abdullah. "Put Whippersnapper in here. Then pick up Midnight and be ready to get out of the window as soon as they come into the inn."

Whippersnapper had chosen that moment to go exploring under an oak settle. Abdullah dived after him. As he backed out on his knees with the kitten squirming in his hand, he could hear distant boots clumping into the taproom. The soldier was undoing the latch on the window. Abdullah dropped Whippersnapper into his outstretched hat and turned round for Midnight. And saw the genie bottle warming on the hearth. Midnight was up on a high shelf across the room. This was hopeless. The boots were now much nearer, tramping towards the parlour door. The soldier was banging at the window, which seemed to be stuck.

Abdullah snatched up the genie bottle. "Come *here*, Midnight!" he said and ran towards the window, where he collided with the soldier backing away.

"Stand clear," said the soldier. "Thing's stuck. Have to kick it."

As Abdullah staggered aside, the parlour door was flung open and three large men in uniform plunged into the room. At the same instant, the soldier's boot met the window frame with a bang. The casement burst open and the soldier went scrambling out over the sill. The three men shouted. Two made for the window and one dived for Abdullah. Abdullah overturned the oak settle in front of all of them and then sprinted for the window, where he hurdled the sill out into the drenching rain without pausing to think.

Then he remembered Midnight. He turned back.

She was huge again, larger than he had ever seen her, looming like a great black shadow in the space below the window, with her immense white fangs bared at the three men. They were falling over one another to get away backwards through the door. Abdullah turned and ran after the soldier, gratefully. He was pelting towards the far corner of the inn. The fourth constable, who was outside holding the horses, started to run after them, then realised that this was stupid and ran back to the horses, which scattered away from him as he ran at them. As Abdullah bounded after the soldier through a sopping kitchen garden, he could hear the shouting of all four constables as they tried to catch their horses.

The soldier was an expert at escapes. He found a way from the vegetable garden into an orchard and from there a gate into a wide field, all without wasting an instant. A wood stood across the field in the distance like a promise of safety, veiled in rain.

"Did you get Midnight?" gasped the soldier, as they trotted through the soaking grass of the field.

"No," said Abdullah. He had no breath to explain.

"*What?*" exclaimed the soldier. He stopped and swung round.

At that moment the four horses, each with a constable in the saddle, came jumping over the orchard hedge into the field. The soldier swore violently. He and Abdullah both sprinted for the wood. By the time they reached its bushy outskirts, the horsemen were well over halfway across the field. Abdullah and the soldier crashed through the bushes and leaped onwards into open woodland where, to Abdullah's amazement, the ground was thick with thousands upon thousands of bright blue flowers, growing like a carpet into far blue distance.

"What – these flowers?" he panted.

"Bluebells," said the soldier. "If you've lost Midnight, I'll kill you."

"I haven't. She'll find us. She grew. Told you. Magic," Abdullah gasped.

The soldier had never seen this trick of Midnight's. He did not believe Abdullah. "Run faster," he said. "We'll have to circle back and collect her."

They rushed forward, crunching bluebells, suffused with the strange wild scent of them. Abdullah could have believed, but for the grey pouring rain and the shouts of the constables, that he was running over the floor of heaven. He was rapidly back in his daydream. When he made his garden for the cottage he would share with Flower-in-the-Night, he would have bluebells in it by the thousand, like these. But this did not blind him to the fact that they were leaving a trampled trail of broken white stems and snapped-off flowers as they ran. Nor did it deafen him to the cracking of twigs as the constables shoved their horses into the wood behind him.

"This is hopeless!" said the soldier. "Get that genie of yours to make the constables lose us."

"Point out – sapphire of soldiers – no wish – day after tomorrow," Abdullah panted.

"He can give you one in advance again," said the soldier.

Blue steam fluttered angrily from the bottle in Abdullah's hand. "I gave you your last wish only on condition you left me alone," said the genie. "All I ask is to be left to sorrow alone in my bottle. And do you let me? No. At the first sign of trouble you start wailing for extra wishes. Doesn't anyone consider *me* around here?"

"Emergency – oh hyacinth – *bluebell* among bottled spirits," Abdullah puffed. "Transport us – far off—"

"Oh no you don't!" said the soldier. "You don't wish us far off without Midnight. Have him make us invisible until we find her."

"Blue jade of genies—" gasped Abdullah.

"If there's one thing I hate," interrupted the genie, bellying gracefully forth in a lavender cloud, "more than this rain and being pestered for wishes in advance all the time, it's being *coaxed* for wishes in flowery language. If you want a wish, talk straight."

"Take us to Kingsbury," puffed Abdullah.

"Make those fellows lose us," the soldier said at the same moment.

They glared at one another as they ran.

"Make up your minds," said the genie. He folded his arms and streamed contemptuously out behind them. "It's all one to me what you choose to waste another wish on. Just let me remind you that it will be your last one for two days."

"I'm not leaving Midnight," said the soldier.

"If we are – waste a wish," panted Abdullah, "then should – usefully – foolish fortune hunter – forward our – quest – Kingsbury."

"Then you can go without me," said the soldier.

"The horsemen are only fifty feet away," remarked the genie.

They looked over their shoulders and discovered this was quite true. Abdullah hurriedly gave in. "Then make them unable to see us," he panted.

"Have us unseen until Midnight finds us," added the soldier. "I know she will. She's that clever."

Abdullah had a glimpse of an evil grin spreading on the genie's smoky face and of smoky arms making certain gestures.

There followed a wet and gluey strangeness. The world suddenly distorted around Abdullah and grew vast and blue and green and out of focus. He crawled, in a slow and toilsome crouch, among what seemed to be giant bluebells, placing each huge and warty hand with extreme care, because, for some reason, he could not look downwards – only up and across. It was such hard work that he wanted to stop and crouch where he was, but the ground was shaking most terribly. He could feel some gigantic creatures galloping towards him, so he crawled on frantically. Even so, he barely got out of their way in time.

A huge hoof, as big as a round tower, with metal underneath it, came smashing down just beside him as he crawled. Abdullah was so frightened by it that he froze and could not move. He could tell that the enormous creatures had stopped too, quite close. There were loud, annoyed sounds that he could not hear properly. They went on for some time. Then the smashing of hooves began again, and went on for some time too, trampling this way and that, always rather near, until, after what seemed most of the day, the creatures seemed to give up looking for him and went crashing and squelching away.

Chapter Thirteen

In which Abdullah challenges fate

Abdullah crouched for a while longer, but when the creatures did not come back he began crawling again, in a vague, vain way, hoping to discover what had happened to him. He knew *something* had happened, but he did not seem to have much of a brain to think with.

While he crawled, the rain stopped, which he was rather sad about, since it was wonderfully refreshing to the skin. On the other hand – a fly circled in a shaft of sunlight and came to sit on a bluebell leaf nearby. Abdullah promptly shot out a long tongue, whipped up that fly and swallowed it. *Very* nice! he thought. Then he thought, But flies are unclean! More troubled than ever, he crawled round another bluebell clump.

And there was another one just like himself.

It was brown and squat and warty, and its yellow eyes were at the top of its head. As soon as it saw him, it opened its wide lipless mouth in a bray of horror and began to swell up. Abdullah did not wait to see more. He turned and crawled off as fast as his distorted legs could take him. He knew what he was now. He was a toad. The malicious genie had fixed things so that he would be a toad until Midnight found him. When she did, he was fairly sure she would eat him.

He crawled under the nearest overarching bluebell leaves and hid...

About an hour later, the bluebell leaves parted to let through a monster black paw. It seemed interested in Abdullah. It kept its claws sheathed and patted at him. Abdullah was so horrified that he tried to hop away backwards.

Whereupon he found himself lying on his back among the bluebells.

He blinked up at the trees first, trying to adjust to the way he suddenly had thoughts in his head again. Some of those thoughts were unpleasant ones, about two bandits crawling beside an oasis pool in the shape of toads, and about eating a fly, and being nearly trodden on by a horse. Then he looked round and found the soldier crouching nearby, looking as bewildered as Abdullah felt. His pack was beside him and, beyond that, Whippersnapper was making determined efforts to climb out of the soldier's hat. The genie bottle stood smugly beside the hat.

The genie was outside the bottle in a small wisp like the flame of a spirit lamp, with his smoky arms propped on the neck of the bottle. "Enjoy yourselves?" he asked jeeringly. "I got you there, didn't I? That'll teach you to pester me for extra wishes!"

Midnight had been extremely alarmed by their sudden transformation. She was in a small angry arch, spitting at both of them.

The soldier stretched out his hand to her and made soothing noises. "You frighten Midnight again like that," he told the genie, "and I'll break your bottle!"

"You said that before," retorted the genie, "and you couldn't, worse luck. The bottle's enchanted."

"Then I'll make sure his next wish is that *you* turn into a toad," the soldier said, jerking his thumb at Abdullah.

The genie shot Abdullah a wary look at this. Abdullah said nothing, but he saw it was a good idea and might keep the genie in order. He sighed. One way and another, he just could not seem to stop wasting wishes.

They picked themselves and their belongings up and resumed their journey. But they went much more cautiously. They kept to the smallest lanes and footpaths they could find and that night, instead of going to an inn, they camped in an old empty barn. Here Midnight suddenly looked alert and interested and shortly slipped away into the shadowy corners. After a while, she came trotting back with a dead mouse, which she laid carefully in the soldier's hat for Whippersnapper. Whippersnapper was not very sure what to do with it. In the end he decided it was the kind of toy you leapt on fiercely and killed. Midnight prowled off again. Abdullah heard the small sounds of her hunting most of the night.

In spite of this, the soldier worried about feeding the cats. Next morning he wanted Abdullah to go to the nearest farm and buy milk.

"You do it if you want it," Abdullah said curtly.

And somehow he found himself on the way to the farm with a can from the soldier's pack on one side of his belt and the genie bottle bumping at the other.

Exactly the same thing happened the next two mornings too, with the small difference that they slept under haystacks both those nights and Abdullah bought a beautiful fresh loaf one morning and some eggs on the next. On the way back to the haystack that third morning, he tried to work out just why he was feeling increasingly bad tempered and put-upon.

It was not just that he was stiff and tired and damp all the time. It was not just that he seemed to spend such a lot of time running errands for the soldier's cats – though that had something to do with it. Some of it was Midnight's fault. Abdullah knew he ought to be grateful to her for defending them from the constables. He *was* grateful, but he still did not get on with Midnight. She rode his shoulder disdainfully every day and contrived to make it quite clear that, as far as she was concerned, Abdullah was only a sort of horse. It was a bit hard to take from a mere animal.

Abdullah brooded on this and other matters all that day, while he tramped country lanes with Midnight draped elegantly around his neck and the soldier trudging cheerfully ahead. It was not that he did not like cats. He was used to them now. Sometimes he found Whippersnapper almost as sweet as the soldier did. No, his bad humour had much more to do with the way the soldier and the genie between them kept contriving to postpone his search for Flower-in-the-Night. If he was not careful, Abdullah could see himself tramping the country lanes for the rest of his life, without ever getting to Kingsbury at all. And when he did get there, he still had to locate a wizard. No, it would not do.

That night, they found the remains of a stone tower to camp in. This was much better than a haystack. They could light a fire and eat hot food from the soldier's packets, and Abdullah could get warm and dry at last. His spirits rose.

The soldier was cheerful too. He sat leaning against the stone wall with Whippersnapper asleep in his hat beside him and gazed out at the sunset. "I've been thinking," he said. "You get a wish from your misty blue friend tomorrow, don't you? You know the most practical wish you could make? You should wish for that magic carpet back. Then we could really get on."

"It would be just as easy to wish ourselves straight to

Kingsbury, intelligent infantryman," Abdullah pointed out – a little sullenly, if the truth be told.

"Ah yes, but I've got that genie's measure now, and I know he'd mess that wish up if he possibly could," the soldier said. "My point is, you know how to work that carpet, and you could get us there with much less trouble *and* a wish in hand for emergencies."

This was sound sense. Nevertheless Abdullah only grunted. This was because the way the soldier put his advice had made Abdullah suddenly see things a whole new way. Of course the soldier had got the genie's measure. The soldier was like that. He was an expert in getting other people to do what he wanted. The only creature who could make the soldier do something he did not want was Midnight, and Midnight did things *she* did not want only when Whippersnapper wanted something. That put the kitten right at the top of the pecking order. A kitten! thought Abdullah. And since the soldier had the genie's measure and the genie was very definitely on top of Abdullah, that put Abdullah right down at the bottom. No wonder he had been feeling so put-upon! It did not make him feel any better to realise that things had been exactly the same way with his father's first wife's relations.

So Abdullah only grunted, which in Zanzib would have counted as shocking rudeness, and the soldier was quite unaware of it. He pointed cheerfully at the sky. "Lovely sunset again. Look, there's another castle."

The soldier was right. There was a glory of yellow lakes

in the sky, and islands and promontories, and one long indigo headland of cloud with a frowning square cloud like a fortress on it. "It is not the same as the other castle," Abdullah said. He felt it was time he asserted himself.

"Of course not. You never get the same cloud twice," said the soldier.

Abdullah contrived to be the first one awake the next morning. Dawn was still flaring across the sky when he sprang up, seized the genie bottle and took it some distance away from the ruins where their camp was. "Genie," he said. "Appear."

A flutter of steam appeared at the mouth of the bottle, grudging and ghostly. "What's this?" it said. "Where's all the talk about jewels and flowers and so forth?"

"You told me you did not like it. I have discontinued it," said Abdullah. "I have now become a realist. The wish I want to make is in accordance with my new outlook."

"Ah," said the wisp of genie. "You're going to ask for the magic carpet back."

"Not at all," said Abdullah. This so surprised the genie that he rose right out of the bottle and regarded Abdullah with wide eyes, which in the dawn light looked solid and shiny and almost like human eyes. "I shall explain," said Abdullah. "Thus. Fate is clearly determined to delay my search for Flower-in-the-Night. This is in spite of the fact that Fate has also decreed that I shall marry her. Any attempt I make to go against Fate causes you to make sure that my wish does no good to anyone, and usually also ensures that I get pursued by persons on camels or horses. Or else the soldier causes me to waste a wish. Since I am tired both of your malice and the soldier so continually getting his own way, I have decided to challenge Fate instead. I intend to waste every wish deliberately from now on. Fate will then be forced to take a hand, or else the prophecy concerning Flower-in-the-Night will never be fulfilled."

"You're being childish," said the genie. "Or heroic. Or possibly mad."

"No – realistic," said Abdullah. "Furthermore I shall challenge *you* by wasting the wishes in a way that might do good somewhere to someone."

The genie looked decidedly sarcastic at this. "And what is your wish today? Homes for orphans? Sight for the blind? Or do you simply want all the money in the world taken away from the rich and given to the poor?"

"I was thinking," said Abdullah, "that I *might* wish that those two bandits whom you transformed into toads should be restored to their own shape."

A look of malicious glee spread over the genie's face. "You might do worse. I could grant you that one with pleasure."

"What is the drawback to that wish?" asked Abdullah.

"Oh, not much," said the genie. "Simply that the Sultan's soldiers are camped in that oasis at the moment. The Sultan is convinced that you are still somewhere in the desert. His men are quartering the entire region for you, but I'm sure they will spare a moment for two bandits, if only to show the Sultan how zealous they are."

Abdullah considered this. "And who else is in the desert who might be in danger from the Sultan's search?"

The genie looked sideways at him. "You *are* anxious to waste a wish, aren't you? Nobody much there except a few carpet weavers and a prophet or so – and Jamal and his dog, of course."

"Ah," said Abdullah. "then I waste this wish on Jamal and his dog. I wish that Jamal and his dog both be instantly transported to a life of ease and prosperity as – let me see – yes, as palace cook and guard dog in the nearest royal palace apart from Zanzib."

"You make it very difficult," the genie said pathetically, "for that wish to go wrong."

"Such was my aim," said Abdullah. "If I could discover how to make *none* of your wishes go wrong, it would be a great relief."

"There is one wish you could make to do that," said the genie.

He sounded rather wistful, from which Abdullah realised what he meant. The genie wanted to be free of the enchantment that bound him to the bottle. It would be easy enough to waste a wish that way, Abdullah reflected, but only if he could count on the genie being grateful enough to help him find Flower-in-the-Night afterwards. With *this* genie, that was most unlikely. And if he freed the genie, then he would have to give up challenging Fate, which he was determined to do. "I shall think about that wish for later," he said. "My wish today is for Jamal and his dog. Are they now safe?"

"Yes," the genie said sulkily. From the look on his smoky face as it vanished inside the bottle, Abdullah had an uneasy feeling that he had somehow contrived to make this wish go wrong too, but of course there was no way to tell.

Abdullah turned round to find the soldier watching him. He had no idea how much the soldier had overheard, but he got ready for an argument.

But all the soldier said was, "Don't quite follow your logic in all that," before suggesting that they walked on until they found a farm where they could buy breakfast.

Abdullah shouldered Midnight again and they trudged off. All that day they wandered deep lanes again. Though there was no sign of any constables, they did not seem to be getting any nearer to Kingsbury. In fact, when the soldier enquired from a man digging a ditch how far it was to Kingsbury, he was told it was four days' walk.

Fate! thought Abdullah.

The next morning he went round to the other side of the haystack where they had slept and wished that the two toads in the oasis should now become men.

The genie was very annoyed. "You heard me say that the first person who opened my bottle would become a toad! Do you want me to undo my good work?"

"Yes," said Abdullah.

"Regardless of the fact that the Sultan's men are still there and will certainly hang them?" asked the genie.

"I think," said Abdullah, remembering his experiences as a toad, "that they would rather be men even so."

"Oh very well then!" the genie said mournfully. "You realise my revenge is in ruins, don't you? But what do *you* care? I'm just a daily wish in a bottle to you!"

CHAPTER FOURTEEN

Which tells how the magic carpet reappeared

Once again, Abdullah turned round to find the soldier watching him, but this time the soldier said nothing at all. Abdullah was fairly sure he was simply biding his time.

That day, as they trudged onwards, the ground climbed. The lush green lanes gave way to sandy tracks bordered with bushes that were dry and spiny. The soldier remarked cheerfully that they seemed to be getting somewhere different at last. Abdullah only grunted. He was determined not to give the soldier an opening.

By nightfall, they were high on an open heath, looking over a new stretch of the plain. A faint pimple on the horizon was, the soldier said, still very cheerful, certainly Kingsbury.

As they settled down to camp, he invited Abdullah, even more cheerfully, to see how charmingly Whippersnapper was playing with the buckles on his pack.

"Doubtless," said Abdullah. "It charms me even less than a lump on the skyline that may be Kingsbury."

There was another huge red sunset. While they ate supper, the soldier pointed it out to Abdullah and drew his attention to a large red castle-shaped cloud. "Isn't that beautiful?" he said.

"It is only a cloud," said Abdullah. "It has no artistic merit."

"Friend," said the soldier, "I think you are letting that genie get to you."

"How so?" said Abdullah.

The soldier pointed with his spoon to the distant dark hummock against the sunset. "See there?" he said. "Kingsbury. Now I have a hunch, and I think you do too, that things are going to start moving when we get there. But we don't seem to get there. Don't think I can't see your point of view – you're a young fellow, disappointed in love, impatient – naturally you think Fate's against you. Take it from me, Fate doesn't care either way most of the time. The genie's not on anyone's side any more than Fate is."

"How do you make that out?" asked Abdullah.

"Because he hates everyone," said the soldier. "Maybe it's his nature – though I daresay being shut in a bottle doesn't help any. But don't forget that, whatever his feelings, he's always got to grant you a wish. Why make it hard for yourself just to spite the genie? Why not make the most useful wish you can, get what *you* want out of it and put up with whatever he does to send it wrong? I've been thinking this through and it seems to me that *whatever* that genie does to send it wrong, your best wish is still to ask for that magic carpet back."

While the soldier was speaking, Midnight – to Abdullah's great surprise – climbed to Abdullah's knees and rubbed herself against his face, purring. Abdullah had to admit he was flattered. He had been letting Midnight get to him as well as the genie and the soldier – not to speak of Fate. "If I wish for the carpet," he said, "I am prepared to bet that the misfortunes the genie sends with it will far outweigh its usefulness."

"You bet, do you?" said the soldier. "I never resist a bet. Bet you a gold piece the carpet will be more use than trouble."

"Done," said Abdullah. "And now you have your own way again. It perplexes me, my friend, that you never rose to command that army of yours."

"Me too," said the soldier. "I'd have made a good general."

Next morning, they woke into a thick mist. Everywhere was white and wet and it was impossible to see beyond the nearest bushes. Midnight coiled against Abdullah, shivering. The genie's bottle, when Abdullah put it down in front of them, had a distinctly sulky look.

"Come out," said Abdullah. "I need to make a wish."

"I can grant it quite as well from in here," the genie retorted hollowly. "I don't like this damp."

"Very well," said Abdullah. "I wish for my magic carpet back again."

"Done," said the genie. "And let that teach you to make silly bets!"

For a while, Abdullah looked up and around expectantly but nothing seemed to happen. Then Midnight sprang to her feet. Whippersnapper's face came out of the soldier's pack, ears cocked sideways to the south. When Abdullah gazed that way, he thought he could just hear a slight whispering, which could have been the wind of something moving through the mist. Shortly, the mist swirled – and swirled harder. The grey oblong of the carpet slid into sight overhead and glided to the ground beside Abdullah.

It had a passenger. Curled up on the carpet, peacefully asleep, was a villainous man with a large moustache. His beak of a nose was pressed into the carpet, but Abdullah could just see the gold ring in it, half hidden by the moustache and a dirty drape of headcloth. One of the man's hands clutched a silver-mounted pistol. There was no question that this was Kabul Aqba again.

"I think I win the bet," Abdullah murmured.

Even that murmur – or maybe the chilliness of the mist – set the bandit stirring and muttering fretfully. The soldier put his finger to his lips and shook his head. Abdullah nodded. If he had been on his own, he would have been wondering what on earth to do now, but with the soldier there he felt almost equal to Kabul Aqba. As quietly as he could, he made a gentle snoring noise and whispered to the carpet, "Come out from underneath that man and hover in front of me."

Ripples ran down the edge of the carpet. Abdullah could see it was trying to obey. It gave a strong wriggle, but Kabul Aqba's weight was evidently just too much to allow it to slide out from under him. So it tried another way. It rose an inch into the air and, before Abdullah realised what it intended to do, it had darted out from under the sleeping bandit.

"*No!*" said Abdullah, but he said it too late. Kabul Aqba thumped down on to the ground and woke. He sat up, waving his pistol and howling in a strange language.

In an alert, leisurely sort of way, the soldier picked up the hovering carpet and wrapped it round Kabul Aqba's head. "Get his pistol," he said, holding the struggling bandit in both brawny arms.

Abdullah plunged to one knee and grasped the strong hand waving the pistol. It was a *very* strong hand. Abdullah could do nothing about taking the pistol away. He could only hang on and go crashing to and fro as the hand tried to shake him off. Beside him, the soldier was also crashing to and fro. Kabul Aqba seemed quite amazingly strong. Abdullah, as he was battered about, tried to take hold of one of the bandit's fingers and uncurl it from round the pistol.

But at this Kabul Aqba roared and rose upwards and Abdullah was flung off backwards with the carpet somehow wrapped round *him* instead of round Kabul Aqba. The soldier hung on. He hung on even though Kabul Aqba went on rising upwards, roaring now like the sky falling, and the soldier, from gripping him round the arms, went to gripping him round the waist and then round the top of the legs. Kabul Aqba shouted as if his voice was the thunder itself and rose up bigger yet, until both his legs were too big to hold at once, and the soldier slid down until he was grimly clutching one of them, just below its vast knee. That leg tried to kick the soldier loose and failed. Whereupon Kabul Aqba spread enormous leathery wings and tried to fly away. But the soldier, though he slid downwards again, hung on still.

Abdullah saw all this while he was struggling out from under the carpet. He also caught a glimpse of Midnight standing protectively over Whippersnapper, larger even than she had been when she faced the constables. But not large enough. What stood there now was one of the mightiest of mighty djinns. Half of him was lost upwards in the mist, which he was beating into swirling smoke with his wings, unable to fly because the soldier was anchoring one of his enormous taloned feet to the ground.

"Explain yourself, mightiest of mighty ones!" Abdullah shouted up into the mist. "By the Seven Great Seals, I conjure you to cease your struggling and explain!"

The djinn stopped roaring and halted the violent fanning

of his wings. "You conjure me, do you, mortal?" the great sullen voice came down.

"I do indeed," said Abdullah. "Say what you were doing with my carpet and in the form of that most ignoble of nomads. You have wronged me at least twice!"

"Very well," said the djinn. He began ponderously to kneel down.

"You can let go now," Abdullah said to the soldier who, not knowing the laws that governed djinns, was still hanging on to the vast foot. "He has to stay and answer me now."

Warily the soldier let go and mopped sweat from his face. He did not seem reassured when the djinn simply folded his wings and knelt. This was not surprising, because the djinn was as high as a house even kneeling and the face coming into view through the mist was hideous. Abdullah had another glimpse of Midnight, now normal size again, scurrying for the bushes with Whippersnapper dangling from her mouth. But the face of the djinn took up most of his attention. He had seen that blank brown glare and the gold ring through that hooked nose – albeit briefly – before, when Flower-in-the-Night was carried off from the garden.

"Correction," Abdullah said. "You have wronged me *three* times."

"Oh, more than that," the djinn rumbled blandly. "So many times that I have lost count."

At this Abdullah found himself angrily folding his arms. "Explain."

"Willingly," said the djinn. "I was indeed hoping to be

asked by someone, although I had supposed the questions most likely to come from the Duke of Farqtan or the three rival princes of Thayack, rather than from you. But none of the rest have proved determined enough – which surprises me somewhat, because you were certainly never my main irons in the fire, either of you. Know then that I am one of the greatest of the host of Good Djinns and my name is Hasruel."

"I didn't know there *were* any good djinns," said the soldier.

"Oh there are, innocent northerner," Abdullah told him. "I have heard this one's name spoken in terms that place him nearly as high as the angels."

The djinn frowned – an unpleasant sight. "Misinformed merchant," he rumbled. "I am *higher* than some angels. Know that some two hundred angels of the lesser air are mine to command. They serve as guards to the entrance of my castle."

Abdullah kept his arms folded and tapped with his foot. "This being the case," he said, "explain why you have seen fit to behave towards me in a manner so far from angelic."

"The blame is not mine, mortal," said the djinn. "Need spurred me on. Understand all, and forgive. Know that my mother, the Great Spirit Dazrah, in a moment of oversight allowed herself to be ravished by a djinn of the Host of Evil some twenty years ago. She then gave birth to my brother Dalzel who – since Good and Evil do not breed well together – proved weak and white and undersized. My mother could not tolerate Dalzel and gave him to me to bring up. I lavished every care upon him as he grew. So you can imagine my horror and sorrow when he proved to inherit the nature of his Evil Sire. His first act, when he came of age, was to steal my life and hide it, thereby making me his slave."

"Come again?" said the soldier. "You mean you're *dead*?"

"Not at all," said Hasruel. "We djinns are not as you mortals, ignorant man. We can only die if one small portion of us is destroyed. For this reason, all djinns prudently remove that small part from our persons and hide it. As I did. But when I instructed Dalzel how to hide his own life, I lovingly and rashly told him where my life was hidden. And he instantly took my life into his power, forcing me to do his bidding or die."

"Now we come to it," said Abdullah. "His bidding was to steal Flower-in-the-Night."

"Correction," said Hasruel. "My brother inherits a grandeur of mind from his mother, great Dazrah. He ordered me to steal every princess in the world. A moment's thought will show you the sense in this. My brother is of an age to marry, but he is of a birth so mixed that no female among djinns will countenance him. He is forced to resort to mortal women. But since he is a djinn, naturally only those females of the highest blood will serve."

"My heart bleeds for your brother," remarked Abdullah. "Could he not be satisfied with less than all?"

"Why should he be?" asked Hasruel. "He commands my power now. He gave the matter careful thought. And, seeing clearly that his princesses would not be able to walk on air as we djinns do, he first ordered me to steal a certain moving castle belonging to a wizard in this land of Ingary, in which to house his brides, and then he ordered me to commence stealing princesses. This I am now engaged in doing. But naturally at the same time I am laying plans of my own. For each princess that I take, I arrange to leave behind at least one injured lover or disappointed prince who might be persuaded to attempt to rescue her. In order to do this, the lover will have to challenge my brother and wrest from him the secret hiding place of my life."

"And is this where I come in, mighty machinator?" Abdullah asked coldly. "I am part of your plans to regain your life, am I?"

"Just barely," answered the djinn. "My hopes were more upon the heir of Alberia or the prince of Peichstan, but both these young men have thrown themselves into hunting instead. Indeed, all of them have shown remarkable lack of spirit, including the king of High Norland, who is merely attempting to catalogue his books on his own, without his daughter's help, and even he was a likelier chance than you. You were, you might say, an outside bet of mine. The prophecy at your birth *was* highly ambiguous, after all. I confess to selling you that magic carpet almost purely out of amusement—"

"You did!" Abdullah exclaimed.

"Yes — amusement at the number and nature of the daydreams proceeding from your booth," said Hasruel.

Abdullah, despite the cold of the mist, found his face was heating up.

"Then," continued Hasruel, "when you surprised me by escaping from the Sultan of Zanzib, it amused me to take on your character of Kabul Aqba and to force you to live out some of your daydreams. I usually try to make appropriate adventures befall each suitor."

Despite his embarrassment, Abdullah could have sworn that the djinn's great gold-brown eyes slanted towards the soldier here. "And how many disappointed princes have you so far put in motion, oh subtle and jesting djinn?" he asked.

"Very nearly thirty," Hasruel said, "but, as I said, most of them are not in motion at all. This strikes me as strange, for their birth and qualifications are all far better than yours. However, I console myself with the thought that there are still one hundred and thirty-two princesses left to steal."

"I think you might have to be satisfied with me," Abdullah said. "Low as my birth is, Fate seems to want it so. I am in a position to assure you of this, since I have recently challenged Fate on this very point."

The djinn smiled — a sight as unpleasant as his frown — and nodded. "This I know," he said. "This is the reason I have stooped to appear before you. Two of my servant angels returned to me yesterday, having just been hanged in the shape of men. Neither was wholly pleased by this and both claimed it was your doing."

Abdullah bowed. "Doubtless when they consider, they will find it preferable to being immortal toads," he said. "Now tell me one last thing, oh thoughtful thief of princesses. Say where Flower-in-the-Night, not to speak of your brother Dalzel, may be found."

The djinn's smile broadened – which made it even more unpleasant, as this revealed a number of extremely long fangs. He pointed upwards with a vast spiked thumb. "Why, earthbound adventurer, they are naturally in the castle you have been seeing in the sunset these last few days," he said. "It used, as I said, to belong to a wizard of this land. You will not find it easy to get there, and if you do, you will do well to remember that I am my brother's slave and forced to act against you."

"Understood," said Abdullah.

The djinn planted his enormous taloned hands on the ground and began to lever himself up. "I must also observe," he said, "that the carpet is under orders not to follow me. May I depart now?"

"No, wait!" cried the soldier. Abdullah, at the same moment, remembered one thing he had forgotten and asked, "And what of the genie?" but the soldier's voice was louder and drowned Abdullah's. "*WAIT, you monster!* Is that castle hanging around in the sky here for any particular reason, monster?"

Hasruel smiled again and paused, balanced on one huge knee. "How perceptive of you, soldier. Indeed yes.

The castle is here because I am preparing to steal the daughter of the king of Ingary, Princess Valeria."

"My princess!" said the soldier.

Hasruel's smile became a laugh. He threw back his head and bellowed into the mist. "I doubt it, soldier! Oh, I doubt it! This princess is only four years old. But though she is of little use to you, I trust that you are going to be of great use to me. I regard both you and your friend from Zanzib as well-placed pawns on my chessboard."

"How do you mean?" the soldier asked indignantly.

"Because the two of you are going to help me steal her!" said the djinn, and sprang away upward into the mist in a whirl of wings, laughing hugely.

CHAPTER FIFTEEN

In which the travellers arrive at Kingsbury

"If you ask me," said the soldier, moodily dumping his pack on the magic carpet, "that creature is as bad as his brother – if he *has* a brother, that is."

"Oh, he has a brother. Djinns do not lie," said Abdullah. "But they are always prone to see themselves as superior to mortals, even the good djinns. And Hasruel's name *is* on the Lists of the Good."

"You could have fooled me!" said the soldier. "Where's Midnight got to? She must have been frightened to death." He made such a pother over hunting for Midnight in the bushes that Abdullah did not try to explain any more of the lore concerning djinns, which every child in Zanzib learnt at school. Besides, he feared the soldier was right. Hasruel might have taken the Seven Vows that made him one of the Host of the Good, but his brother had given him the perfect excuse to break all seven of them. Good or not, Hasruel was clearly enjoying himself hugely.

Abdullah picked up the genie bottle and put it on the carpet. It promptly fell on its side and rolled off. "No, no!" the genie cried from inside. "I'm not going on *that*! Why do you think I fell off it before? I hate heights!"

"Oh don't *you* start!" said the soldier. He had Midnight wrapped around one arm, kicking and scratching and biting, and demonstrating in every way she could that cats and flying carpets do not mix. This in itself was enough to make anyone irritable, but Abdullah suspected that most of the soldier's ill humour had to do with the fact that Princess Valeria was only four years old. The soldier had been thinking of himself as engaged to Princess Valeria. Now, not unnaturally, he was feeling a fool.

Abdullah seized the genie bottle, very firmly, and settled himself on the carpet. Tactfully, he said nothing about their bet, although it was fairly clear to him that he had won it hands down. True, they had the carpet back, but since it was forbidden to follow the djinn it was no use at all for rescuing Flower-in-the-Night.

After a prolonged struggle, the soldier got himself and his hat and Midnight and Whippersnapper more or less securely on the carpet too. "Give your orders," he said. His brown face was flushed.

Abdullah snored. The carpet rose a gentle foot in the air, whereupon Midnight howled and struggled and the genie bottle shook in his hands. "Oh elegant tapestry of enchantment," Abdullah said, "oh carpet compiled of the most complex cantrips, I pray you to move at a sedate speed towards Kingsbury, but to exercise the great wisdom woven into your fabric to make sure that we are not seen by anyone on the way."

Obediently, the carpet climbed through the mist, upwards and south. The soldier clamped Midnight in his arms. A hoarse and trembling voice said from the bottle, "Do you *have* to flatter it so disgustingly?"

"This carpet," said Abdullah, "unlike you, is of an ensorcellment so pure and excellent that it will listen only to the finest language. It is at heart a poet among carpets."

A certain smugness spread through the pile of the carpet. It held its tattered edges proudly straight and sailed sweetly forward into the golden sunlight above the mist. A small blue jet came out of the bottle and disappeared again with a yip of panic. "Well, *I* wouldn't do it!" said the genie.

At first it was easy for the carpet not to be seen. It simply flew above the mist, which lay below them white and solid as milk. But as the sun climbed, golden-green fields began to appear shimmeringly through it, then white roads and occasional houses. Whippersnapper was frankly fascinated. He stood at the edge staring downwards and looked so likely to tip off head first that the soldier kept one hand strongly round his small bushy tail.

This was just as well. The carpet banked away towards a line of trees that followed a river. Midnight dug all her claws in and Abdullah only just saved the soldier's pack.

The soldier looked a little seasick. "Do we have to be this careful not to be seen?" he asked as they went gliding beside the trees like a tramp lurking in a hedge.

"I think so," said Abdullah. "In my experience, to see this eagle among carpets is to wish to steal it." And he told the soldier about the person on the camel.

The soldier agreed that Abdullah had a point. "It's just that it's going to slow us down," he said. "My feeling is that we ought to get to Kingsbury and warn the king that there's a djinn after his daughter. Kings give big rewards for that kind of information." Clearly, now he had been forced to give up the idea of marrying Princess Valeria, the soldier was thinking of other ways of making his fortune.

"We shall do that, never fear," said Abdullah, and once again did not mention their bet.

It took most of that day to reach Kingsbury. The carpet followed rivers, slid from wood to forest, and only put on speed where the land below was empty. When, in the late afternoon, they reached the city, a wide cluster of towers inside high walls that was easily three times the size of Zanzib, if not larger, Abdullah directed the carpet to find a good inn near the king's palace and to set them down somewhere where no one would suspect how they had travelled.

The carpet obeyed by sliding over the great walls like a snake. After that it kept to the roofs, following the shape of each roof the way a flounder follows the sea bottom. Abdullah and the soldier and the cats too stared down and around in wonder. The streets, wide or narrow, were choked with richly dressed people and expensive carriages. Every house seemed to Abdullah like a palace. He saw towers, domes, rich carvings, golden cupolas and marble courts the Sultan of Zanzib would have been glad to call his own. The poorer houses – if you could call such richness poor – were decorated with painted patterns, quite exquisitely. As for the shops, the wealth and quantity of the wares they had for sale made Abdullah realise that the Bazaar at Zanzib was really shabby and second-rate. No wonder the Sultan had been so anxious for an alliance with the prince of Ingary!

The inn the carpet found for them, near the great marble buildings at the centre of Kingsbury, had been plastered by a master in raised designs of fruit, which had then been painted in the most glowing colours with much gold leaf. The carpet landed gently on the sloping roof of the inn stables, hiding them cunningly beside a gold spire with a gilded weathercock on the top. They sat and looked round at all this magnificence while they waited for the yard below to be empty. There were two servants down there, cleaning a gilded carriage, gossiping as they worked.

Most of what they said was about the landlord of this inn, who was clearly a man who loved money. But, when they had finished complaining how little they were paid, one man said, "Any news of that Strangian soldier who robbed all those people up north? Someone told me he was heading this way."

To which the other replied, "He's sure to make for Kingsbury. They all do. But they're watching for him at the city gates. He won't get far."

The soldier's eyes met Abdullah's.

Abdullah murmured, "Do you have a change of clothes?"

The soldier nodded and dug furiously in his pack. Shortly, he produced two peasant-style shirts with smocked embroidery on the chests and backs. Abdullah wondered how he had come by those.

"Clothes-line," murmured the soldier, bringing out a clothes-brush and his razor. There on the roof, he changed into one of the shirts and did his best to brush his trousers without making a noise. The noisiest part was when he was trying to shave without anything but the razor. The two servants kept glancing towards the dry scratching from the roof.

"Must be a bird," said one.

Abdullah put the second shirt on over his jacket, which was by now looking like anything but his best one. He was rather hot like that, but there was no way he could remove the money hidden in his jacket without letting the soldier see how much he had. He brushed his hair with the clothes-brush, smoothed his moustache – it now felt as if there were at least twelve hairs there – and then brushed his trousers with the clothes-brush too. When he was done, the soldier passed Abdullah the razor and silently stretched out his pigtail.

"A great sacrifice, but a wise one, I think, my friend," Abdullah murmured. He sawed the pigtail off and hid it in the golden weathercock. This made quite a transformation. The soldier now looked like a bushy-headed prosperous farmer. Abdullah hoped he would pass for the farmer's young brother himself.

While they were doing this, the two servants finished cleaning the carriage and began pushing it into the coach house. As they passed under the roof where the carpet was, one of them asked, "And what do you think to this story that someone's trying to steal the princess?"

"Well, I think it's true," the other one said, "if that's what you're asking. They say the Royal Wizard risked a lot to send a warning, poor fellow, and he's not the kind to take a risk for nothing."

The soldier's eyes met Abdullah's again. His mouth formed a hearty curse.

"Never mind," Abdullah murmured. "There are other ways to earn a reward."

They waited until the servants had gone back across the yard and into the inn. Then Abdullah requested the carpet to land in the yard. It glided obediently down. Abdullah picked the carpet up and wrapped the genie bottle inside it, while the soldier carried his pack and both cats. They went into the inn trying hard to look dull and respectable.

The landlord met them there. Warned by what the servants had said, Abdullah met the landlord with a gold piece casually between his finger and thumb. The landlord looked at that. His flinty eyes stared at the gold piece so fixedly that Abdullah doubted if he even saw their faces. Abdullah was extremely polite. So was the landlord. He showed them to a nice spacious room on the second floor. He agreed to send up supper and provide baths.

"And the cats will need—" the soldier began.

Abdullah kicked the soldier's ankle, hard. "And that will be all, oh lion among landlords," he said. "Although, most helpful of hosts, if your active and vigilant staff could provide a basket, a cushion and a dish of salmon, the powerful witch to whom we are to deliver tomorrow this pair of exceptionally gifted cats, will undoubtedly reward whoever brings these things most bountifully."

"I'll see what I can do, sir," the landlord said. Abdullah carelessly tossed him the gold piece. The man bowed deeply and backed out of the room, leaving Abdullah feeling decidedly pleased with himself.

"There's no need to look so smug!" the soldier said angrily. "What are we supposed to do now? I'm a wanted man here and the king seems to know all about the djinn."

It was a pleasant feeling to Abdullah to find that he was in command of events instead of the soldier. "Ah, but does the king know that there is a castle full of stolen princesses hovering overhead to receive his daughter?" he said. "You are forgetting, my friend, that the king cannot have had the advantage of speaking personally to the djinn. We might make use of this fact."

"How?" demanded the soldier. "Can you think of a way to stop that djinn stealing the child? Or a way to get to the castle, for that matter!"

"No, but it seems to me that a wizard might know these things," said Abdullah. "I think we should modify the idea you had earlier. Instead of finding one of this king's wizards and strangling him, we might enquire which wizard is the best and pay him a fee for his help."

"All right, but you'll have to do that," said the soldier. "Any wizard worth his salt would spot me for a Strangian at once and call the constables before I could move."

The landlord brought the food for the cats himself. He hurried in with a bowl of cream, a carefully boned salmon and a dish of whitebait. He was followed by his wife, a woman as flinty-eyed as himself, carrying a soft rush basket and an embroidered cushion. Abdullah tried not to look smug again. "Generous thanks, most illustrious of innkeepers," he said. "I will tell the witch of your great care."

"That's all right, sir," the landlady said. "We know how to respect those that use magic, here in Kingsbury."

Abdullah went from smug to mortified. He saw now that he should have pretended to be a wizard himself. He relieved his feelings by saying, "That cushion *is* stuffed only with peacock feathers, I hope? The witch is most particular."

"Yes, sir," said the landlady. "I know all about that."

The soldier coughed. Abdullah gave up. He said grandly, "As well as the cats, my friend and I have been entrusted with a message for a wizard. We would prefer to deliver it to a Royal Wizard – but we heard rumours on the way that the Royal Wizard had met with some sort of misfortune."

"That's right," said the landlord, pushing his wife aside. "One of the Royal Wizards *has* disappeared, sir, but fortunately there are two. I can direct you to the other one – Royal Wizard Suliman – if you want, sir." He looked meaningly at Abdullah's hands.

Abdullah sighed and fetched out his largest silver piece. That seemed to be the right amount. The landlord gave him very careful directions and took the silver piece, promising baths and supper shortly. The baths, when they came, were hot and the supper was good. Abdullah was glad. While the soldier was bathing himself and Whippersnapper, Abdullah transferred his wealth from his jacket to his money belt, which made him feel much better.

The soldier must have felt better too. He sat after supper with his feet up on a table, smoking that long clay pipe of his. Cheerfully, he untied the bootlace from the neck of the genie bottle and dangled it for Whippersnapper to play with.

"There's no doubt about it," he said. "Money talks in this town. Are you going to talk to the Royal Wizard this evening? The sooner the better, to my mind."

Abdullah agreed. "I wonder what his fee will be," he said.

"Big," said the soldier. "Unless you can work it that you're doing *him* a favour by telling him what the djinn said. All the same," he went on thoughtfully, whisking the bootlace out of Whippersnapper's pouncing paws, "I reckon you shouldn't tell him about the genie or the carpet if you can help it. These magical gentlemen love magical items the way this innkeeper loves gold. You don't want him asking for those for his fee. Why don't you leave them here when you go? I'll look after them for you."

Abdullah hesitated. It seemed sound sense. Yet he did not trust the soldier.

"By the way," said the soldier, "I owe you a gold piece."

"You do?" said Abdullah. "Then this is the most surprising news I have had since Flower-in-the-Night told me I was a woman!"

"That bet of ours," said the soldier. "The carpet brought the djinn, and he's even bigger trouble than the genie usually manages. You win. Here." He tossed a gold piece across the room at Abdullah.

Abdullah caught it, pocketed it and laughed. The soldier *was* honest, after his own fashion. He went cheerfully downstairs, full of thoughts of being soon on the trail of Flower-in-the-Night, where the landlady caught him and told him all over again how to get to Wizard Suliman's house. Abdullah was so cheerful that he parted with another silver piece almost without a pang.

The house was not far from the inn, but it was in the Old Quarter, which meant that the way was mostly through confusing small alleys and hidden courts. It was twilight now, with one or two large liquid stars already in the dark blue sky above the domes and towers, but Kingsbury was well lit by big silver globes of light, floating overhead like moons.

Abdullah was looking up at them, wondering if they were magical devices, when he happened to notice a black four-legged shadow stealing along the roofs beside him. It could have been any black cat out for a hunt on the tiles, but Abdullah knew it was Midnight. There was no mistaking the way she moved. At first, when she vanished into the deep black shadow of a gable, he supposed she was after a roosting pigeon to make another unsuitable meal for Whippersnapper. But she reappeared again when he was halfway down the next alley, creeping along a parapet above him, and he began to think she was following him.

When he went through a narrow court with trees in tubs down the centre and he saw her jump across the sky, from one gutter to another, in order to get into that court too, he knew she was certainly following him. He had no idea why. He kept an eye out for her as he went down the next two alleys, but he only saw her once, on an arch over a doorway. When he turned into the cobbled court where the Royal Wizard's house was, there was no sign of her. Abdullah shrugged and went to the door of the house.

It was a handsome narrow house with diamond-paned windows and interwoven magic signs painted on its old irregular walls. There were tall spires of yellow flame burning in brass stands on either side of the front door. Abdullah seized the knocker, which was a leering face with a ring in its mouth, and boldly knocked.

The door was opened by a manservant with a long dour face. "I'm afraid the wizard is extremely busy, sir," he said. "He is receiving no clients until further notice." And he started to shut the door.

"No, wait, faithful footman and loveliest of lackeys!" Abdullah protested. "What I have to say concerns no less than a threat to the king's daughter!"

"The wizard knows all about that, sir," said the man, and went on shutting the door.

Abdullah deftly put his foot in the space. "You must hear me, most sapient servant," he began. "I come—"

Behind the manservant, a young woman's voice said, "Just a moment, Manfred. I know this is important." The door swung open again.

Abdullah gaped rather as the servant vanished from the doorway and reappeared some way back in the hall inside. His place at the door was taken by an extremely lovely young woman with dark curls and a vivid face. Abdullah saw enough of her in one glance to realise that, in her foreign northern way, she was as beautiful as Flower-in-the-Night, but after that he felt bound to look modestly away from her. She was obviously going to have a baby. Ladies in Zanzib did not show themselves in this interesting condition. Abdullah scarcely knew where to look.

"I'm the wizard's wife, Lettie Suliman," this young woman said. "What did you come about?"

Abdullah bowed. It helped to keep his eyes on the doorstep. "Oh fruitful moon of lovely Kingsbury," he said, "know that I am Abdullah, son of Abdullah, carpet merchant from distant Zanzib, with news that your husband will wish to hear. Tell him, oh splendour of a sorcerous house, that this morning I spoke with the mighty djinn Hasruel concerning the king's most precious daughter."

Lettie Suliman was clearly not at all used to the manners of Zanzib. "Good heavens!" she said. "I mean – how polite! And you're speaking the exact truth, aren't you? I think you ought to talk to Ben at once. Please come in."

She backed away from the doorway to give Abdullah room to enter. Abdullah, still with his eyes modestly lowered, stepped forward into the house. As soon as he did, something landed on his back. Then it took off again with a heavy rip of claws, and went sailing over his head to land with a thump on Lettie's prominent front. A noise like a metal pulley filled the air.

"Midnight!" Abdullah said crossly, staggering forward.

"*Sophie!*" screamed Lettie, staggering backwards with the cat in her arms. "Oh Sophie, I've been worried *sick*! Manfred, get Ben at once. I don't care what he's doing – this is *urgent*!"

CHAPTER SIXTEEN

In which strange things befall Midnight and Whippersnapper

There was a great deal of confusion and rushing about. Two other servants appeared, followed by first one and then a second young man in long blue gowns, who seemed to be the wizard's apprentices. All these people ran about, while Lettie ran back and forth in the hall with Midnight in her arms, screaming orders. In the midst of it all, Abdullah found Manfred showing him to a seat and solemnly giving him a glass of wine. Since this seemed what he was expected to do, Abdullah sat down and sipped the wine, rather bemused by the confusion.

Just as he was thinking it was going to go on for ever, it all stopped. A tall commanding man in a black robe had appeared from somewhere. "What on *earth* is going on?" said this man.

Since this summed up Abdullah's feelings entirely, he found himself rather taking to this man. He had faded red hair and a tired, craggy face. The black robe made Abdullah certain that this must be Wizard Suliman – he would have looked like a wizard whatever he was wearing. Abdullah rose from his chair and bowed. The wizard shot him a look of craggy mystification and turned to Lettie.

"He's from Zanzib, Ben," said Lettie, "and he knows something about the threat to the princess. And he brought Sophie with him. She's the *cat*! Look! Ben, you've got to change her back at *once*!"

Lettie was one of those ladies who look lovelier the more distraught they get. Abdullah was not surprised when Wizard Suliman took her gently by the elbows and said, "Yes, of course, my love," and followed that by kissing her forehead. It made Abdullah wonder miserably whether he would ever have a chance to kiss Flower-in-the-Night like that, or to add like the wizard added, "Calm down – remember the baby."

After this the wizard said over his shoulder, "And can't someone shut the front door? Half Kingsbury must know what's happened by now."

This endeared the wizard to Abdullah more than ever. The one thing which had prevented him getting up and shutting the door was a fear that it might be the custom here to leave your front door open in a crisis. He bowed again, and found the wizard swinging round to face him.

"And what *has* happened, young man?" asked the wizard. "How did you know this cat was my wife's sister?"

Abdullah was somewhat taken aback by this question. He explained – several times – that he had no idea Midnight was human, let alone that she was the Royal Wizard's sister-in-law, but he was not at all sure that anyone listened. They all seemed so glad to see Midnight that they simply assumed that Abdullah had brought her to the house out of pure friendship. Far from demanding a large fee, Wizard Suliman seemed to think that *he* owed Abdullah something and, when Abdullah protested that this was not so, he said, "Well, come along and see her changed back anyway."

He said this in such a friendly and trusting way that Abdullah warmed to him even more and let himself be swept along with everyone else to a large room that *seemed* to be at the back of the house – except that Abdullah had a feeling that it was somehow somewhere else entirely. The floor and the walls sloped in a way that was not usual.

Abdullah had never seen any working wizardry before. He gazed around with interest, for the room was crowded with intricate magical devices. Nearest to him were filigree shapes with delicate smokes wreathing about them. Beside that, large and peculiar candles stood inside complicated signs, and beyond those were strange images made of wet clay. Further off, he saw a fountain of five jets that fell in odd geometric patterns, and that half hid many much odder things, crowded into the distance beyond.

"No room to work in here," Wizard Suliman said, sweeping through. "These should hold by themselves while we set up in the next room. Hurry, all of you."

Everyone whirled on into a smaller room beyond, which was empty apart from some round mirrors hanging on the walls. Here Lettie set Midnight carefully down on a blue-green stone in the middle, where she sat seriously washing the inside of her front legs and looking totally unconcerned, while everyone else, including Lettie and the servants, worked away feverishly at building a sort of tent round her out of long silver rods.

Abdullah stood prudently against the wall, watching. By now he was rather regretting assuring the wizard that he owed him nothing. He should have taken the opportunity to ask how to reach the castle in the sky. But he reckoned that, since nobody seemed to have listened to him then, it was better to wait until things calmed down. Meanwhile, the silver rods grew into a pattern of skeletal silver stars and Abdullah watched the bustle, somewhat confused at the way the scene was reflected in all the mirrors, small and busy and bulging. The mirrors bent as oddly as the walls and floors did.

At length Wizard Suliman clapped his large bony hands. "Right," he said. "Lettie can help me here. The rest of you get to the other room and make sure the wards for the princess stay in place."

The apprentices and the servants hurried away. Wizard Suliman spread his arms. Abdullah intended to watch closely and remember clearly what happened. But somehow, as soon as the magic-working started, he was not at all sure what was going on. He knew things were happening, but they did not *seem* to happen. It was like listening to music when you were tone-deaf. Every so often, Wizard Suliman uttered a deep strange word that blurred the room and the inside of Abdullah's head with it, which made it even harder to see what was happening. But most of Abdullah's difficulty came from the mirrors on the walls.

They kept showing small round pictures which looked like reflections but were not – or not quite. Every time one of the mirrors caught Abdullah's eye, it showed the framework of rods glowing with silvery light in a new pattern – a star, a triangle, a hexagon, or some other symbol angular and secret – while the real rods in front of him did not glow at all. Once or twice a mirror showed Wizard Suliman with his arms spread when, in the room, his arms were by his sides. Several times a mirror showed Lettie standing still with her hands clasped, looking vividly nervous. But each time Abdullah looked at the real Lettie, she was moving about, making strange gestures and perfectly calm. Midnight never appeared in the mirrors at all. Her small black shape in the middle of the rods was oddly hard to see in reality too.

Then all the rods suddenly glowed misty silver and the

space inside filled with a haze. The wizard spoke a final deep word and stepped back.

"Confound it!" said someone inside the rods. "I can't smell you at all now!"

This made the wizard grin and Lettie laugh outright. Abdullah looked for the person who was amusing them so and was forced to look away almost at once. The young woman crouching inside the framework, understandably enough, had no clothes on at all. The glimpse he caught told him that the young woman was as fair as Lettie was dark, but otherwise quite like her. Lettie ran to the side of the room and came back with a wizardly green gown. When Abdullah dared to look, the young woman was wearing the gown like a dressing-gown and Lettie was trying to hug her and help her out of the framework at the same time.

"Oh *Sophie*! What *happened*?" she kept saying.

"One moment," gasped Sophie. She seemed to have difficulty balancing on two feet at first, but she hugged Lettie and then staggered to the wizard and hugged him too. "It feels so odd without a tail!" she said. "But thanks awfully, Ben." Then she advanced on Abdullah, walking rather more easily now. Abdullah backed against the wall, afraid she was going to hug him too, but all Sophie said was, "You must have wondered why I was following you. The truth is, I *always* get lost in Kingsbury."

"I am happy to have been of service, most charming of changelings," Abdullah said, rather stiffly. He was not sure he was going to get on with Sophie any more than he had got on with Midnight. She struck him as uncomfortably strong-minded for a young woman – almost as bad as his father's first wife's sister Fatima.

Lettie was still demanding to know what had turned Sophie into a cat and Wizard Suliman was saying anxiously, "Sophie, does this mean that Howl's wandering about as an animal too?"

"No, no," Sophie said, and suddenly looked desperately anxious. "I've no idea where Howl is. He was the one who turned me into a cat, you see."

"*What*? Your own husband turned you into a cat!" Lettie exclaimed. "Is this another of your quarrels then?"

"Yes, but it was all perfectly reasonable," said Sophie. "It was when someone stole the moving castle, you see. We only had about half a day's notice, and that was only because Howl happened to be working on a divining spell for the king. It showed something very powerful stealing the castle and then stealing Princess Valeria. Howl said he'd warn the king at once. Did he?"

"He certainly did," said Wizard Suliman. "The princess is guarded every second. I invoked demons and set up wards in the next room. Whatever being is threatening her has no chance of getting through."

"Thank goodness!" said Sophie. "That's a weight off my mind. It's a djinn, did you know?"

"Even a djinn couldn't get through," said Wizard Suliman. "But what did Howl do?"

"He swore," said Sophie. "In Welsh. Then he sent

Michael and the new apprentice away. He wanted to send me away too. But I said if he and Calcifer were staying, then so was I, and couldn't he put a spell on me that would simply make the djinn not notice I was there? And we argued about that—"

Lettie chuckled. "Now why doesn't that surprise me?" she said.

Sophie's face became somewhat pink and she put her head up defiantly. "Well, Howl would keep saying I'd be safest right out of the way in Wales with his sister, and he *knows* I don't get on with her, and I kept saying I'd be more use if I could be in the castle without the thief noticing. Anyway—" she put her face in her hands "—I'm afraid we were still arguing when the djinn came. There was an enormous noise and everything went dark and confused. I remember Howl shouting the words of the cat-spell – he had to gabble them in a hurry – and then yelling to Calcifer—"

"Calcifer's their fire demon," Lettie explained politely to Abdullah.

"—yelling to Calcifer to get out and save himself because the djinn was too strong for either of them," Sophie went on. "Then the castle came off from on top of me like the lid off a cheese dish. Next thing I knew I was a cat in the mountains north of Kingsbury."

Lettie and the Royal Wizard exchanged puzzled looks over Sophie's bent head. "Why those mountains?" Wizard Suliman wondered. "The castle wasn't anywhere near there."

"No, it was in four places at once," Sophie said. "I think I was thrown somewhere midway between. It could have been worse. There were plenty of mice and birds to eat."

Lettie's lovely face twisted in disgust. "*Sophie!*" she exclaimed. "Mice!"

"Why not? That's what cats eat," Sophie said, lifting her head defiantly again. "Mice are delicious. But I'm not so fond of birds. The feathers choke you. But—" She gulped and put her head in her hands again. "But it happened at a rather bad time for me. Morgan was born about a week after that, and of course he was a kitten—"

This caused Lettie, if possible, even more consternation than the thought of her sister eating mice. She burst into tears and flung her arms around Sophie. "Oh Sophie! What did you *do*?"

"What cats always do, of course," Sophie said. "Fed him and washed him a lot. Don't worry, Lettie. I left him with Abdullah's friend the soldier. That man would kill anyone who harmed his kitten. But," she said to Wizard Suliman, "I think I ought to fetch Morgan now so that you can turn him back too."

Wizard Suliman was looking almost as distraught as Lettie. "I wish I'd known!" he said. "If he was born a cat as part of the same spell, he may be changed back already. We'd better find out." He strode to one of the round mirrors and made circular gestures with both hands.

The mirror – all the mirrors – at once seemed to be reflecting the room at the inn, each from a different viewpoint, as if they were hanging on the wall there. Abdullah stared from one to the other and was as alarmed at what he saw as the other three were. The magic carpet had, for some reason, been unrolled upon the floor. On it lay a plump naked pink baby. Young as this baby was, Abdullah could see he had a personality as strong as Sophie's. And he was asserting that personality. His legs and arms were punching the air, his face was contorted with fury and his mouth was a square angry hole. Though the pictures in the mirrors were silent, it was clear that Morgan was being very noisy indeed.

"Who is that man?" said Wizard Suliman. "I've seen him before."

"A Strangian soldier, worker of wonders," Abdullah said helplessly.

"Then he must remind me of someone I know," said the wizard.

The soldier was standing beside the screaming baby looking horrified and useless. Perhaps he was hoping the genie would do something. At any rate, he had the genie bottle in one hand. But the genie was hanging out of the bottle in several spouts of distracted blue smoke, each spout a face with its hand over its ears, as helpless as the soldier.

"Oh the poor darling child!" said Lettie.

"The poor blessed soldier, you mean," said Sophie. "Morgan's furious. He's never *been* anything but a kitten and kittens can do so much more than babies can. He's angry because he can't walk. Ben, do you think you can—?"

The rest of Sophie's question was drowned in a noise like a giant piece of silk tearing. The room shook. Wizard Suliman exclaimed something and made for the door – and then had to dodge hastily. A whole crowd of screaming, wailing *somethings* swept through the wall beside the door, swooped across the room and vanished through the opposite wall. They were going too fast to be seen clearly, but none of them seemed to be human. Abdullah had a blurred glimpse of multiple clawed legs, of something streaming along on no legs at all, of beings with one wild eye and of others with many eyes in clusters. He saw fanged heads, flowing tongues, flaming tails. One, moving swiftest of all, was a rolling ball of mud.

Then they were gone. The door was thrown open by an agitated apprentice. "Sir, sir! The wards are down! We couldn't hold—"

Wizard Suliman seized the young man's arm and hurried him back into the next room, calling over his shoulder, "I'll be back when I can! The princess is in danger!"

Abdullah looked to see what was happening to the soldier and the baby, but the round mirrors now showed nothing but his own anxious face, and Sophie's and Lettie's, all staring upwards into them.

"Drat!" said Sophie. "Lettie, can you work them?"

"No. They're Ben's special thing," said Lettie.

Abdullah thought of the carpet unrolled and the genie bottle in the soldier's hand. "Then in that case, oh pair of twinned pearls," he said, "most lovely ladies, I will, with your permission, hasten back to the inn before too many complaints are made about the noise."

Sophie and Lettie replied in chorus that they were coming too. Abdullah could scarcely blame them, but he came precious near it in the next few minutes. Lettie, it seemed, was not up to hurrying through the streets in her interesting condition. As the three of them rushed through the jumble and chaos of broken spells in the next room, Wizard Suliman spared a second from frantically setting up new things in the ruins to order Manfred to get the carriage out. While Manfred raced off to do that, Lettie took Sophie upstairs to get her some proper clothes.

Abdullah was left pacing the hall. To everyone's credit, he only waited there less than five minutes, but during that time he tried the front door at least ten times, only to find there was a spell holding it shut. He thought he would go mad. It seemed like a century before Sophie and Lettie came downstairs, both in elegant going-out clothes, and Manfred opened the front door to show a small open carriage drawn by a nice bay gelding, waiting outside on the cobbles. Abdullah wanted to take a flying leap into that carriage and whip up that gelding. But of course that was not polite. He had to wait while Manfred helped the ladies up into it and then climbed to the driver's seat. The carriage set off smartly clattering across the cobbles while Abdullah was still squeezing himself into the seat beside Sophie, but even that was not quick enough for him. He could hardly bear to think of what the soldier might be doing.

"I hope Ben can get some wards back on the princess soon," Lettie said anxiously as they rolled spankingly across an open square.

The words were scarcely out of her mouth when there came a hurried volley of explosions, like very mismanaged fireworks. A bell began to ring somewhere, dismal and hasty – gong-gong-gong.

"What's all that?" asked Sophie, and then answered her own question, pointing and crying out, "Oh confound it! Look, look, look!"

Abdullah craned round where she pointed. He was in time to see a black spread of wings blotting out the stars above the nearest domes and towers. Below, from the tops of several towers, came little flashes and a number of bangs as the soldiers there fired at those wings. Abdullah could have told them that that kind of thing was no use at all against a djinn. The wings wheeled imperturbably and circled upwards, and then vanished into the dark blue of the night sky.

"Your friend the djinn," Sophie said. "I think we distracted Ben at a crucial moment."

"The djinn intended that you should, oh former feline," Abdullah said. "If you recollect, he remarked as he was leaving that he expected one of us to help him steal the princess."

Other bells round the city had joined in ringing the alarm now. People ran into the streets and stared upwards. The carriage jingled on through an increasing clamour and was forced to go slower and slower as more people gathered in the streets. Everyone seemed to know exactly what had happened. "The princess is gone!" Abdullah heard. "A devil has stolen Princess Valeria!" Most people seemed awed and frightened, but one or two were saying, "That Royal Wizard ought to be hanged! What's he *paid* for?"

"Oh dear!" said Lettie. "The king won't believe for a moment how hard Ben's been working to stop this happening!"

"Don't worry," said Sophie. "As soon as we've fetched Morgan, I'll go and tell the king. I'm good at telling the king things."

Abdullah believed her. He sat and jittered with impatience.

After what seemed another century but was probably only five minutes, the carriage pushed its way into the crowded inn yard. It was full of people all staring upwards. "Saw its wings," he heard a man saying. "It was a monstrous bird with the princess clutched in its talons."

The carriage stopped. Abdullah could give way to his impatience at last. He sprang down, shouting, "Clear the way, clear the way, oh people! Here are two witches on important business!" By repeated shouting and pushing, he managed to get Sophie and Lettie to the inn door and shove them inside. Lettie was very embarrassed.

"I wish you wouldn't *say* that!" she said. "Ben doesn't like people to know I'm a witch."

"He will have no time to think of it just now," Abdullah

said. He pushed the two of them past the staring landlord and to the stairs. "Here are the witches I spoke to you about, most heavenly host," he told the man. "They are anxious about their cats." He leapt up the stairs. He overtook Lettie, then Sophie, and raced on up the next flight. He flung open the door of the room. "Do nothing rash—" he began, and then stopped as he realised there was complete silence inside.

The room was empty.

CHAPTER SEVENTEEN

In which Abdullah at last reaches the Castle in the Air

There was a cushion in a basket among the remains of supper on the table. There was a rumpled dent in one of the beds and a cloud of tobacco smoke above it, as if the soldier had been lying there smoking until very recently. The window was closed. Abdullah rushed towards it, intending to fling it open and look out – for no real reason except that it was all he could think of – and found himself tripping over a saucer full of cream. The saucer overturned, slewing thick yellow-white cream in a long streak across the magic carpet.

Abdullah stood staring down at it. At least the carpet was still there. What did that mean? There was no sign of the soldier and certainly no sign of a noisy baby anywhere in the room. Nor, he realised, turning his eyes rapidly towards every place he could think of, was there any sign of the genie bottle.

"Oh *no*!" Sophie said, arriving at the door. "Where *is* he? He can't have gone far if the carpet's still here."

Abdullah wished he could be so certain of that. "Without desiring to alarm you, mother of a most mobile baby," he said, "I have to observe that the genie appears to be missing also."

A small vague frown creased the skin of Sophie's forehead. "What genie?"

While Abdullah was remembering that, as Midnight, Sophie had always seemed quite unaware that the genie existed, Lettie arrived in the room too, panting, with one hand pressed to her side. "What's the matter?" she gasped.

"They're not here," said Sophie. "I suppose the soldier must have taken Morgan to the landlady. She must know about babies."

With a feeling of grasping at straws, Abdullah said, "I will go and see." It was always just possible that Sophie was right, he thought, as he sped down the first flight of stairs. It was what most men would do faced with a screaming baby suddenly – always supposing that man did not have a genie bottle in his hand.

The lower flight of stairs was full of people coming up,

men wearing tramping boots and some kind of uniform. The landlord was leading them upwards, saying. "On the second floor, gentlemen. Your description fits the Strangian, if he had cut off his pigtail, and the younger fellow is obviously the accomplice you speak of."

Abdullah turned and ran back upstairs on tiptoe, two stairs at a time.

"There is general disaster, most bewitching pair of women!" he gasped to Sophie and Lettie. "The landlord – a perfidious publican – is bringing constables to arrest myself and the soldier. Now what can we do?"

It was time for a strong-minded woman to take charge. Abdullah was quite glad that Sophie was one. She acted at once. She shut the door and shot its bolt. "Lend me your handkerchief," she said to Lettie, and when Lettie passed it over, Sophie knelt and mopped the cream off the magic carpet with it. "You come over here," she told Abdullah. "Get on this carpet with me and tell it to take us to wherever Morgan is. You stay here, Lettie, and hold the constables up. I don't think the carpet would carry you."

"Fine," said Lettie. "I want to get back to Ben before the king starts blaming him anyway. But I'll give that landlord a piece of my mind first. It'll be good practice for the king." As strong-minded as her sister, she squared her shoulders and stuck out her elbows in a way that promised a bad time for the landlord and the constables as well.

Abdullah was glad about Lettie too. He crouched on the carpet and snored gently. The carpet quivered. It was a reluctant quiver. "Oh fabulous fabric, carbuncle and chrysolite among carpets," Abdullah said, "this miserable clumsy churl apologises profoundly for spilling cream upon your priceless surface—"

Heavy knocking came at the door. "Open, in the king's name!" bellowed someone outside.

There was no time to flatter the carpet any further. "Carpet, I implore you," Abdullah whispered, "transport myself and this lady to the place where the soldier has taken the baby."

The carpet shook itself irritably, but it obeyed. It shot forwards in its usual way, straight through the closed window. Abdullah was alert enough this time actually to see the glass and the dark frame of the window for an instant, like the surface of water, as they passed through it and then soared above the silver globes that lit the street. But he doubted if Sophie saw. She clutched Abdullah's arm with both hands and he rather thought her eyes were shut.

"I hate heights!" she said. "It had better not be far."

"This excellent carpet will carry us with all possible speed, worshipful witch," Abdullah said, trying to reassure her and the carpet together. He was not sure it worked with either of them. Sophie continued to cling painfully to his arm, uttering little short gasps of panic, while the carpet, having made one brisk, giddy sweep just above the towers and lights of Kingsbury, swung dizzily around what seemed to be the domes of the palace and began on another circuit of the city.

"What is it *doing*?" gasped Sophie. Evidently her eyes were not quite shut.

"Peace, most serene sorceress," Abdullah reassured her. "It does but circle to gain height as birds do." Privately he was sure the carpet had lost the trail. But, as the lights and domes of Kingsbury went by underneath for the third time, he saw he had accidentally guessed right. They were now several hundred feet higher. On the fourth circuit, which was wider than the third – though quite as giddy – Kingsbury was a little jewelled cluster of lights far, far below.

Sophie's head bobbed as she took a downwards peep. Her grip on Abdullah became even tighter, if that was possible. "Oh goodness and awfulness!" she said. "We're still going *up*! I do believe that wretched soldier has taken Morgan after the djinn!"

They were now so high that Abdullah feared she was right. "He no doubt wished to rescue the princess," he said, "in hope of a large reward."

"He had no business to take my baby along too!" Sophie declared. "Just wait till I see him! But how did he *do* it without the carpet?"

"He must have ordered the genie to follow the djinn, oh moon of motherhood," Abdullah explained.

To which Sophie said again, "What genie?"

"I assure you, sharpest of sorcerous minds, that I owned a genie as well as this carpet, though you never appeared to see it," Abdullah said.

"Then I take your word for it," said Sophie. "Keep talking. Talk – or I shall look down and if I look down I *know* I'll fall off!"

Since she was still clinging mightily to Abdullah's arm, he knew that if she fell then so would he. Kingsbury was now a bright hazy dot, appearing on this side and then on that, as the carpet continued to spiral upwards. The rest of Ingary was laid out around it like a huge dark blue dish. The thought of plunging all that way down made Abdullah almost as frightened as Sophie. He began hastily to tell her all his adventures, how he had met Flower-in-the-Night, how the Sultan had put him in prison, how the genie had been fished out of the oasis pool by Kabul Aqba's men – who were really angels – and how hard it was to make a wish that the genie's malice did not spoil.

By this time he could see the desert as a pale sea south of Ingary, though they were so high that it was quite hard to make out anything below. "I see now that the soldier agreed I had won that bet in order to convince me of his honesty," Abdullah said ruefully. "I think he always meant to steal the genie and probably the carpet too."

Sophie was interested. Her grip on his arm relaxed slightly, to Abdullah's great relief. "You can't blame that genie for hating everyone," she said. "Think how you felt shut in that dungeon."

"But the soldier—" said Abdullah.

"Is another matter!" Sophie declared. "Just *wait* till I get my hands on him! I can't *abide* people who go soft over animals and then cheat every human they come across! But, to get back to this genie you say you had – it looks as if the djinn meant you to have it. Do you think it was part of his scheme to have disappointed lovers help him get the better of his brother?"

"I believe so," said Abdullah.

"Then when we get to the cloud castle, *if* that's where we're going," Sophie said, "then we might be able to count on other disappointed lovers arriving to help."

"Maybe," Abdullah said cautiously. "But I recollect, most curious of cats, that you were fleeing to the bushes while the djinn spoke, and the djinn himself expected only myself."

Nevertheless, he looked upwards. It was growing chilly now and the stars seemed uncomfortably close. There was a sort of silveriness to the dark blue of the sky which suggested moonlight trying to break through from somewhere. It was very beautiful. Abdullah's heart swelled with the thought that he might be, at last, on the way to rescue Flower-in-the-Night.

Unfortunately, Sophie looked up too. Her grip on his arm tightened. "Talk," she said, "I'm terrified."

"Then you must talk too, courageous caster of spells," said Abdullah. "Close your eyes and tell me of the prince of Ochinstan to whom Flower-in-the-Night was betrothed."

"I don't think she could have been," Sophie said, babbling rather. She was truly terrified. "The king's son is only a baby. Of course there's the king's *brother*, Prince

Justin, but *he* was supposed to be marrying Princess Beatrice of Strangia – except that she refused to hear of it and ran away. Do you think the djinn's got her? I think your Sultan was just after some of the weapons our wizards have been making here – and he wouldn't have got them. They don't let the mercenaries take them south when they go. In fact, Howl says they shouldn't even send mercenaries. Howl—" Her voice faded. Her hands on Abdullah's arm shook. "Talk!" she croaked.

It was getting hard to breathe. "I barely can, strong-handed sultana," Abdullah gasped. "I think the air is thin here. Can you not make some witchly weaving that might help us to breathe?"

"Probably not. You keep calling me a witch, but I'm really quite new to it," Sophie protested. "You saw. When I was a cat, all I could do was get larger." But she let go of Abdullah for a moment in order to make short jerky gestures overhead. "Really, air!" she said. "This is disgraceful! You are going to have to let us breathe a bit better than this or we won't last out. Gather round and let us breathe you!" She clutched Abdullah again. "Is that any better?"

There really did seem to be more air now, though it was colder than ever. Abdullah was surprised, because Sophie's method of casting a spell struck him as most unwitch-like – in fact it was not much different from his own way of persuading the carpet to move – but he had to admit that it worked. "Yes. Many thanks, speaker of spells."

"*Talk!*" said Sophie.

They were so high that the world below was out of sight. Abdullah had no trouble understanding Sophie's terror. The carpet was sailing through dark emptiness, up and up, and Abdullah knew that if he had been alone he might have been screaming. "*You* talk, mighty mistress of magics," he quavered. "Tell me of this Wizard Howl of yours."

Sophie's teeth chattered, but she said proudly, "He's the best wizard in Ingary or anywhere else. If he'd only had time, he would have defeated that djinn. And he's sly and selfish and vain as a peacock and cowardly and you can't pin him down to anything."

"Indeed?" asked Abdullah. "Strange that you should speak so proudly such a list of vices, most loving of ladies."

"What do you mean – vices?" Sophie asked angrily. "I was just *describing* Howl. He comes from another world entirely, you know, called Wales, and I refuse to believe he's dead— Ooh!"

She ended in a moan as the carpet plunged upwards into what had seemed to be a gauzy veil of cloud. Inside the cloud, the gauziness proved to be flakes of ice, which peppered them in slivers and chunks and rounds like a hailstorm. They were both gasping as the carpet burst upwards out of it. Then they both gasped again, in wonder.

They were in a new country that was bathed in moonlight – moonlight that had the golden tinge of a harvest moon to it. But when Abdullah spared an instant to look for the moon, he could not see it anywhere. The light seemed to come from the silver-blue sky itself, studded with great limpid golden stars. But he could only spare that one glance. The carpet had come out beside a hazy, transparent sea and was labouring alongside soft rollers breaking on cloudy rocks. Regardless of the fact that they could see through each wave as if it were gold-green silk, its water was wet and threatened to overwhelm the carpet. The air was warm. And the carpet, not to speak of their own clothes and hair, was loaded with piles of melting ice. Sophie and Abdullah, for the first few minutes, were entirely occupied in sweeping ice over the edges of the carpet into the translucent ocean, where it sank through into the sky beneath and vanished.

When the carpet bobbed up lighter and they had a chance to look around, they gasped again. For here were the islands and promontories and bays of dim gold that Abdullah had seen in the sunset, spreading out from beside them into the far silver distance, where they lay hushed and still and enchanted like a vista of paradise itself. The pellucid waves broke on the cloud shore with only the faintest of whispers, which seemed to add to the silence.

It seemed wrong to speak in such a place. Sophie nudged Abdullah and pointed. There, on the nearest cloudy headland, stood a castle, a mass of proud, soaring towers with dim silvery windows showing in them. It was made of cloud. As they looked, several of the taller towers streamed sideways and shredded out of existence, while others shrank and broadened. Under their eyes, it grew like a blot into a massive frowning fortress, and then began to change again.

But it was still there and still a castle and it seemed to be the place where the carpet was taking them.

The carpet was going at a swift walking pace, but gently, keeping to the shoreline as if it was not at all anxious to be seen. There were cloudy bushes beyond the waves, tinged red and silver like the aftermath of sunset. The carpet lurked in the cover of these, just as it had lurked behind trees in Kingsbury Plain, while it circled the bay to come to the promontory.

As it went there were new vistas of golden seas, where far-off smoky shapes moved that could have been ships, or may have been cloudy creatures on business of their own. Still in utter, whispering silence, the carpet crept out on to the headland, where there were no more bushes. Here it slunk close to the cloudy ground, much as it had followed the shapes of the roofs in Kingsbury. Abdullah did not blame it. Ahead of them, the castle was changing again, stretching out until it had become a mighty pavilion. As the carpet entered the long avenue leading to its gates, domes were rising and bulging, and it had protruded a dim gold minaret as if it was watching them coming.

The avenue was lined with cloudy shapes which also seemed to watch them coming. The shapes grew out of the cloud-ground in the way that one often sees a tuft of cloud curl upwards out of the main mass. But, unlike the castle, they did not change shape. Each one ramped proudly upwards, somewhat in the shape of a seahorse, or the knights in a game of chess, except that their faces were blanker and flatter than the faces of horses, and surrounded by curling tendrils that were neither cloud nor hair.

Sophie looked at each one as they passed it with increasing disfavour. "I don't think much of his taste in statues," she said.

"Oh hush, most outspoken lady!" Abdullah whispered. "These are no statues, but the two hundred attendant angels spoken of by the djinn!"

The sound of their voices attracted the attention of the nearest cloudy shape. It stirred mistily, opened a pair of immense moonstone eyes and bent to survey the carpet as it slunk past it.

"Don't you dare to try to stop us!" Sophie said to it. "We're only coming to get my baby."

The huge eyes blinked. Evidently the angel was not used to being spoken to so sharply. Cloudy white wings began to spread from its sides.

Hastily, Abdullah stood up on the carpet and bowed. "Greetings, most noble messenger of the heavens," he said. "What the lady says so bluntly is the truth. Pray forgive her. She is from the north. But she, like me, comes in peace. The djinns are minding her child and we do but come to collect him and render them our most humble and devout thanks."

This seemed to placate the angel. Its wings melted back into its cloudy sides and, though its strange head turned to watch them as the carpet slunk on, it did not try to stop them. But by now the angel across the way had its eyes open too, and the two next were turned to stare as well.

Abdullah did not dare sit down again. He braced his feet for balance and bowed to each pair of angels as they came to it. This was not easy to do. The carpet knew how dangerous the angels could be as well as Abdullah did and it was moving faster and faster.

Even Sophie realised that a little politeness would help. She nodded to each angel as they whipped past. "Evening," she said. "Lovely sunset today. Evening." She had no time for more, because the carpet was fairly scuttling up the last stretch of avenue. When it reached the castle gates – which were shut – it dived through like a rat up a drainpipe. Abdullah and Sophie were suffused with foggy damp and then out into calm goldish light.

They found they were in a garden. Here the carpet fell to the floor, limp as a dishrag, where it stayed. It had little shivers running through the length of it, as a carpet might that was shaking with fear, or panting with effort, or both.

Since the ground in the garden was solid and did not seem to be made of cloud, Sophie and Abdullah cautiously stepped on to it. It was firm turf, growing silver-green grass. In the distance, among formal hedges, a marble fountain played. Sophie looked at this, and looked round, and began to frown.

Abdullah stooped and considerately rolled the carpet up, patting it and speaking soothingly. "Bravely done, most daring of damasks," he told it. "There, there. Never fear. I will not allow any djinn, however mighty, to harm so much as a thread of your treasured fabric or a fringe from your border."

"You sound like that soldier making a fuss of Morgan when he was Whippersnapper," Sophie said. "The castle's over there."

They set off towards it, Sophie staring alertly round and uttering one or two snorts, Abdullah with the carpet tenderly over his shoulder. He patted it from time to time and felt the quivers die out of it as they went. They walked for some time, for the garden, although it was not made of cloud, changed and enlarged around them. The hedges became artistic banks of pale pink flowers and the fountain – which they could see clearly in the distance all the time – now appeared to be crystal or possibly chrysolite. A few steps more, and everything was in jewelled pots, and frondy, with creepers trained up lacquered pillars. Sophie's snorts became louder. The fountain, as far as they could tell, was of silver inset with sapphires.

"That djinn has taken liberties with a person's castle," Sophie said. "Unless I'm entirely turned round, this used to be our bathroom."

Abdullah felt his face heat up. Sophie's bathroom or not, these were the gardens out of his daydreams. Hasruel was mocking him, as he had mocked Abdullah all along. When the fountain ahead turned to gold, glinting wine dark with rubies, Abdullah became as annoyed as Sophie was.

"This is not the way a garden should be, even if we disregard the confusing changes," he said angrily. "A garden should be natural-seeming, with wild sections, including a large area of bluebells."

"Quite right," said Sophie. "Look at that fountain now! *What* a way to treat a bathroom!"

The fountain was platinum, with emeralds. "Ridiculously flashy!" said Abdullah. "When I design *my* garden—"

He was interrupted by a child screaming. Both of them began to run.

CHAPTER EIGHTEEN

Which is rather full of princesses

The child's screams rose. There was no doubt about the direction. As Sophie and Abdullah ran that way, along a pillared cloister, Sophie panted, "It's not Morgan – it's an older child!"

Abdullah thought she was right. He could hear words in the screams, although he could not pick out what they were. And surely Morgan, even howling his loudest, did not possess big enough lungs to make this kind of noise. After getting almost too loud to bear, the screams became grating sobs. Those sank to a steady, nagging wah-wah-wah! and, just as the sound became truly intolerable, the child raised his or her voice into hysterical screams again.

Sophie and Abdullah followed the noise to the end of the cloister and out into a huge cloudy hall. There they stopped prudently behind a pillar and Sophie said, "Our main room. They must have blown it up like a balloon!"

It was a very big hall. The screaming child was in the middle of it. She was about four years old, with fair curls and wearing a white nightdress. Her face was red, her mouth was a black square, and she was alternately throwing herself down on the green porphyry floor and standing up in order to throw herself down again. If ever there was a child in a paddy it was this one. The echoes in the huge hall yelled with it.

"It's Princess Valeria," Sophie murmured to Abdullah. "I thought it might be."

Hovering over the howling princess was the huge shape of Hasruel. Another djinn, much smaller and paler, was dodging about behind him. "*Do* something!" this small djinn shouted. Only the fact that he had a voice like silver trumpets made him audible. "She's driving me insane!"

Hasruel bent his great visage down to Valeria's screaming face. "Little princess," he boomingly cooed, "stop crying. You will not be hurt."

Princess Valeria's answer was first to stand up and scream in Hasruel's face, then to throw herself flat on the floor and roll and kick there.

"Wah-wah-wah!" she vociferated. "I want *home*! I want my *dad*! I want my *nurse*! I want my *Uncle Ju-stin*! WaaaAH!"

"Little princess!" Hasruel cooed desperately.

"Don't just *coo* at her!" trumpeted the other djinn, who was clearly Dalzel. "Work some magic! Sweet dreams, a spell of silence, a thousand teddies, a ton of toffee! *Anything!*"

Hasruel turned round on his brother. His spread wings fanned agitated gales which flapped Valeria's hair and fluttered her nightdress. Sophie and Abdullah had to cling to the pillar or the force of the wind would have blown them backwards.

But it made no difference to Princess Valeria's tantrum. If anything, she screamed harder. "I have *tried* all that, brother of mine!" Hasruel boomed.

Princess Valeria was now producing steady yells of "*MOTHER! MOTHER! THEY'RE BEING HORRID TO ME!*" Hasruel had to raise his voice to a perfect thunder.

"Don't you know," he thundered, "that there is almost no magic that will stop a child in this kind of temper?"

Dalzel clapped his pale hands across his ears – pointed ears with a look of fungus to them. "Well, I can't stand it!" he shrilled. "Put her to sleep for a hundred years!"

Hasruel nodded. He turned back to Princess Valeria as she screamed and thrashed upon the floor and spread his huge hand above her.

"Oh dear!" said Sophie to Abdullah. "*Do* something!"

Since Abdullah had no idea what to do, and since he privately felt that *anything* that stopped this horrible noise was a good idea, he did nothing but edge uncertainly away from the pillar. And, fortunately, before Hasruel's magic had any noticeable effect on Princess Valeria, a crowd of other people arrived. A loud, rather rasping voice cut through the din.

"What is all this noise about?"

Both djinns started backwards. The new arrivals were all female and they all looked extremely displeased, but when you had said that, you seemed to have said the only two things they had in common. They stood in a row, thirty or so of them, glaring accusingly at the two djinns, and they were tall, short, stout, skinny, young and old, and of every colour the human race produces. Abdullah's eyes scudded along the row in amazement. These must be the kidnapped princesses. That was the third thing they had in common. They ranged from a tiny frail yellow princess nearest to him, to an elderly bent princess in the mid-distance. And they were wearing every possible kind of clothing, from a ball dress to tweeds.

The one who had called out was a solidly built middle-sized princess standing slightly in front of the rest. She was wearing riding clothes. Her face, besides being tanned and a little lined from outdoor activity, was downright and sensible. She looked at the two djinns with utter contempt. "Of all the ridiculous things!" she said. "Two great powerful creatures like you, and you can't even stop a child crying!" And she stepped up to Valeria and gave her a sharp slap on her threshing behind. "Shut up!"

It worked. Valeria had never been slapped in her life before. She rolled over and sat up as if she had been shot. She stared at the downright princess out of astonished, swollen eyes. "You *hit* me!"

"And I shall hit you again if you ask for it," said the downright princess.

"I shall scream," said Valeria. Her mouth went square again. She drew a deep breath.

"No you won't," said the downright princess. She picked Valeria up and bundled her briskly into the arms of the two princesses behind her. They, and several more, closed around Valeria in a huddle, making soothing noises. From the midst of the huddle, Valeria began screaming again, but in a way that was not quite convinced. The downright princess put her hands on her hips and turned contemptuously to the djinns.

"See?" she said. "All you need is a bit of firmness and some kindness – but neither of you can be expected to understand *that*!"

Dalzel stepped towards her. Now that he was not so anguished, Abdullah saw with surprise that Dalzel was beautiful. Apart from his fungoid ears and taloned feet, he could have been a tall angelic man. Golden curls grew on his head and his wings, though small and stunted-looking, were golden too. His very red mouth spread into a sweet smile. Altogether, he had an unearthly beauty that matched the strange cloud kingdom where he lived. "Pray take the child away," he said, "and comfort her, oh Princess Beatrice, most excellent of my wives."

Downright Princess Beatrice was gesturing to the other princesses to take Valeria away, but she turned back sharply at this. "I've told you, my lad," she said, "that *none* of us is any wife of yours. You can call us that until you're blue in the face, but it won't make the slightest difference. We are *not* your wives and we never will be!"

"Exactly!" said most of the other princesses, in a firm but ragged chorus. All of them, except for one, turned and swept away, taking the sobbing Princess Valeria with them.

Sophie's face was lit with a delighted smile. She whispered, "It looks as if the princesses are holding their own!"

Abdullah could not attend to her. The remaining princess was Flower-in-the-Night. She was, as always, twice as beautiful as he remembered her, looking very sweet and grave, with her great dark eyes fixed seriously on Dalzel. She bowed politely. Abdullah's senses sang at the sight of her. The cloudy pillars around him seemed to sway in and out of existence. His heart pounded for joy. She was safe! She was here! She was speaking to Dalzel.

"Forgive me, great djinn, if I remain to ask you a question," she said and her voice, even more than Abdullah remembered it, was melodious and merry as a cool fountain.

To Abdullah's outrage, Dalzel reacted with what seemed to be horror.

"Oh not *you* again!" he trumpeted – at which Hasruel, standing like a dark column in the background, folded his arms and grinned maliciously.

"Yes it is I, stern stealer of the daughters of the Sultans," Flower-in-the-Night said, with her head bowed politely. "I am here merely to ask what thing it was which started the child crying."

"How should *I* know?" Dalzel demanded. "You're always asking me questions I can't answer! Why are you asking this one?"

"Because," Flower-in-the-Night answered, "oh robber of the offspring of rulers, the easiest way to calm the child is to deal with the cause of her temper. This I know from my own childhood, for I was much given to tantrums myself."

Surely not! Abdullah thought. She is lying for a purpose. No nature as sweet as hers could ever have screamed for anything! Yet, as he was outraged to see, Dalzel had no difficulty believing this.

"I'll *bet* you were!" Dalzel said.

"So what was the cause, bereaver of the brave?" Flower-in-the-Night persisted. "Was it that she wished to be back in her own palace, or to have her own particular doll, or was she simply frightened by your face, or—?"

"I'm not sending her back, if that's what you're aiming for," Dalzel interrupted. "She's one of my wives now."

"Then I adjure you to find out what set her off screaming, captor of the righteous," Flower-in-the-Night said politely, "for without that knowledge, even thirty princesses may not silence her." Indeed, Princess Valeria's voice was rising again in the distance – wah-*wah*-WAH – as she spoke. "I speak from experience," Flower-in-the-Night observed. "I once screamed night and day, for a whole week, until my voice was gone, because I had grown out of my favourite shoes."

Abdullah could see Flower-in-the-Night was telling the exact truth. He tried to believe it, but, try as he might, he just could not imagine his lovely Flower-in-the-Night lying on the floor kicking and screaming.

Dalzel again had no difficulty at all. He shuddered and turned angrily to Hasruel. "Think, can't you? You brought her in. You must have noticed what set her off."

Hasruel's great brown visage crumpled helplessly. "Brother mine, I brought her in through the kitchen, for she was silent and white with fear and I thought maybe a sweetmeat would make her happy. But she threw the sweetmeats at the cook's dog and remained silent. Her cries only began, as you know, after I placed her among the other princesses, and her screams only when you had her brought—"

Flower-in-the-Night raised a finger. "Ah!" she said.

Both djinns turned to her.

"I have it," she said. "It must be the cook's dog. It is often an animal with children. She is used to being given all she wants and she wants the dog. Instruct your cook, king of kidnappers, to bring his animal to our quarters and the noise will cease, this I promise you."

"Very well," said Dalzel. "*Do* it!" he trumpeted at Hasruel.

Flower-in-the-Night bowed. "I thank you," she said and

turned and walked gracefully away.

Sophie shook Abdullah's arm. "Let's follow her."

Abdullah did not move or reply. He stared after Flower-in-the-Night, hardly able to believe he was really seeing her, and equally unable to believe that Dalzel did not fall at her feet and adore her. He had to admit that this was a relief, but all the same—!

"She's yours, is she?" Sophie said after one look at his face. Abdullah nodded raptly. "Then you've got good taste," said Sophie. "Now come *on* before they notice us!"

They edged behind the pillars in the direction Flower-in-the-Night had gone, keeping a wary eye on the huge hall as they went. In the far distance, Dalzel was moodily settling into an enormous throne at the top of a flight of steps. When Hasruel returned from wherever the kitchens were, Dalzel motioned him to kneel by the throne. Neither looked their way. Sophie and Abdullah tiptoed to an archway where a curtain was still swaying after Flower-in-the-Night had lifted it to go through. They pushed the curtain aside and followed.

There was a large well-lit room beyond, confusingly full of princesses. From somewhere in the midst of them, Princess Valeria sobbed, "I want to go home now!"

"Hush, dear. You shall soon," someone answered.

Princess Beatrice's voice said, "You cried beautifully, Valeria. We're all proud of you. But do stop crying now, there's a good girl."

"Can't!" sobbed Valeria. "I'm in the *habit*!"

Sophie was staring round the room in growing outrage. "This is our *broom* cupboard!" she said. "Really!"

Abdullah could not attend to her because Flower-in-the-Night was quite near, softly calling, "Beatrice!"

Princess Beatrice heard and plunged out of the crowd. "Don't tell me," she said. "You did it. Good. Those djinns don't know what hits them when you get after them, Flower. Then things are coming along beautifully, if that man agrees—"

At this point she noticed Sophie and Abdullah. "Where did you two spring from?" she said.

Flower-in-the-Night whirled round. For a moment, when she saw Abdullah, there was everything in her face he could have wished for: recognition, delight, love and pride. *I knew you'd come to rescue me!* said her big dark eyes. Then, to his hurt and perplexity, it all went. Her face became smooth and polite. She bowed courteously. "This is Prince Abdullah from Zanzib," she said, "but I'm not acquainted with the lady."

Flower-in-the-Night's behaviour shook Abdullah from his daze. It must be jealousy of Sophie, he thought. He too bowed and made haste to explain.

"This lady, oh pearls in many a king's diadems, is wife to the Royal Wizard Howl and comes here in search of her child."

Princess Beatrice turned her keen, weathered face to Sophie.

"Oh, it's *your* baby!" she said. "Howl with you, by any chance?"

"No," Sophie said miserably. "I hoped he'd be here."

"Not a trace of him, I'm afraid," said Princess Beatrice. "Pity. He'd be useful even if he did help conquer my country. But we've got your baby. Come this way."

Princess Beatrice led the way to the back of the room, past the group of princesses trying to comfort Valeria. Since Flower-in-the-Night went with her, Abdullah followed. To his increasing distress, Flower-in-the-Night was now barely looking at him, only inclining her head politely at each princess they passed. "The princess of Alberia," she said formally. "The princess of Farqtan. The Lady Heiress of Thayack. This is the princess of Peichstan and beside her the Paragon of Inhico. Beyond her, you see the Damoiselle of Dorimynde."

So if it was not jealousy, what *was* it? Abdullah wondered unhappily.

There was a wide bench at the back of the room with cushions on it. "My oddments shelf!" Sophie growled. There were three princesses sitting on the bench: the elderly princess Abdullah had noticed before, a lumpish princess swaddled in a coat, and the tiny yellow princess perched in the middle between them. The tiny princess's twig-like arms were wrapped round the chubby pink body of Morgan.

"She is, as far as we can pronounce it, High Princess of Tsapfan," Flower-in-the-Night said formally. "On her right is the Princess of High Norland. On her left the Jharine of Jham."

The tiny High Princess of Tsapfan looked like a child

with a doll too big for her, but, in the most expert and experienced way, she was giving Morgan a feed from a large baby bottle.

"He's fine with her," said Princess Beatrice. "Good thing for her. Stopped her moping. She says she's had fourteen babies of her own."

The tiny princess glanced up with a shy smile, "Boyth, all," she said, in a small lisping voice.

Morgan's toes and hands were curling and uncurling. He looked the picture of a satisfied baby. Sophie gazed for a moment.

"Where did she get that bottle?" she asked, as if she were afraid it might be poisoned.

The tiny princess looked up again. She smiled and spared a minute finger to point.

"Doesn't speak our language very well," Princess Beatrice explained. "But that genie seemed to understand her."

The princess's twig-like finger was pointing to the floor by the bench, where, below her small dangling feet, stood a familiar blue-mauve bottle. Abdullah dived for it. The lumpish Jharine of Jham dived for it at the same moment, with an unexpectedly big strong hand.

"Stop it!" the genie howled from inside as they tussled for it. "I'm *not* coming out! Those djinns will kill me this time for sure!"

Abdullah took hold of the bottle in both hands and jerked. The jerk caused the swaddling coat to fall away from the Jharine. Abdullah found himself looking into wide blue eyes in a lined face inside a bush of grizzled hair. The face wrinkled innocently as the old soldier gave him a sheepish smile and let go of the genie bottle.

"You!" Abdullah said disgustedly.

"Loyal subject of mine," Princess Beatrice explained. "Turned up to rescue me. Rather awkward actually. We had to disguise him."

Sophie swept Abdullah and Princess Beatrice aside. "Let me get at him," she said.

CHAPTER NINETEEN

In which a soldier, a cook and a carpet seller all state their price

There was a brief time of noise so loud that it drowned Princess Valeria completely. Most of it came from Sophie, who started with mild words like "thief" and "liar" and worked up to screaming accusations at the soldier of crimes Abdullah had never heard of, and perhaps even the soldier had never thought to commit. Listening, Abdullah thought the metal-pulley noise Sophie used to make as Midnight was actually nicer than the noise she was making now. But some of the noise came from the soldier, who had one knee up and both hands in front of his face and was bellowing, louder and louder, "Midnight – I mean, madam! Let me *explain*, Midnight – er – madam!"

To this, Princess Beatrice kept adding raspingly, "No, let *me* explain!"

And various princesses added to the clamour by crying out, "Oh please be quiet or the djinns will hear!"

Abdullah tried to stop Sophie by shaking imploringly at her arm. But probably nothing would have stopped her, had not Morgan taken his mouth from the bottle, gazed round in distress, and started to cry too. Sophie shut her mouth with a snap and then opened it to say, "All right then. Explain."

In the comparative quiet, the tiny princess hushed Morgan and he went back to feeding again.

"I didn't mean to bring the baby," said the soldier.

"*What?*" said Sophie. "You were going to desert my—"

"No, no," said the soldier. "I told the genie to put him where someone would look after him and take me after the princess of Ingary. I won't deny I was after a reward." He appealed to Abdullah. "But you know what that genie's like, don't you? Next thing I knew, we were both here."

Abdullah held the genie bottle up and looked at it. "He got his wish," the genie said sulkily from inside.

"And the infant was yelling blue murder," said Princess Beatrice. "Dalzel sent Hasruel to find out what the noise was, and all I could think of to say was that Princess Valeria was in a paddy. Then of course we had to get Valeria to scream. That was when Flower here started to make plans."

She turned to Flower-in-the-Night, who was obviously thinking of something else – and that something else had nothing to do with Abdullah, Abdullah noted dismally. She was staring across the room. "Beatrice, I think the cook is here with the dog," she said.

"Oh good!" said Princess Beatrice. "Come along, all of you." She strode towards the middle of the room.

A man in a tall chef's hat was standing there. He was a seamed and hoary fellow with only one eye. His dog was pressed close to his legs, growling at any princess who came near. This probably expressed the way the cook was feeling too. He looked thoroughly suspicious of everything.

"Jamal!" shouted Abdullah. After which he held the genie bottle up and looked at it again.

"Well, it *was* the nearest palace that wasn't Zanzib," the genie protested.

Abdullah was so delighted to see his old friend safe that he did not argue with the genie. He barged past ten princesses, entirely forgetting his manners, and seized Jamal by the hand. "My friend!"

Jamal's one eye stared. A tear came out of it as he wrung Abdullah's hand hard in return. "You are safe!" he said. Jamal's dog bounced to its hind legs and planted its front paws on Abdullah's stomach, panting lovingly. A familiar squiddy breath filled the air.

And Valeria promptly began screaming again. "I don't want that doggie! He SMELLS!"

"Oh hush!" said at least six princesses. "Pretend, dear. We need the man's help."

"I – DON'T – WANT – !" yelled Princess Valeria.

Sophie tore herself away from where she was leaning critically over the tiny princess and marched down upon Valeria. "Stop it, Valeria," she said. "You remember me, don't you?"

It was clear Valeria did. She rushed at Sophie and wrapped her arms round her legs, where she burst into much more genuine tears. "Sophie, Sophie, Sophie! Take me *home*!"

Sophie sat down on the floor and hugged her. "There, there. Of course we'll take you home. We've just got to arrange it first. It's very odd," she remarked to the surrounding princesses. "I feel quite expert with Valeria, but I'm scared stiff of dropping Morgan."

"You'll learn," said the elderly princess of High Norland, sitting stiffly down beside her. "I'm told they all do."

Flower-in-the-Night stepped to the centre of the room. "My friends," she said, "and all three kind gentlemen, we must now put our heads together to discuss the plight in which we find ourselves and make plans for our early release. First, however, it would be prudent to put a spell of silence upon the doorway. It would not do for our kidnappers to overhear." Her eyes, in the most thoughtful and neutral way, went to the genie bottle in Abdullah's hand.

"No!" said the genie. "Try to make me do anything and you're all toads!"

"I'll do it," said Sophie. She scrambled up with Valeria still clinging to her skirts and went over to the doorway, where she took hold of a handful of the curtain there. "Now you're not the kind of cloth to let any sound through, are you?" she remarked to the curtain. "I suggest you have a word with the walls and make that quite clear. Tell them no one's going to be able to hear a word we say inside this room."

A murmur of relief and approval came from most of the princesses at this. But Flower-in-the-Night said, "My pardon for being critical, skilful sorceress, but I think the djinns should be able to hear *something* or else they will become suspicious."

The tiny princess from Tsapfan wandered up with Morgan looking huge in her arms. Carefully she passed the baby to Sophie. Sophie looked terrified and held Morgan as if he was a bomb about to blow up. This seemed to displease Morgan. He waved his arms. While the tiny princess was laying both small hands on the curtain, several looks of utter distaste chased themselves across his face. "BURP!" he remarked.

Sophie jumped and all but dropped Morgan. "Heavens!" she said. "I'd no idea they did that!"

Valeria laughed heartily. "My brother does – all the time."

The tiny princess made gestures to show that she had now dealt with Flower-in-the-Night's objection. Everyone listened closely. In the distance somewhere they could hear the pleasant ringing hum of princesses chatting together.

There was even an occasional yell that sounded like Valeria.

"Most perfect," said Flower-in-the-Night. She smiled warmly at the tiny princess and Abdullah wished she would only smile like that at him. "Now if every person could sit down, we can lay some plans to escape."

Everyone obeyed in their own way. Jamal squatted with his dog in his arms, looking suspicious. Sophie sat on the floor with Morgan clumsily in her arms and Valeria leaning against her. Valeria was quite happy now. Abdullah sat cross-legged beside Jamal. The soldier came and sat about two places away, whereupon Abdullah took tight hold of the genie bottle and gripped the carpet over his shoulder with the other hand.

"That girl Flower-in-the-Night is a real marvel," Princess Beatrice remarked as she sat herself between Abdullah and the soldier. "She came here knowing nothing unless she'd read it out of a book. And she learns all the time. Took her two days to get the measure of Dalzel – wretched djinn's scared stiff of her now. Before she arrived all I'd managed was to make it clear to the creature that we weren't going to be his wives. But she thinks big. Had her mind on escaping right from the start. She's been plotting all along to get that cook in to help. Now she's done it. Look at her! Looks fit to rule an empire, doesn't she."

Abdullah nodded sadly and watched Flower-in-the-Night as she stood waiting for everyone to get settled. She was still wearing the gauzy clothes she had been wearing when Hasruel snatched her from the night garden. She was still as slim, as graceful, and as beautiful. Her clothes were now crushed and a little tattered. Abdullah had no doubt that every crease, every three-cornered tear, and every hanging thread meant some new thing that Flower-in-the-Night had learnt. Fit to rule an empire indeed! he thought. If he compared Flower-in-the-Night with Sophie, who had displeased him for being so strong-minded, he knew Flower-in-the-Night had twice Sophie's strength of mind. And as far as Abdullah was concerned, this only made Flower-in-the-Night more excellent. What made him wretched was the way she carefully and politely avoided singling him out in any way. And he wished he knew *why*.

"The problem we face," Flower-in-the-Night was saying, when Abdullah started to attend, "is that we are in a place where it does no good simply to get *out*. If we could sneak out of the castle without the djinns becoming aware of it, or the angels of Hasruel preventing us, we should only sink through the clouds and fall heavily to earth, which is a very long way below. Even if we can overcome those difficulties in some way—" Here her eyes turned to the bottle in Abdullah's hand and, thoughtfully, to the carpet over his shoulder, but not, alas, to Abdullah himself "—there seems nothing to stop Dalzel sending his brother to bring us all back. Therefore the essence of any plan we make has to be the defeat of Dalzel. We know that his chief power derives from the fact that he has stolen the life of his brother Hasruel, so that Hasruel must obey him or die. So it follows that, in order to escape, we must find Hasruel's life and restore it to him. Noble ladies, excellent gentlemen and esteemed dog, I invite your ideas on this matter."

Excellently put, oh flower of my desire! Abdullah thought sadly as Flower-in-the-Night gracefully sat down.

"But we still don't know where Hasruel's life can be!" bleated the fat princess of Farqtan.

"Exactly," said Princess Beatrice. "Only Dalzel knows that."

"But the beastly creature's always dropping hints," complained the blonde princess from Thayack.

"To let us know how clever he is!" the dark-skinned princess of Alberia said bitterly.

Sophie looked up. "What hints?" she said.

There was a confused clamour as at least twenty princesses all tried to tell Sophie at once. Abdullah was straining his ears to catch at least one of the hints and Flower-in-the-Night was getting up to restore order, when the soldier said loudly, "Oh shut up, the lot of you!"

This caused complete silence. The eyes of every single princess turned to him in freezing royal outrage.

The soldier found this very amusing. "Hoity-toity!" he said. "Look at me how you please, ladies. But while you do, think whether I ever agreed to help you escape. I did not. Why should I? Dalzel never did me any harm."

"That," said the elderly princess of High Norland, "is because he's not found you yet, my good man. Do you wish to wait and see what happens when he does?"

"I'll risk it," said the soldier. "On the other hand I *might* help – and I reckon you won't get too far if I don't – provided one of you can make it worth my while."

Flower-in-the-Night, poised on her knees ready to stand, said with beautiful haughtiness, "Worth your while in what way, menial mercenary? All of us have fathers who are very rich. Rewards will shower on you once they have us back. Do you wish to be assured of a certain sum from each? That can be arranged."

"And I wouldn't say no," said the soldier. "But that's not what I meant, my pretty. When I started on this caper, I was promised I'd get a princess of my own out of it. That's what I want – a princess to marry. One of you ought to be able to accommodate me. And if you can't or won't, then you can count me out and I'll be off to make my peace with Dalzel. He can hire me to guard you."

This caused a silence, if possible more frozen, outraged and royal than before, until Flower-in-the-Night pulled herself together and rose to her feet again. "My friends," she said, "we all need the help of this man – if only for his ruthless low cunning. What we do not want is to have a beast like him set over us to guard us. Therefore I vote that he be allowed to choose a wife from among us. Who disagrees?"

It was clear that every other princess disagreed mightily. Further freezing looks were turned on the soldier, who grinned and said, "If I go to Dalzel and offer myself to guard you, rest assured you'll *never* get away. I'm up to every trick. Isn't that true?" he asked Abdullah.

"It is true, most cunning corporal," Abdullah said.

There was a small murmuring from the tiny princess. "She says she's married already – those fourteen children, you know," said the elderly princess, who seemed to understand the murmur.

"Then let all who are as yet unmarried please raise their hands," said Flower-in-the-Night and, most determinedly, raised her own.

Waveringly, reluctantly, two-thirds of the other princesses put their hands up also. The soldier's head turned slowly as he looked round them, and the look on his face reminded Abdullah of Sophie when, as Midnight, she was about to feast on salmon and cream. Abdullah's heart stood still as the man's blue eyes travelled from princess to princess. It was obvious he would choose Flower-in-the-Night. Her beauty stood out like a lily in the moonlight.

"You," said the soldier at last, and pointed. To Abdullah's astonished relief, he was pointing at Princess Beatrice.

Princess Beatrice was equally astonished. "*Me?*" she said.

"Yes, you," said the soldier. "I've always fancied a nice bossy, downright princess like you. Fact that you're a Strangian too makes it ideal."

Princess Beatrice's face had become a bright beety red. It did not improve her looks. "But – but—" she said, and then pulled herself together. "My good soldier, I'll have you know I'm supposed to be marrying Prince Justin of Ingary."

"Then you'll just have to tell him you're spoken for,"

said the soldier. "Politics, wasn't it? It seems to me you'll be glad to get out of it."

"Well, I —" began Princess Beatrice. To Abdullah's surprise, there were tears in her eyes and she had to start again. "You don't *mean* it!" she said. "I'm not good looking or any of those things."

"That suits me," said the soldier, "down to the ground. What would I do with a flimsy, pretty little princess? I can see you'd back me up whatever scam I got up to – and I bet you can darn socks too."

"Believe it or not, I can darn," said Princess Beatrice. "*And* mend boots. You *really* mean it?"

"Yes," said the soldier.

The two of them had swung round to face one another and it was clear that both were entirely in earnest. And the rest of the princesses had somehow forgotten to be frozen and royal. Every one of them was leaning forwards to watch with a tender, approving smile. There was the same smile on Flower-in-the-Night's face as she said, "Now may we continue our discussion, if no one else objects?"

"Me... I do," said Jamal. "I object."

All the princesses groaned. Jamal's face was almost as red as Princess Beatrice's and his one eye was screwed up – but the soldier's example had made him bold.

"Lovely ladies," he said, "we are frightened, me and my dog. Until we got snatched away up here to do your cooking for you, we were on the run in the desert with the Sultan's camels at our heels. We don't want to be sent back to that. But if all you perfect princesses get away from here, what *do* we do? Djinns don't eat the kind of food I can cook. Meaning no disrespect to anyone, if I help you to get away, my dog and I are out of a job. It's as simple as that."

"Oh dear," said Flower-in-the-Night, and seemed not to know what else to say.

"Such a shame. He's a very good cook," remarked a plump princess in a loose red gown, who was probably the Paragon of Inhico.

"He certainly is!" said the elderly princess of High Norland. "I shudder to remember the food those djinns kept stealing for us until he came." She turned to Jamal. "My grandfather once had a cook from Rashpuht," she said, "and, until you got here, I'd never tasted anything like that man's fried squid! And yours is even better. You help us to escape, my man, and I'll employ you like a shot, dog and all. But," she added, as a grin brightened on Jamal's leathery face, "please remember that my old father only rules a very small Principality. You'll get board and lodging, but I can't afford a big wage."

The grin remained broadly fixed on Jamal's features. "My great, great lady," he said, "it is not wages I want, only safety. For this I will cook you food fit for angels."

"Hm," said the elderly princess. "I'm not at all sure what those angels eat – but that's settled then. Do either of you other two want anything before you'll help?"

Everyone looked at Sophie.

"Not really," Sophie said, rather sadly. "I've got Morgan,

and since Howl doesn't seem to be here, there's nothing else I need. I'll help you anyway."

Everyone looked at Abdullah then.

He rose to his feet and bowed. "Oh moons of many monarchs' eyes," he said, "far be it from one as unworthy as me to impose any kind of conditions for my help on such as you. Help freely given is best, as the books tell us." He had got this far in his magnificent and generous speech when he realised it was all nonsense. There *was* something he did want – very much indeed. He hastily changed his tack. "And freely given my help will be," he said, "as free as air blows or rain bedews the flowers. I will work myself to extinction for your noble sakes and crave only in return one small boon, most simply granted—"

"Get *on* with it, young man!" said the princess of High Norland. "What *do* you want?"

"Five minutes' talk in private with Flower-in-the-Night," Abdullah admitted.

Everyone looked at Flower-in-the-Night. Her head went up, rather dangerously.

"Come off it, Flower!" said Princess Beatrice. "Five minutes won't kill you!"

Flower-in-the-Night seemed fairly clear that it *might* kill her. She said, like a princess going to her execution, "Very well," and, with a more than usually freezing look in the direction of Abdullah, she asked, "Now?"

"Or sooner, dove of my desire," he said, bowing firmly.

Flower-in-the-Night nodded frigidly and stalked away to

the side of the room, looking positively martyred. "Here," she said as Abdullah followed her.

He bowed again, even more firmly. "I said, in private, oh starry subject of my sighs," he pointed out.

Flower-in-the-Night irritably twitched aside one of the curtains hanging beside her. "They can probably still hear," she said coldly, beckoning him after her.

"But not see, princess of my passion," Abdullah said, edging behind the curtain.

He found himself in a tiny alcove. Sophie's voice came to him clearly. "That's the loose brick where I used to hide money. I hope they have *room*." Whatever the place once had been, it now seemed to be the princesses' wardrobe. There was a riding jacket hanging behind Flower-in-the-Night as she folded her arms and faced Abdullah. Cloaks, coats and a hooped petticoat that evidently went under the loose red garment worn by the Paragon of Inhico dangled around Abdullah as he faced Flower-in-the-Night. Still, Abdullah reflected, it was not much smaller or more crowded than his own booth in Zanzib and that was usually private enough.

"What did you want to say?" Flower-in-the-Night asked freezingly.

"To ask the reason for this very coldness!" Abdullah answered heatedly. "What have I done that you will barely look at me and barely speak? Have I not come here, expressly to rescue you? Have I not, alone of all the disappointed lovers, braved every peril in order to reach this castle? Have I not gone through the most strenuous adventures, allowing your father to threaten me, the soldier to cheat me and the genie to mock me, solely in order to bring you my aid? What more do I have to do? Or should I conclude that you have fallen in love with Dalzel?"

"*Dalzel!*" exclaimed Flower-in-the-Night. "Now you insult me! Now you add insult to injury! Now I see Beatrice was right and you do indeed not love me!"

"*Beatrice!*" thundered Abdullah. "What has *she* to say about how I feel?"

Flower-in-the-Night hung her head a little, although she looked more sulky than ashamed. There was a dead silence. In fact the silence was so *very* dead that Abdullah realised that the sixty ears of all the other thirty princesses – no, sixty-*eight* ears, if you counted Sophie, the soldier, Jamal and his dog and assumed Morgan was asleep – anyway that all these ears were at that moment focused entirely upon what he and Flower-in-the-Night were saying.

"Talk among yourselves!" he shouted.

The silence became uneasy. It was broken by the elderly princess saying, "The most distressing thing about being up here above the clouds is that there is no *weather* to make conversation out of."

Abdullah waited until this statement was followed by a reluctant hum of other voices and then turned back to Flower-in-the-Night. "Well? What *did* Princess Beatrice say?"

Flower-in-the-Night raised her head haughtily. "She said

that portraits of other men and pretty speeches were all very well, but she couldn't help noticing you'd never made the slightest attempt to kiss me."

"Impertinent woman!" said Abdullah. "When I first saw you, I assumed you were a dream. I assumed you would only melt."

"But," said Flower-in-the-Night, "the second time you saw me, you seemed quite sure I was real."

"Certainly," said Abdullah, "but then it would have been unfair, because, if you recall, you had then seen no other living men but your father and myself."

"Beatrice," said Flower-in-the-Night, "says that men who do nothing but make fine speeches make very poor husbands."

"*Bother* Princess Beatrice!" said Abdullah. "What do *you* think?"

"I think," said Flower-in-the-Night, "*I* think I want to know why you found me too unattractive to be worth kissing."

"*I DIDN'T find you unattractive!*" bawled Abdullah. Then he remembered the sixty-eight ears beyond the curtain and added in a fierce whisper, "If you must know I – I had never in my life kissed a young lady, and you are far too beautiful for me to want to get it wrong!"

A small smile, heralded by a deep dimple, stole across Flower-in-the-Night's mouth. "And how many young ladies have you kissed by now?"

"None!" groaned Abdullah. "I am still a total amateur!"

"So am I," admitted Flower-in-the-Night. "Though at least I know enough not to mistake you for a woman now. That was very stupid!"

She gave a gurgle of laughter. Abdullah gave another gurgle. In no time at all, both of them were laughing heartily, until Abdullah gasped, "I think we should practise!"

After that, there was silence from behind the curtain. This silence went on so long that all the princesses ran out of small talk, except Princess Beatrice, who seemed to have a lot to say to the soldier. At length, Sophie called out, "Are you two finished?"

"Certainly," Flower-in-the-Night and Abdullah called out. "Absolutely!"

"Then let's make some plans," said Sophie.

Plans were no problem at all to Abdullah in the state of mind he was in just then. He came out from behind the curtain holding Flower-in-the-Night's hand and, if the castle had chanced to vanish at that moment, he knew he could have walked on the clouds beneath, or failing that, on air. As it was, he walked across what seemed a very unworthy marble floor and simply took charge.

CHAPTER TWENTY

In which a djinn's life is found and then hidden

Ten minutes later, Abdullah said, "There, most eminent and intelligent persons, are our plans laid. It only remains for the genie—"

Purple smoke poured from the bottle and trailed in agitated waves along the marble floor. "You do *not* use me!" cried the genie. "I said toads and I *mean* toads! Hasruel put me in this bottle, don't you understand? If I do anything against him, he'll put me somewhere even worse!"

Sophie looked up and frowned at the smoke. "There really is a genie!"

"But I merely require your powers of divination to tell

me where Hasruel's life is hidden," Abdullah explained. "I am not asking for a wish."

"*No!*" howled the mauve smoke.

Flower-in-the-Night picked the bottle up and balanced it on her knee. Smoke flowed downwards in puffs and seemed to try to seep into the cracks in the marble floor. "It stands to reason," Flower-in-the-Night said, "that since every man we asked to help has had his price, then the genie has his price also. It must be a male characteristic. Genie, if you agree to help Abdullah in this, I will promise you what logic assures me is the correct reward."

Grudgingly, the mauve smoke began to seep backwards towards the bottle again. "Oh very well," said the genie.

Two minutes after this, the charmed curtain in the doorway to the princesses' room was swept aside and everyone streamed out into the great hall, clamouring for Dalzel's attention and dragging Abdullah in their midst, a helpless prisoner.

"Dalzel! Dalzel!" clamoured the thirty princesses. "Is *this* the way you guard us? You ought to be ashamed of yourself!"

Dalzel looked up. He was leaning over the side of his great throne to play chess with Hasruel. He blenched a bit at what he saw and signed to his brother to remove the chess set. Fortunately, the crowd of princesses was too thick for him to notice Sophie and the Jharine of Jham huddled in the midst of it, though his lovely eyes did fall on Jamal and narrow with astonishment. "What is it *now*?" he said.

"A *man* in our room!" screamed the princesses. "A terrible, awful *man*!"

"What man?" trumpeted Dalzel. "What man would dare?"

"*This one!*" shrieked the princesses.

Abdullah was dragged forward between Princess Beatrice and the princess of Alberia, most shamefully clothed in almost nothing but the hooped petticoat that had hung behind the curtain. This petticoat was an essential part of the plan. Two of the things underneath it were the genie's bottle and the magic carpet. Abdullah was glad he had taken these precautions when Dalzel glared at him. He had not known before that a djinn's eyes could actually flame. Dalzel's eyes were like two bluish furnaces.

Hasruel's behaviour made Abdullah even more uncomfortable. A mean grin spread over Hasruel's huge features and he said, "Ah! You again!" Then he folded his great arms and looked very sarcastic indeed.

"How did this fellow get in here?" Dalzel demanded in his trumpet voice.

Before anyone could answer, Flower-in-the-Night performed her part in the plan by bursting out from among the other princesses and throwing herself gracefully down on the steps of the throne. "Have mercy, great djinn!" she cried out. "He only came to rescue me!"

Dalzel laughed contemptuously. "Then the fellow's a fool. I shall throw him straight back to earth."

"Do that, great djinn, and I shall never leave you in peace!" Flower-in-the-Night declared.

She was not acting. She really meant it. Dalzel knew she did. A shiver ran through his narrow, pale body and his gold-taloned fingers gripped the arms of the throne. But his eyes still flamed with rage. "I shall do what I want!" he trumpeted.

"Then desire to be merciful!" cried Flower-in-the-Night. "Give him at least a chance!"

"Be quiet, woman!" trumpeted Dalzel. "I haven't decided yet. I want to know how he managed to get in here first."

"Disguised as the cook's dog, of course," said Princess Beatrice.

"And quite naked when he turned into a man!" said the princess of Alberia.

"Shocking business," said Princess Beatrice. "We had to put him in the Paragon's petticoat."

"Bring him closer," commanded Dalzel.

Princess Beatrice and her assistant lugged Abdullah towards the steps of the throne, Abdullah walking with little mincing steps that he hoped the djinns would put down to the petticoat. The reason, in fact, was that the third thing under the petticoat was Jamal's dog. It was gripped rather firmly between Abdullah's knees in case it escaped. This part of the plan made it necessary to be minus one dog, and none of the princesses had trusted Dalzel not to send Hasruel looking for it and prove that everyone was lying.

Dalzel glared down at Abdullah, and Abdullah hoped very much that Dalzel truly had almost no powers of his own. Hasruel had called his brother weak. But it occurred to Abdullah that even a weak djinn was several times stronger than a man. "You came here as a dog?" Dalzel trumpeted. "How?"

"By magic, great djinn," Abdullah said. He had intended to make a detailed explanation at this point, but, under the Paragon's petticoat, a hidden struggle was developing. Jamal's dog turned out to hate djinns even more than it hated most of the human race. It wanted to go for Dalzel. "I disguised myself as the dog of your cook," Abdullah began to explain. At this point, Jamal's dog became so eager to go for Dalzel that Abdullah was afraid it would get loose. He was forced to grip his knees together tighter yet. The dog's response was a huge snarling growl. "Your pardon!" panted Abdullah. Sweat was standing on his brow. "I am still so much of a dog that I cannot refrain from growling from time to time."

Flower-in-the-Night recognised that Abdullah was having problems and burst into lamentations. "Oh most noble prince! To suffer the shape of a dog for my sake! Spare him, noble djinn! Spare him!"

"Be quiet, woman," said Dalzel. "Where is that cook? Bring him forward."

Jamal was dragged forward by the princess of Farqtan and the Heiress of Thayack, wringing his hands and cringing. "Honoured djinn, it was nothing to do with me, I swear!" Jamal wailed. "Do not hurt me! I never knew he was not a real dog!" Abdullah could have sworn that Jamal was in a state of true terror. Maybe he was, but he had the presence of mind, all the same, to pat Abdullah on the head. "Nice dog," he said. "Good fellow." After which he fell down and grovelled on the steps of the throne in the manner of Zanzib. "I am innocent, great one!" he blubbered. "Innocent! Harm me not!"

The dog was soothed by its master's voice. Its growls stopped. Abdullah was able to relax his knees a little. "I am innocent too, oh collector of royal maidens," he said. "I came only to rescue the one I love. You must surely feel kindly towards my devotion, since you love so many princesses yourself!"

Dalzel rubbed his chin in a perplexed way. "Love?" he said. "No, I can't say I understand love. I can't understand how *anything* could make someone put themselves in your position, mortal."

Hasruel, squatting vast and dark beside the throne, grinned more meanly than ever. "What do you want me to do with the creature, brother?" he rumbled. "Roast him? Extract his soul and make it part of the floor? Take him apart—?"

"No, no! Be merciful, great Dalzel!" Flower-in-the-Night promptly cried out. "Give him at least a chance! If you do, I will never ask you questions, or complain, or lecture you again. I will be meek and polite!"

Dalzel grasped his chin again and looked uncertain. Abdullah felt much relieved. Dalzel was indeed a weak djinn – weak in character anyway. "If I were to give him a chance—" he began.

"If you'll take my advice, brother," Hasruel cut in, "you won't. He's tricky, this one."

At this, Flower-in-the-Night raised another great wail and beat her breast. Abdullah cried out through the noise, "Let me try to guess where you hid your brother's life, great Dalzel. If I fail to guess, kill me, If I guess right, let me depart in peace."

This amused Dalzel highly. His mouth opened, showing pointed silvery teeth, and his laughter rang round the cloudy hall like a fanfare of trumpets. "But you'll never guess, little mortal!" he laughed. Then, as the princesses had repeatedly assured Abdullah, Dalzel was unable to resist giving hints. "I've hidden that life so cleverly," he said gleefully, "that you can look at it and not see it. Hasruel can't see it, and he is a djinn. So what hope have you? But I think for the fun of it I will give you three guesses before I kill you. Guess away. Where *have* I hidden my brother's life?"

Abdullah shot a swift look at Hasruel in case Hasruel decided to interfere. But Hasruel was simply squatting there, looking inscrutable. So far, the plan was succeeding. It was in Hasruel's interest not to interfere. Abdullah had been counting on that. He took a firmer grip on the dog with his knees and hitched at the Paragon's petticoat, while he pretended to think. What he was really doing was jogging the genie bottle. "For my first guess, great djinn—" he said, and stared at the floor as if the green porphyry might inspire him. Would the genie go back on his word? For one scared and miserable moment, Abdullah thought that the genie had let him down as usual and that he was going to have to risk guessing on his own. Then to his great relief, he saw a tiny tendril of purple smoke creep out from under the Paragon's petticoat, where it lay, still and watchful, beside Abdullah's bare foot. "My first guess is that you hid Hasruel's life on the moon," Abdullah said.

Dalzel laughed delightedly. "Wrong! He would have found it there! No, it's much more obvious than that, and much *less* obvious. Consider the game of Hunt-the-Slipper, mortal!"

This told Abdullah that Hasruel's life was here in the castle, as most of the princesses had thought it was. He made a great show of thinking hard. "My second guess is that you gave it to one of the guardian angels to keep," he said.

"Wrong again!" said Dalzel, more delighted than ever. "The angels would have given it back straight away. It's *much* cleverer than that, little mortal. You'll never guess. It's amazing how no one can see what's under their own noses!"

At this, in a burst of inspiration, Abdullah was sure he knew where Hasruel's life really was. Flower-in-the-Night loved him. He was still walking on air. His mind was inspired and he *knew*. But he was mortally afraid of making a mistake. When the time shortly came when he had to take hold of Hasruel's life himself, he knew he would have to go straight to it, because Dalzel would give him no second chance. That was why he needed the genie to confirm the guess. The tendril of smoke was still lying there, near invisible, and if Abdullah had guessed, surely the genie knew too?

"Er—" Abdullah said. "Um—"

The tendril of smoke crept noiselessly back inside the Paragon's petticoat and bellied up inside, where it must have tickled the nose of Jamal's dog. The dog sneezed.

"Atishoo!" cried Abdullah, and almost drowned the thread of the genie's voice whispering, "*It's the ring in Hasruel's nose!*"

"Atishoo!" said Abdullah and pretended to guess wrong. This was where his plan was distinctly risky. "Your brother's life is one of your teeth, great Dalzel."

"*Wrong!*" trumpeted Dalzel. "Hasruel, roast him!"

"Spare him!" wailed Flower-in-the-Night as Hasruel, with disgust and disappointment written all over him, began to get up.

The princesses were ready for this moment. Ten royal hands instantly pushed Princess Valeria out of the crowd to the steps of the throne.

"*I want my doggie!*" Valeria announced. This was her big moment. As Sophie had pointed out to her, she had found thirty new aunties and three new uncles, and all of them had begged her to scream as hard as she could. No one had ever *wanted* her to scream before. In addition, all the new aunties had promised her a box of sweeties if she made this a really good tantrum. Thirty boxes. It was worth the best she could do. She made her mouth square.

She expanded her chest. She gave it everything she had.

"*I WANT MY DOGGIE! I DON'T WANT ABDULLAH! I WANT MY DOGGIE BACK!*" She hurled herself at the throne steps, fell over Jamal, threw herself to her feet again and flung herself at the throne. Dalzel hastily jumped on to the throne seat to get out of her way. "*GIVE ME MY DOGGIE!*" Valeria bellowed.

At the same moment, the tiny yellow princess of Tsapfan gave Morgan a shrewd nip, just in the right place. Morgan had been asleep in her tiny arms, dreaming he was a kitten again. He woke with a jump and found he was still a helpless baby. His fury knew no bounds. He opened his mouth and he roared. His feet pedalled with anger. His hands pumped. And his roars were so lusty that, had it been a competition between himself and Valeria, Morgan might have won. As it was, the noise was unspeakable. The echoes in the hall picked it up, doubled the screams and rolled it all back at the throne.

"Echo at those djinns," Sophie was saying in her conversational magical way. "Don't just double it. *Treble* it."

The hall was a madhouse. Both djinns clapped their hands over their pointed ears. Dalzel hooted, "Stop it! Stop them! Where did that baby come from?"

To which Hasruel howled, "Women have babies, fool of a djinn! What did you expect?"

"*I WANT MY DOGGIE BACK!*" stated Valeria, beating the seat of the throne with her fists.

Dalzel's trumpet voice fought to be heard. "*Give* her a doggie, Hasruel, or I'll kill you!"

At this stage in Abdullah's plans he had confidently expected – if he had not been killed by then – to be turned into a dog. It was what he had been leading up to. This, he had calculated, would also have released Jamal's dog. He had counted on the sight of not one dog but two, dashing from beneath the Paragon's petticoat, to add to the confusion. But Hasruel was as distracted by the screams, and the triple echoes of screams, as his brother was. He turned this way and that, clutching his ears and yelling with pain, the picture of a djinn at his wits' end. Finally he folded his great wings and became a dog himself.

He was a very huge dog, something between a donkey and a bulldog, brown and grey in patches, with a golden ring in his snub nose. This huge dog put its gigantic forepaws on the arm of the throne and stretched an enormous slavering tongue out towards Valeria's face. Hasruel was trying to seem friendly. But at the sight of something so big and so ugly, Valeria, not unnaturally, screamed harder than ever. The noise frightened Morgan. He screamed harder too.

Abdullah had a moment when he was quite at a loss what to do, and then another moment when he was sure no one would hear him shout. "*Soldier!*" he roared. "Hold Hasruel! Someone hold Dalzel!"

Luckily the soldier was alert. He was good at that. The Jharine of Jham vanished in a flurry of old clothes and the soldier leapt up the steps of the throne. Sophie rushed after him, beckoning to the princesses. She threw her arms round Dalzel's slender white knees, while the soldier wrapped his brawny arms round the neck of the dog. The princesses stampeded up the steps behind them, where most of them threw themselves on Dalzel too, with the air of princesses badly in need of revenge – all except Princess Beatrice, who dragged Valeria out of the brawl and began the difficult task of shutting her up. The tiny princess of Tsapfan meanwhile sat calmly on the porphyry floor, rocking Morgan back to sleep.

Abdullah tried to run towards Hasruel. But, no sooner did he move, than Jamal's dog seized its chance and got away. It burst out from under the Paragon's petticoat to see a fight in progress. It loved fights. It also saw another dog. If anything, it hated dogs even more than djinns or the human race. No matter what size the dog was. It sped snarling to the attack. While Abdullah was still trying to kick his way out of the Paragon's petticoat, Jamal's dog sprang for Hasruel's throat.

This was too much for Hasruel, already beset by the soldier. He became a djinn again. He made an angry gesture. And the dog went sailing away, end over end, to land with a yelp on the other side of the hall. After that Hasruel tried to stand up, but the soldier was on his back by then, preventing him spreading his leathery wings. Hasruel heaved and surged.

"Hold your head down, Hasruel, I conjure you!" Abdullah shouted, kicking free of the Paragon's petticoat at last. He leapt up the steps wearing nothing but his loincloth and seized hold of Hasruel's great left ear. At this Flower-in-the-Night understood where Hasruel's life was and, to Abdullah's great joy, she jumped up and hung on to Hasruel's right ear. And there they hung, raised in the air from time to time when Hasruel got the better of the soldier, and slammed to the floor when the soldier got the better of Hasruel, with the soldier's straining arms wrapped round the djinn's neck just beside them and Hasruel's great snarling face between them. From time to time, Abdullah caught glimpses of Dalzel standing on the seat of his throne under a pile of princesses. He had spread his weak golden wings. They did not seem much use for flying with, but he was battering at the princesses with them and shouting to Hasruel for help.

Dalzel's trumpet shouts seemed to inspire Hasruel. He began to get the better of the soldier. Abdullah tried to get a hand loose so that he could reach out to the golden ring, dangling just by his shoulder, under Hasruel's hooked nose. Abdullah freed his left hand. But his right hand was sweating and slipping off Hasruel's ear. He grabbed – desperately – before he slipped off.

He had reckoned without Jamal's dog. After lying dazed for most of a minute, it stood up, angrier than ever and full of hatred for djinns. It saw Hasruel and knew its enemy. Back across the hall it raced, hackles up and snarling, past the tiny princess and Morgan, past Princess Beatrice and Valeria, through the princesses eddying round the throne, past the crouching figure of its master, and sprang at the easiest piece of djinn to reach. Abdullah snatched his hand away just in time.

SNAP! went the dog's teeth. *Gulp* went the dog's throat. After which a puzzled look crossed the dog's face and it dropped to the floor, hiccuping uneasily. Hasruel howled with pain and sprang upright with both hands clapped to his nose. The soldier was hurled to the floor. Abdullah and Flower-in-the-Night were flung off to either side. Abdullah dived for the hiccuping dog, but Jamal got there first and picked it up tenderly.

"Poor dog, my poor dog! Better soon!" he crooned to it and carried it carefully away down the steps.

Abdullah dragged the dazed soldier with him and put them both in front of Jamal. "Stop, everyone!" he shouted. "Dalzel, I conjure you to stop! We have your brother's life!"

The struggle on the throne stilled. Dalzel stood with spread wings and his eyes like furnaces again. "I don't believe you," he said. "Where?"

"Inside the dog," said Abdullah.

"But only until tomorrow," Jamal said soothingly, thinking only of his hiccuping dog. "It has an irritable gut from eating too much squid. Be thankful—"

Abdullah kicked him to shut him up. "The dog has eaten the ring in Hasruel's nose," he said.

The dismay on Dalzel's face told him that the genie had been right. He had guessed correctly. "Oh!" said the princesses. All eyes turned to Hasruel, huge and bowed over, with tears in his fiery eyes and both hands clasped to his nose. Djinn-blood, which was clear and greenish, dripped between his great horned fingers.

"I shold hab dode," Hasruel said dismally. "It wad right udder by dose."

The elderly princess of High Norland detached herself from the crowd round the throne, felt in her sleeve and reached up to Hasruel with a small lacy handkerchief. "Here you are," she said. "No hard feelings."

Hasruel took the handkerchief with a grateful "Thang you," and pressed it to the torn end of his nose. The dog had not really eaten much except the ring. Having mopped the place carefully, Hasruel knelt ponderously down and beckoned Abdullah up the steps of the throne. "What would you have me do now I am good again?" he asked mournfully.

CHAPTER TWENTY-ONE

In which the castle comes down to earth

Abdullah did not need to give Hasruel's question much thought. "You must exile your brother, mighty djinn, to a place from which he will not return," he said.

Dalzel at once burst into melting blue tears. "It's not *fair*!" he wept, and stamped his foot on the throne. "Everyone's always against me! You don't love me, Hasruel! You cheated me! You didn't even try to get rid of those three people hanging on to you!"

Abdullah was sure Dalzel was right about that. Knowing the power a djinn had, Abdullah was sure Hasruel could have flung the soldier, not to speak of himself and Flower-

266

in-the-Night, to the ends of the earth if he had wanted to.

"It wasn't as if I was doing any harm!" Dalzel shouted. "I have a right to get married, don't I?"

While he shouted and stamped, Hasruel murmured to Abdullah, "There is a wandering island in the ocean to the south, which is only to be found once in a hundred years. It has a palace and many fruit trees. May I send my brother there?"

"And now you're going to send me away!" Dalzel screamed. "None of you care how lonely I shall be!"

"By the way," Hasruel murmured to Abdullah, "your father's first wife's relatives made a pact with the mercenaries, which allowed them to flee from Zanzib to escape the Sultan's wrath, but they left the two nieces behind. The Sultan has locked the unfortunate girls up, they being the nearest of your family he could find."

"Most shocking," Abdullah said. He saw what Hasruel was driving at. "Perhaps, mighty djinn, you might celebrate your return to goodness by fetching the two damsels here?"

Hasruel's hideous face brightened. He raised his great clawed hand. There was a clap of thunder followed by some girlish squealing, and the two fat nieces stood before the throne. It was as simple as that. Abdullah saw that Hasruel had indeed been holding back his strength before. Looking into the djinn's great slanting eyes – which still had tears in the corners from the dog's attack – he saw that Hasruel knew he knew.

"Not *more* princesses!" Princess Beatrice said. She was kneeling by Valeria looking rather harassed.

"Nothing of the sort, I assure you," said Abdullah.

The two nieces could hardly have looked less like princesses. They were in their oldest clothes, practical pink and workaday yellow, torn and stained from their experiences, and the hair of both had come unfrizzed. They took one look at Dalzel stamping and weeping above them on the throne, another look at the huge shape of Hasruel, and then a third look at Abdullah wearing nothing but a loincloth, and they screamed. After which each tried to hide her face in the other's plump shoulder.

"Poor girls," stated the princess of High Norland. "Hardly royal behaviour."

"Dalzel!" Abdullah shouted up at the sobbing djinn. "Beauteous Dalzel, poacher of princesses, be peaceful a moment and look upon the gift I have given you to take with you into exile."

Dalzel stopped in mid-sob. "Gift?"

Abdullah pointed. "Behold two brides, young and succulent and sorely in need of a bridegroom."

Dalzel wiped luminous tears from his cheeks and surveyed the nieces in much the same way that Abdullah's cannier customers used to inspect his carpets. "A matching pair!" he said. "And wonderfully fat! Where's the catch? Are they perhaps not yours to give away?"

"No catch, shining djinn," said Abdullah. It seemed to him that, now the girls' other relatives had deserted them, they were surely his to dispose of. But to be on the safe side, he added, "They are yours for the stealing, mighty Dalzel." He went up to the nieces and patted each on her plump arm. "Ladies," he said. "Fullest moons of Zanzib, pray forgive me that unfortunate vow which prevents me forever from enjoying your largeness. Look up instead and behold the husband I have found you in my place."

The heads of both nieces came up as soon as they heard the word *husband*. They gazed at Dalzel. "He's ever so handsome," said the pink one.

"I like them with wings," said the yellow one. "It's different."

"Fangs are rather sexy," mused the pink one. "So are claws, provided he's careful with them on the carpets."

Dalzel beamed wider with each remark. "I shall steal these at once," he said. "I like them better than princesses. Why didn't I collect fat ladies instead, Hasruel?"

A fond smile bared Hasruel's fangs. "It was your decision, brother." His smile faded. "If you are quite ready, it is my duty to send you into exile now."

"I don't mind so much now," Dalzel said, with his eyes still on the two nieces.

Hasruel stretched out his hand again, slowly, regretfully, and slowly, in three long rolls of thunder, Dalzel and the two nieces faded out of sight. There was a slight smell of the sea and a faint noise of seagulls. Both Morgan and Valeria started crying again. Everyone else sighed, Hasruel deepest of all. Abdullah realised with some surprise that Hasruel truly loved his brother. Although it was hard to understand how anyone could love Dalzel, Abdullah could hardly blame him. Who am I to criticise? he thought, as Flower-in-the-Night came up and put her arm through his.

Hasruel heaved up an even heavier sigh and sat down on the throne – which fitted his size far better than Dalzel's – with his great wings drooping sadly to either side. "There is other business," he said, touching his nose gingerly. It seemed to be healing already.

"Yes, there certainly *is*!" said Sophie. She had been waiting on the throne steps for her chance to speak. "When you stole our moving castle, you disappeared my husband Howl. Where is he? I want him back."

Hasruel raised his head sadly, but before he could reply there were alarmed noises from the princesses. Everyone at the bottom of the steps retreated from the Paragon's petticoat. It was bulging and bellying up and down on its hoops like a concertina. "Help!" cried the genie inside. "Let me out! You promised!"

Flower-in-the-Night's hand leapt to her mouth. "Oh! I clean forgot!" she said and darted away from Abdullah, down the steps. She threw aside the petticoat in a roll of purple smoke. "I wish," she cried out, "that you be released from your bottle, genie, and be free for ever more!"

As usual, the genie did not waste time in thanks. The bottle burst with a resounding SMACK. Inside the rolls of smoke, a decidedly more solid figure climbed to its feet.

Sophie gave a scream at the sight. "Oh bless the girl!

Thank you, *thank you*!" She arrived in the vanishing smoke so fast that she nearly knocked the solid man there over. He did not seem to mind. He picked Sophie up and swung her round and round. "Oh why didn't I *know*? Why didn't I *realise*?" Sophie panted, staggering about on broken glass.

"Because that was the enchantment," Hasruel said gloomily. "If he was known to be Wizard Howl, someone would have released him. You could not know who he was, nor could he tell anyone."

The Royal Wizard Howl was a younger man than Wizard Suliman, and a good deal more elegant. He was richly dressed in a suit of mauve satin, against which his hair showed a rather improbable shade of yellow. Abdullah stared at the wizard's light eyes in the wizard's bony face. He had seen those eyes clearly, one early morning. He felt he should have guessed. He felt himself altogether in an awkward position. He had used the genie. He felt he knew the genie very well. Did that mean he also knew the wizard? Or not?

For this reason, Abdullah did not join in when everyone, including the soldier, gathered round Wizard Howl, exclaiming and congratulating him. He watched the tiny princess of Tsapfan walk quietly among the exclaiming crowd and gravely put Morgan into Howl's arms. "Thanks," said Howl. "I thought I'd better bring him along where I could keep an eye on him," he explained to Sophie. "Sorry if I gave you a fright." Howl seemed more used to holding babies than Sophie was. He rocked Morgan soothingly and stared at him. Morgan stared, rather balefully, back. "My word, he's ugly!" Howl said. "Chip off the old block."

"*Howl!*" said Sophie. But she did not sound angry.

"One moment," said Howl. He advanced to the steps of the throne and looked up at Hasruel. "Look here, djinn," he said, "I've a bone to pick with you. What do you mean by pinching my castle and shutting me up in a bottle?"

Hasruel's eyes lit to an angry orange. "Wizard, do you imagine your power is equal to mine?"

"No," said Howl. "I just want an explanation." Abdullah found himself admiring the man. Knowing what a coward the genie had been, he had no doubt that Howl was a jelly of terror inside. But he showed no sign of it. He hoisted Morgan over his mauve silk shoulder and glared back at Hasruel.

"Very well," said Hasruel. "My brother ordered me to steal the castle. In this I had no choice. But Dalzel gave no orders concerning you, except that I ensure you could not steal the castle back again. Had you been a blameless man, I would simply have transported you to the island where my brother is now. But I knew you had been using your wizardry to conquer a neighbouring country—"

"That's not fair!" said Howl. "The king *ordered* me—!" He sounded for a moment just like Dalzel and he must have realised that he did. He stopped. He thought. Then he said ruefully, "I daresay I could have redirected His Majesty's mind, if it had occurred to me. You're right. But don't ever let me catch you where I can put *you* in a bottle, that's all."

"That I might deserve," Hasruel agreed. "And I deserve it the more as I took pains to let everyone involved meet with the most fitting fate I could devise." His eyes slanted towards Abdullah. "Did I not?"

"Most painfully, great djinn," Abdullah agreed. "ALL my dreams came true, not only the pleasant ones."

Hasruel nodded. "And now," he said, "I must leave you, when I have performed one more small needful act." His wings rose and his hands gestured. Instantly he was in the midst of a swarm of strange, winged shapes. They hovered over his head and around the throne like transparent sea horses, completely silent except for the faint whisper of their whirling wings.

"His angels," Princess Beatrice explained to Princess Valeria.

Hasruel whispered to the winged shapes and they departed from him as suddenly as they had appeared, to reappear in the same swarm, whispering around Jamal's head. Jamal backed away from them, horrified, but it did no good. The swarm followed him. One after another, the winged shapes went to perch on different parts of Jamal's dog. As each landed, it shrank and disappeared among the hairs of the dog's coat, until only two were left.

Abdullah suddenly found these two shapes hovering level with his eyes. He ducked, but the shapes followed. Two small cold voices spoke, in a way that seemed for his ears alone. "After long thought," they said, "we find we prefer this shape to that of toads. We think in the light of eternity and we therefore thank you." So saying, the two shapes darted away to perch on Jamal's dog, where they too shrank and disappeared into the gnarled skin of its ears.

Jamal stared at the dog in his arms. "Why am I holding a dog full of angels?" he asked Hasruel.

"They will not harm you or your beast," said Hasruel. "They will simply wait for the gold ring to reappear. Tomorrow, I believe you said? You must see that I am naturally anxious to keep track of my life. When my angels find it, they will bring it to me wherever I am." He sighed, heavily enough to stir everyone's hair. "And I do not know where I shall be," he said. "I shall have to find some place of exile in the far deeps. I have been wicked. I cannot again join the ranks of the Good Djinns."

"Oh come now, great djinn!" said Flower-in-the-Night. "It was taught to me that goodness is forgiveness. Surely the Good Djinns will welcome you back?"

Hasruel shook his great head. "Intelligent princess, you do not understand."

Abdullah found that he understood Hasruel very well. Perhaps his understanding had something to do with the way he had been less than polite to his father's first wife's relatives. "Hush, love," he said. "Hasruel means that he enjoyed his wickedness and does not regret it."

"It is true," said Hasruel. "I had more fun these last months than I had in many hundreds of years before that. Dalzel taught me this. Now I must go away for fear I start having the same fun among the Good Djinns. If I only knew where to go."

A thought seemed to strike Howl. He coughed. "Why not go to another world?" he suggested. "There are many hundreds of other worlds, you know."

Hasruel's wings rose and beat with excitement, whirling the hair and dresses of every princess in the hall. "There are? Where? Show me how I may get to another world."

Howl put Morgan into Sophie's awkward arms and bounded up the steps of the throne. What he showed Hasruel was a matter of a few strange gestures and a nod or so. Hasruel seemed to understand perfectly. He nodded in return. Then he rose from the throne and simply walked away, without another word, across the hall and through the wall as if it was so much mist. The huge hall suddenly felt empty.

"Good riddance!" said Howl.

"Did you send him to *your* world?" Sophie asked.

"No way!" said Howl. "They've got enough to worry about there. I sent him in the opposite direction. I took a risk that the castle wouldn't just disappear." He turned round slowly, staring out at the cloudy reaches of the hall. "It's all still here," he said. "That means Calcifer must be here somewhere. He's the one who keeps it going." He gave out a ringing shout. "*Calcifer! Where are you?*"

The Paragon's petticoat once more seemed to take on a life of its own. This time it bowled away sideways on its hoops to let the magic carpet float free of it. The carpet shook itself, in rather the same way as Jamal's dog was now doing. Then, to everyone's surprise, it flopped to the floor and began to unravel. Abdullah nearly cried out at the waste. The long thread whirling free was blue and curiously bright, as if the carpet was not made of the usual wool at all. The free thread, darting back and forth across the carpet, rose higher and higher as it grew longer, until it was stretched between the high cloudy ceiling and the almost bare canvas it had been woven into.

At last, with an impatient flip, the other end tore free from the canvas and shrank upwards into the rest, where it spread in a flickering sort of way, and shrank again, and finally spread into a new shape like an upside-down teardrop, or maybe a flame. This shape came drifting downwards, steadily and purposefully. When it was near, Abdullah could see a face on the front of it composed of little purple or green or orange flames. Abdullah shrugged fatalistically. It seemed that he had parted with all those gold pieces to buy a fire demon and not a magic carpet at all.

The fire demon spoke, with a purple flickering mouth. "Thank goodness!" it said. "Why didn't someone call my name before? I *hurt*."

"Oh poor Calcifer!" said Sophie. "I didn't *know*!"

"I'm not speaking to you," retorted the strange flame-shaped being. "You stuck your claws into me. Nor," it said as it floated past Howl, "to you either. You let me in for this. It wasn't me that wanted to help the king's army. I'm only speaking to *him*," it said, bobbing up beside Abdullah's shoulder. He heard his hair frizzle gently. The flame was hot. "He's the only person who ever tried to flatter me."

"Since when," Howl asked acidly, "have you needed flattery?"

"Since I discovered how nice it is to be told I'm nice," said Calcifer.

"But I don't think you are nice," said Howl. "*Be* like that then!" He turned his back on Calcifer with a fling of mauve satin sleeves.

"Do you want to be a toad?" Calcifer asked. "You're not the *only* one who can do toads, you know!"

Howl tapped with one mauve-booted foot, angrily. "Perhaps," he said, "your new friend might ask you to get this castle down where it belongs then."

Abdullah felt a little sad. Howl seemed to be making it plain that he and Abdullah did *not* know one another. But he took the hint. He bowed. "Oh sapphire among sorcerous beings," he said, "flame of festivity and candle among carpets, magnificent more by a hundred times in your true form than ever you were as treasured tapestry—"

"Get *on* with it!" muttered Howl.

"—would you graciously consent to replace this castle on earth?" Abdullah finished.

"With pleasure," said Calcifer.

They all felt the castle going down. It went so fast at first that Sophie clutched Howl's arm and a number of princesses cried out. For, as Valeria loudly said, a person's stomach got left behind in the sky. It was possible that Calcifer was out of practice after being in the wrong shape for so long. Whatever the reason was, the descent slowed after a minute and became so gentle that everyone hardly noticed it. This was just as well because, as it descended, the castle became noticeably smaller. Everyone was jostled towards everyone else and had to fight for room in which to balance.

The walls moved inwards, turning from cloudy porphyry to plain plaster as they came. The ceiling moved down and its vaulting turned to large black beams, and a window appeared behind the place where the throne had been. It was shadowy at first. Abdullah turned towards it eagerly, hoping for one more glimpse of the transparent sea with its sunset islands, but, by the time the window was a real solid window, there was only sky outside, flooding the cottage-sized room with clear yellow dawn. By this time, princess was crowded against princess, Sophie was squashed in a corner grasping Howl in one arm and Morgan with the other, and Abdullah found himself squeezed between Flower-in-the-Night and the soldier.

The soldier, Abdullah realised, had not said a word in a very long time. In fact, he was behaving decidedly oddly. He had pulled his borrowed veils back over his head and was sitting bowed over on a small stool which had appeared beside the hearth as the castle shrank.

"Are you quite well?" Abdullah asked him.

"Perfectly," said the soldier. Even his voice sounded odd.

Princess Beatrice pushed her way through to him. "Oh *there* you are!" she said. "Whatever is the matter with you?

Afraid I'm going to go back on my promise now we're getting back to normal? Is that it?"

"No," said the soldier. "Or rather – yes. It'll bother you."

"It will bother me not at all!" snapped Princess Beatrice. "When I make a promise I keep it. Prince Justin can just go to – whistle."

"But I *am* Prince Justin," said the soldier.

"*What?*" said Princess Beatrice.

Very slowly and sheepishly the soldier put away his veils and looked up. It was still the same face, with the same blue eyes that were either utterly innocent or deeply dishonest, or both, but it was a smoother and more educated face. A different sort of soldierliness looked out of it.

"That damned djinn enchanted me too," he said. "I remember it now. I was waiting in a wood for the search parties to report back." He looked rather apologetic. "We were hunting for Princess Beatrice – er – you, you know, without much luck, and suddenly my tent blew away and there was the djinn, squeezing himself in among the trees. 'I'm taking the princess,' he said. 'And since you defeated her country by unfair use of magic, you can be one of the defeated soldiers and see how *you* like it.' And, next thing I knew, I was wandering about on the battlefield thinking I was a Strangian soldier."

"And did you hate it?" asked Princess Beatrice.

"Well," said the prince, "it was hard. But I sort of got on with it and picked up everything useful I could and made a few plans. I see I shall have to do something for all those defeated soldiers. But—" a grin that was purely that of the old soldier spread across his face "—to tell the truth, I enjoyed myself rather a lot, wandering through Ingary. I had fun being wicked. I'm like that djinn really. It's getting back to ruling again that's depressing me."

"Well, I can help you there," said Princess Beatrice. "I know the ropes, after all."

"Really?" said the prince, and he looked up at her in the same way that, as the soldier, he had looked at the kitten in his hat.

Flower-in-the-Night nudged Abdullah, softly and delightedly. "The prince of Ochinstan!" she whispered. "No need to fear him!"

Shortly after, the castle came to earth as lightly as a feather. Calcifer, floating against the low beams of the ceiling, announced that he had set it down in the fields outside Kingsbury. "And I sent a message to one of Suliman's mirrors," he said smugly.

This seemed to exasperate Howl. "So did I," he said angrily. "Take a lot on yourself, don't you?"

"Then he got two messages," said Sophie. "What of it?"

"How stupid!" said Howl and began to laugh. At which Calcifer sizzled with laughter too and they seemed to be friends again. Thinking about it, Abdullah could see how Howl felt. He had been bursting with anger all the time he was a genie, and he was still bursting with anger now, with no one except Calcifer to take it out on. Probably Calcifer felt the same. Both of them had magic that was too powerful to risk being angry with ordinary people.

Clearly both messages had arrived. Someone beside the window shouted, "Look!" and everyone crowded to it to watch the gates of Kingsbury opening to let the king's coach hasten out behind a squad of soldiers. In fact it was a procession. The coaches of numerous ambassadors followed the king's, emblazoned with the arms of most of the countries where Hasruel had collected princesses.

Howl turned towards Abdullah. "I felt I got to know you rather well," he said. They looked at one another awkwardly. "Do you know me?" Howl asked.

Abdullah bowed. "At least as well as you know me."

"That's what I was afraid of," Howl said ruefully. "Well then, I know I can rely on you to do some good fast talking when it's needed. When all those coaches get here, it may be necessary."

It was. It was a most confusing time, during the course of which Abdullah grew rather hoarse. But the most confusing part, as far as Abdullah was concerned, was that every single princess, not to speak of Sophie, Howl and Prince Justin, all insisted on telling the king how brave and intelligent Abdullah had been. Abdullah kept wanting to put them right. He had not been brave – just walking on air because Flower-in-the-Night loved him.

Prince Justin took Abdullah aside, into one of the many antechambers of the palace. "Accept it," he said. "Nobody ever gets praised for the right reasons. Look at me. The Strangians here are all over me because I'm giving money to their old soldiers, and my royal brother is delighted because I've stopped making difficulties about marrying Princess Beatrice. Everyone thinks I'm a model prince."

"*Did* you object to marrying her?" asked Abdullah.

"Oh yes," said the prince. "I hadn't met her then of course. The king and I had one of our quarrels about it and I threatened to throw him over the palace roof. When I disappeared, he thought I'd just gone off in a huff for a while. He hadn't even started to worry."

The king was so pleased with his brother, and with Abdullah for bringing Valeria and his other Royal Wizard back, that he ordered a magnificent double wedding for the next day. This added a great deal of urgency to the confusion. Howl hurriedly made a strange simulacrum – constructed mostly of parchment – of a King's Messenger, which was sent by magic to the Sultan of Zanzib, to offer him transport to his daughter's wedding. This simulacrum came back half an hour later, looking decidedly tattered, with the news that the Sultan had a fifty-foot stake ready for Abdullah if he ever showed his face in Zanzib again.

This being so, Sophie and Howl went and talked to the king. The king created two new posts called Ambassadors Extraordinary For The Realm of Ingary and gave those posts to Abdullah and Flower-in-the-Night that same evening.

The wedding of the Prince and the Ambassador made history, for Princess Beatrice and Flower-in-the-Night had fourteen princesses each as bridesmaids, and the king himself gave the brides away. Jamal was Abdullah's best man. As he passed Abdullah the wedding ring, he reported in a whisper that the angels had departed earlier that morning, taking Hasruel's life with them.

"And a good thing too!" Jamal said. "Now my poor dog will stop scratching."

Almost the only persons of note who did *not* attend the wedding were Wizard Suliman and his wife. This had only indirectly to do with the king's anger. It seemed that Lettie had spoken so strong-mindedly to the king, when the king wished to arrest Wizard Suliman, that she had gone into labour rather earlier than her time. Wizard Suliman was afraid to leave her side. But on the very day of the wedding, Lettie gave birth to a daughter with no ill effects at all.

"Oh good!" said Sophie. "I knew I was cut out to be an aunt."

The first task of the two new Ambassadors was to conduct numbers of the kidnapped princesses to their homes. Some of them – like the tiny princess of Tsapfan – lived so far away that their countries had barely been heard of. The Ambassadors had instructions to make trading alliances and also to note all other strange places on the way, with a view to later exploration. Howl had talked to the king. Now – for some reason – all Ingary was talking about mapping the globe. Exploring parties were being chosen and trained.

What with journeying, and pampering princesses, and arguing with foreign kings, Abdullah was somehow always too busy to make his confession to Flower-in-the-Night. It always seemed that there would be a more promising moment the next day. But at last, when they were about to arrive in far-distant Tsapfan, he realised that he could delay no longer.

He took a deep breath. He felt the colour leave his face. "I am not really a prince," he blurted out. There. It was said.

Flower-in-the-Night looked up from the map she was drawing. The shaded lamp in the tent made her face almost more beautiful than usual. "Oh, I know *that*," she said.

"What?" whispered Abdullah.

"Well, naturally, while I was in the castle in the air, I had plenty of time to think about you," she said. "And I soon realised you were romancing, because it was so like *my* daydream, only the other way round. I used to dream that I was just an ordinary girl, you see, and that my father was a carpet merchant in the Bazaar. I used to imagine that I managed the business for him."

"You are a marvel!" said Abdullah.

"Then so are you," she said, and went back to her map.

They returned to Ingary in due time with an extra pack-horse loaded with the boxes of sweets the princesses had promised Valeria. There were chocolates and candied oranges and coconut ices and honeyed nuts; but the most wonderful of all were the sweets from the tiny princess – layer upon layer of paper-thin candy that the tiny princess called Summer Leaves. These came in a box so beautiful that Valeria used it for jewellery when she grew older. Strangely enough, she had almost given up screaming. The king could not understand it, but, as Valeria explained to Sophie, when thirty people all tell you you've *got* to scream, it rather puts you off the whole idea.

Sophie and Howl were living – somewhat quarrelsomely it must be confessed, although they were said to be happiest that way – in the moving castle again. One of its aspects was a fine mansion in the Chipping Valley. When Abdullah and Flower-in-the-Night returned, the king gave them land in the Chipping Valley too, and permission to build a palace there. The house they had built was quite modest: it even had a thatched roof. But their gardens soon became one of the wonders of the land. It was said that Abdullah had help in their design from at least one of the Royal Wizards – for how else could even an Ambassador have a bluebell wood that grew bluebells all the year round?

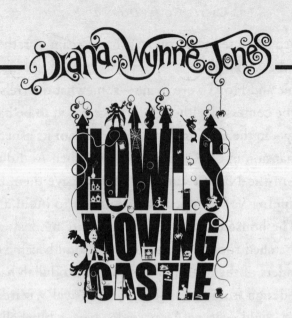

Diana Wynne Jones

HOWL'S MOVING CASTLE

"How about making a bargain with me?" said the demon. *"I'll break your spell if you agree to break this contract I'm under."*

In the land of Ingary, where seven-league boots and cloaks of invisibility exist, pretty Sophie Hatter is cursed into the shape of an old woman. Determined to make the best of things, she travels to the one place where she might find help – the moving castle on the nearby hills.

But the castle belongs to the dreaded Wizard Howl whose appetite, they say, is satisfied only by the hearts of young girls…

HarperCollins *Children's Books*

Diana Wynne Jones

House of Many Ways

"You are rather lost, my dear. Turn round once, clockwise. Then, still turning, open the door with your left hand only. Go through and let the door shut behind you. Then take two long steps sideways to your left. This will bring you back beside the bathroom."

Charmain Baker is in over her head. Looking after Great Uncle William's tiny cottage should have been easy, but he is the Royal Wizard Norland whose house bends space and time. Its single door leads to any number of places: the bedrooms, the kitchen, the caves under the mountains – even the past!

In no time at all, Charmain becomes involved with a magical stray dog, a muddled apprentice wizard and a box of the King's most treasured documents, as well as irritating a clan of small blue creatures.

HarperCollins *Children's Books*

*"There's one absolute rule," said Chrestomanci.
"No witchcraft of any kind is to be practised by
children without supervision. Is that understood?"*

No witchcraft? Gwendolen Chant – a gifted witch
in the making – has other ideas and
is determined to get the better of the great
enchanter. Her brother Cat, who has no
magical gift, is powerless to stop her.

Winner of the Guardian Award.

HarperCollins *Children's Books*